Murder in Marin County

Derek Wade

ISBN: 978-1-62420-417-3

Credits

Cover Artist: Designs by Ms G
Edited by Deborah C. Day

Dedication
For Stephanie

Chapter One

I awake to the sound of heavy air in the sailboat's rigging, in the mast and the shroud, slapping halyards and ruffling canvas covers, uneasy sounds, chaotic. Everything feels wrong and sounds wrong.

A boat sailing at sea has a rhythm. It moves through the wind and waves smoothly. A sailboat can tell you if all is well, even in the roughest weather. You know right away when something breaks or something goes wrong. The sails will slap and halyards will bang. This boat doesn't feel right.

A loud screech resonates from overhead. I can't shake this sleep. I'm stuck in the in-between. The rigging shrieks louder now. I can't be at sea. I'm not on my sailboat in Sausalito. I'm still in the woods.

I yank my head out of the quicksand and get my bearings. The sky is purple, giving way to royal blue. I sense movement…everywhere. I sit up, resting my head against a thousand year old tree. The bushes and ferns are outlined by the rising sun. Foot tall black shapes are moving all around me. They bounce from side to side and up and down. I am in the woods above one of the most expensive suburbs in the country, a quick bridge crossing from San Francisco.

Dark images take shape and squawk as they move about. They're crows, ten or twenty of them. Their cawing builds to a crescendo until it completely devours the quiet. I shift my weight, pulling myself up against the tree. The birds startle and take flight and blacken the sky. They leave behind a mass in the half-light.

A pile of branches just a few feet from where I slept covers something gray and white. The crows settle in nearby branches in anticipation of my departure, their cawing persists. I shake the stiffness from my legs as I become aware of a putrid smell. The odor overpowers me and reaches into my very being. My nose runs. My throat closes up and even my stomach rejects it. My gag reflex kicks in as I quickly turn away. I pull my shirt up to my mouth and try to suck as much air through it as I can, but it doesn't do any good. I lose the Kripsy Kreme flavored bile from the previous night's poor dinner decision.

I know this smell and I know where it's coming from. I turn back to the mass hidden beneath redwood and cedar branches. The crows have returned and are picking tentatively at exposed flesh. They're like sharks in the South Pacific. They keep their distance, constantly sizing you up. Then at the perfect opportunity, they swoop back to take their prey. In this case it's human.

My sinuses are numbed by the stench of the body. My instinctual desire to regurgitate my dinner passes. I step forward and wave my arms, sending the crows into the air. I get a closer look, trying not to disturb the remains. The gray light of morning is filling in the details and hardening the edges. The body is fresh, but I can't really tell more than that. It's mangled arms and legs akimbo. The clothing is torn away in some places, wrapped and twisted in others. There are no shoes present. The twisted legs are beginning to balloon from the internal gases and the trauma. The bloodied hands are devoid of skin and the ends of the fingers are torn open. I look closer at what's left. I can't tell if it is a man or a woman.

I think about what animal could have done this. Mountain lions have long since disappeared from these hills and the last Grizzly was shot here around the turn of the century.

I've seen dead bodies before. I've dragged them from rivers and I've found them lying in their own blood. Some looked peaceful as if it were all part of the process, while others have the look of surprise. I can't see this person's face. I can only imagine the pure shock that it might have registered before meeting its end.

I have stumbled on to something a bit more complicated than a simple surveillance. My work from last night, spying on a married surgeon, is moved to the back burner. It was not my intention to be standing over a body today. I want to be cleaning my boat, polishing the stainless or starting a new maintenance project. I often complain about not being busy enough but when busy comes I complain about that too.

The crows alight to higher branches and continue their eerie calls. I step back from the body and offer a moment of silence. This discovery is an unknowable rite of passage for the victim, a moment when life or death takes a turn and changes everything and everyone connected to him or her.

I lift my camera but the battery is dead.

Chapter Two

The fog is playing tricks on me, seeping into my head, bringing with it self-doubt. The freakish thought of discovering other bodies moves in and out of my head. I don't know the circumstances behind the death, so I don't know what to expect. This can't be the work of a serial killer or rapist. The perpetrator would never mutilate the body like this. To a serial killer the body is the trophy and the morgue is the trophy shelf. He wants everybody to see and know his work. This doesn't make sense.

I begin to contemplate the possibility that a killer might be nearby. I listen. I scan the perimeter. There are bushes and ferns where there was only darkness last night. A grove of tall redwoods and cedars surrounds me. A creek runs toward the bay in the canyon bottom below. There is no one, if there was I'd probably be dead by now.

Could this have happened while I slept? I brace myself against the big redwood tree and reach out to the lifeless form. I reach for the bare skin of one of the mangled limbs. The body is ice cold. This victim of some unbelievable accident or heinous crime met its death sometime before I arrived on the scene.

I ponder the silence a moment before my focus moves to my own feet. I wiggle my toes in my dirty boots. My footprints are everywhere. Fibers from my clothes are probably embedded in the redwoods and in the leaves on the forest floor. My jeans are covered in the same mud and leaves and would leave an indelible impression on a detective investigating the murder scene.

I check my phone for a signal, but of course there's nothing. There's never one when you need it, another dead spot. I take a few pictures with my phone. Now there is nothing I can do except climb out and go for help.

The canyon is a completely different place in the daylight. The climb out takes me longer than anticipated. A cold dense fog has moved in, making it difficult to get my bearings. Once again I am forced to be wary of my every step. I feel uncomfortable leaving the body to the crows, but there is nothing I can do. They'll be back on it in a matter of minutes.

Being in the thick fog is like being under water. Sounds come from everywhere, wrapping around you until you lose your sense of direction. I can hear the distant hum of commuters on Paradise Road in Tiburon which I know to be several canyons away. The crows are still arguing in the canyon, but it sounds like they're everywhere. Maybe they are.

I can sail madly into the night with only the stars for direction, but fill the arena with fog and even the daylight becomes a confusing muddle. I stagger along, growing disoriented, waiting for the hit.

I hear car doors slam. Voices rise from the bay a mile away. A ferry boat leaves the dock at Tiburon, pressing its hindquarters against the metal piers. I hear the booming foghorn that hangs beneath the roadway of the Golden Gate Bridge. I hear all of this. Then I hear the crows again. I continue on until I reach the top of the hill.

It's close to 6:30 A.M. The signal on the phone is weak, low battery. This is not an easy call to make. I call Tom Ricketts, an old friend.

One of my personal and professional goals is to avoid the media. Getting my face plastered on the news and in the papers doesn't exactly do my business any good; my clients expect anonymity. Keeping it off the radio keeps it off the scanners, which means more time to clear out before the *San Francisco Chronicle* and the *Marin Independent Journal* set up camp and before the news helicopters begin their lazy circles overhead.

I call Tom's house and his wife tells me that he is running on the high school track nearby. I find it hard to believe. He hasn't had a runner's physique in years, at least since the invention of the value meal. He carries most of his weight above his belt like all the guys our age. I picture him running; huffing and puffing, sweat pouring down his red face. It isn't like him but we all have to get into shape sometime.

I walk down the narrow path to my Chevy Suburban which is parked at a construction site beneath a grassy slope surrounded by eucalyptus trees. Thankfully, the aroma of eucalyptus oil in the fallen leaves clears the scent of death from my sinuses. I quickly eject the SD card from my SLR, loaded with last night's bread and butter job. I tuck the memory card into my pocket. I look at the contents of my truck; a sail bag is the perfect means by which to transport a body to the dump site, heavy wrenches and tools, solvents and adhesives. My truck looks like it either belongs to a sailor or a serial killer. I'm going to need an alibi.

I give myself the once-over. I'm covered in dirt and mud. My clothes are soiled and damp and I'm emitting an odor I'm not comfortable with and I can't do much about. My cell phone rings. It's Tom Ricketts.

Tom was the kid on the block who your parents didn't want you to play with. He was a thirteen year old joy-rider behind the wheel of his father's Caprice wagon. He was the kid who always got you in trouble and let you take the fall. He was small, sinewy and strong. He was the best friend that you got into fist fights with one day and had the time of your life with the next. He was fearless.

Tom is a little less than thrilled that I'm interrupting his morning run, but he understands the urgency. He's a lieutenant for the San Rafael Police Department. I rarely call him with a false alarm. I tell him what happened moment by moment; including the run in with the security guards on the hill last night, my interrupted surveillance of the doctor and his paramour and the chase that led me to sleep next to a dead body. I'd rather risk a slap on the wrist for trespassing than have to explain away my reason for sleeping in the woods and smelling like an errant slaughterhouse knife sharpener.

Ricketts says he'll make the calls and for me to stay put. He said that it was out of his jurisdiction, but local agencies tend to help each other out in circumstances like this. They all pretty much work together. He would try to get to the scene as fast as he could.

In less than three minutes I hear the sirens racing up the hill. Four Tiburon police cars pour into the construction site with lights ablaze. Gravel flies and a cloud of dust coats everything that is damp, mainly me. Doors fly open and guns are drawn. The cops talk into their shoulder mikes.

I slowly put my hands in the air and step away from the Suburban. The officers have taken up defensive positions behind open patrol car doors with their guns pointed at my kill zone. I turn around and back toward them as directed. They leave their positions to give me a quick pat-down then they approach the Suburban.

My truck is given a light search.

"Clear here!" shouts an officer kneeling on the front seat of my suburban while he points his gun toward the backseat.

"Clear over here!" another officer shouts from a nearby bush.

"I'm clear, you clear?" one officer says to another.

"Clear back here." The last officer shouts in my ear as he leans me against his car.

"We're all clear," I say annoyed. Then we wait.

The cops have been instructed to stand by. We stand around kicking at the dirt. Nobody is talking.

The Tiburon Police Chief, John Lemley, is the first in management to arrive. He slides into the lot driving an older blue Chevy Tahoe that looks like it has seen more soccer field parking lots than crime scenes. The faded bumper sticker in the rear window alludes to the fact that his kids were on the honor roll, and thus were smarter than everyone else and richer than half the rest simply because they went to a school that could afford to spend money on senseless bumper stickers.

Now that the chief's children have left the nest and are studying in distant colleges, save for the one who is trying to find 'herself' while working at a dive shop in a Belize resort town, his wife drives the fun car.

The chief musters. He's in his fifties and carries a daily reminder of his increasing appetite and slowing metabolism in front of him. His height somewhat hides his true girth, but it's his badge that is totally invisible.

The Chief talks to his staff sergeant who puts the boots into action. Two of the police cruisers block the site as other officers grab their shotguns and police tape. The chief looks at me but doesn't say anything.

The sheriff deputies arrive along with the county detective. Their lights are wigwagging with the new state of the art LED strobes that could send the unaware epileptic into grand mal seizures. Once again the dust settles, with most of it sticking to me. If more cars arrive I will become completely camouflaged in dirt and will be able to walk out of here without having to talk to anyone.

The Chief doesn't seem thrilled by the deputies' arrival either but that's what you get in Marin County, numerous jurisdictions all piled up against each other. You call the station about a barking dog and four police agencies show up. At this point, the Chief waves the dust away from his face as he confers with the detective out of earshot, and finally, he motions me over.

"Good morning, Jack." The chief says, wiping his brow, he has a voice like a wrestling match announcer.

"Good morning, Chief." I try to dust off my shirt and pants but it's impossible. The county investigator seems to be watching my futile attempts with disdain. This looks like this is going to be fun.

The chief turns to the investigator, "Homicide Detective Ellen Jacobs of Marin County, this is Jack Brubaker, of the Brubaker Agency in Sausalito and I am sure that he has a very good explanation for being here."

"Detective." I offer my hand but there are no takers. The Chief looks away and Ellen Jacobs grimaces. Could the cool reception be the result of me sleeping with a dead body in the woods last night?

I know of Ellen Jacobs through the occasional news blurb and she knows me because…well, who doesn't. Jacobs is a climber. She started at a podunk valley agency where she supposedly solved the crime of the decade. Her discovery of a pregnant murder victim next to a real estate office here in the Bay Area must have sealed the deal. That was her ticket out of the smoggy Valley and into the hot-tub community. I don't remember her looking this good, but I guess what they say is true: climbing is the best form of exercise.

Ellen looks great with her straight dirty blonde hair pulled back into a burgeoning pony tail. She goes for the conservative navy blue jacket and casual Friday jeans look along with black pumps which will prove to be grossly inappropriate for what we are about to encounter. The dead body doesn't care how she comes dressed to the party.

"I'm going to get out of these shoes." Ellen says looking down at her feet.

"Huh," I mumble. I look down at mine feeling rugged and outdoorsy.

I watch the chief show his young officers how to tie a knot in the police tape while Ellen pulls on a pair of hiking boots. I prefer to watch Ellen.

I know from her ambition that she is probably a man-eater, but then that's my type. Each time I promise myself, no more man-eaters, but I always fall for the man-eater and end up on their menu.

Ellen returns to where I have been standing, alone, like an idiot. There is a long pregnant pause. I can't muster anything more than a nod, she a glare. We're on the right track.

The chief, no longer distracted by his team's inability to tie two lengths of police tape together, rejoins us. "I am glad to see that you've gotten to know each other a little better."

Ellen and I look at each other. This isn't going to be easy.

I know the chief from some previous work I did for him regarding his kid in Belize. And, as a matter of fact, I really don't consider today to be work, I call it real bad luck for me and the dead body in the woods.

"Brubaker," she nods, "I'm sure we will have plenty of time to get acquainted."

"In what, an interview room?" I still can't get a shot at her eyes behind her dark sunglasses. I believe I mentioned that it was foggy, so I don't know why the sunglasses. She must think it gives her the upper hand or maybe she's hiding a hang-over.

The chief looks up the hill and says, "I'm going in with one man. Jacobs, you can follow behind with two of your men. We won't touch anything or leave the trail, assuming we don't have to. Avoid stepping on any footprints. We'll get photos as we go. Once we secure the scene we'll back out, at which time we will hand it over to the county crime scene guys. Brubaker, you can show us where it is. Please restrain from your usual banter. It's too early, and frankly I don't want to hear it."

"Assuming it is a crime scene." Ellen rubs her eyes behind her dark sunglasses.

"It's a crime scene, all right." I say. "Let's cut the protocol."

"We are cutting the protocol. You should be sitting in the back of a patrol car right now," Ellen barks. "So keep your mouth shut."

"Wow, the thought of me being locked up with you, barking orders at me, is a turn on." I put out my wrists mocking a desire for handcuffs.

"Knock it off you two. Brubaker isn't a threat to anyone. And Ellen, don't forget this is still my town and my investigation. No banter!"

There it is. We've been scolded. Ellen lets out a huff of resentment. It puts a smile on my grubby face.

"This will be base camp unless we find something in closer proximity." The Chief looks at his men one more time. Several men are rocking on their heels while another untangles a roll of crime scene tape. "Very well, let's go." Chief Lemley and Detective Jacobs wave their men over as we begin our procession up the hill.

We walk in silence. Camera flashes illuminate the white misty backdrop. We make our way along a trail bordered by the low shrubs and thick grass that run along the crest of a hilltop. I recognize an area blanketed in soft grass and foamy soil. If I had only seen it last night, it would have been the perfect hiding place. The body would have been left for some other rube to find. The trail leads off toward the narrow canyon and a thickening wood.

Deputy Ansell Adams is taking pictures of everything, turning the evidence into a documentary entitled, "What I did before I got fired for burning through this year's photo processing budget." With one of the flashes comes a crash.

"Detective Jacobs, are you alright?" I peer over the bushes while hanging on to the cedar branch that cleaned her clock. She is sprawled spread-eagle among the ferns. As she tries to raise herself up, her hands sink into the damp earth.

I offer my hand and this time she takes it. "Careful of the footprints, they're evidence." I add without the slightest hint of sarcasm.

"I'm okay." Detective Jacobs brushes herself off. As she tries to restore her balance, her diminutive feet sink in the mud. She plunges forward pulling at her mud-caked boots as if she were walking into hurricane force winds. Soon she is back on the trail.

I scan for footprints on the trail, but nothing was left behind, not even my own. Chief Lemley has already passed the point where I left the trail last night. I call after him. He returns and we sort out the procedure beneath the location of the body.

Ellen Jacobs approaches the body, while the chief and I wait below.

"Where were you?" Jacob's asks. Her jeans are muddied and torn. She rubs her forehead where the branch nailed her then presses a handkerchief over her mouth and nose. She stares at the body.

"I was next to that big freaking tree," I answer with an intended impatient tone. I point to one of the giant redwoods. The rotting odor drifts over the group. The photographer is the first to lose it and the other newbies follow suit. The sounds of gagging and retching scatter the birds from the limbs above. The chief seems to inhale the odor, as if he were determining the sex, age and cause of death at that very moment.

I am not sure that Jacobs is interested in my answer because she is focused on the corpse. She is like the Horse Whisperer for dead bodies. At one point I thought she was going to put her ear right up to the decedent's lips.

"So you ran up here, and, as you said, you 'hunkered down next to this tree.' You said you smelled the corpse this morning but you didn't smell anything last night when you were breathing the hardest and when you fell asleep."

The Marin detective seems to have started her interrogation without me. "Right, that's what I said." There are three officers standing down on the path wondering what the hell they are doing there, and so am I. "I was sleeping against the trunk of that big redwood rather than using the body as a pillow." I point to a flattened area of bark on the forest floor.

"Let's keep this on a professional level, Brubaker." The chief speaks.

"Gotcha," I say.

The chief shifts his weight as he scans the nearby terrain. He ponders a moment before asking the obvious. "So you're telling us you didn't know it was here until sunrise. You didn't smell it until this morning?"

"I find it hard to believe, Mr. Brubaker." Ellen doesn't look up from the body.

"That's what I said, chief. I woke up with a goddamned body at my feet and I called it in. You are here and so is everyone else. I have to get to work."

The chief cracks a half-smile. "Calm down."

He hates guys like me, but he also hates the Sheriff's office for taking over his investigations.

"We'll call you. Watch your step on your way out." The chief puts an unlit cigarette in his mouth.

"We'll be in touch." Ellen Jacob's eyes are still on the body. "And leave your shoes."

"What's that?" Is she some kind of sicko?

"Leave 'em." She crosses her arms.

"Here?" I look down at my soiled boots.

"Drop them at base camp before you leave."

"Now or never," I say, pulling my feet out of my boots as I kick them toward the officers on the trail below. One flies through the air and lands perfectly in the rookie's meaty hands while the other slices left and nearly cuts down the chief before landing in distant a bush.

"Don't go anywhere." Jacobs tries to get the last word.

"I am confused. Should I stay or should I go?" I ask.

The chief looks at Ellen with the same question written in the expression on his face. Ellen teeters awkwardly, "Go, but don't go anywhere." She pronounces the last word very slowly, as if conveying a meaning that only I can understand.

The chief and I look to her for clarification.

"You know what I mean!"

The chief and I look at each other and shake our heads very slowly.

"Where in the hell would I go? I'm not wearing any shoes!"

"Just don't sail anywhere. I've heard you have a boat." Fluster leaks through her professional demeanor.

Who has she been talking to? "Right!" The bulb just went off. I don't envy the chief if this is what he is in for.

"Brubaker? We want your photos too," Ellen adds.

"I almost forgot." I look to the chief and he okays it with a nod. I reach into my pocket and give the SD chip to Chief Lemley's guy. I could have feigned ignorance but then I would have been without an alibi.

I push past the other two officers still waiting for orders. I watch my step as I move among the footprints, which are now up to eleven pairs. There goes that evidence.

Chapter Three

Tom Ricketts is climbing the path as I begin my decent into the construction site. Tom and I have come a long way from ripping off candy from the corner liquor store back in the eighties. We used to pile it up on the front seat between us in his father's Caprice station wagon. We were thirteen and Tom could barely see over the wheel. He was considered a troublemaker then, but now I think of him as an adventurer who likes to test the limits including right and wrong.

I rely on Tom for his knowledge of protocol. He's been around some of the trickier cases. Tom is in his mid-thirties, my age. He wears the usual dark glasses that scream law enforcement in any social situation other than the Policeman's Ball. Tom has a thick head of salt and pepper hair which is getting saltier every year. He's got a stoic face that hides the Gulf War years and two failed marriages. He wears a moustache because he's a cop.

"Thanks for the tip. If it turns out to be a serial killer we're already ahead of the game." Tom never says hello.

I was thinking self-preservation. I lean in close to the detective. "I don't know how this guy bought it but it doesn't look like a human did it. This guy is messed up," I say.

Ricketts gives me a nod of mock interest. "Hungry?" He extends a box of Krispy Kreme donuts.

What's left of dinner in my stomach wants to join its friends in the box. "Pass."

"What are you saying?"

The nausea clears. "Go have a look. It's almost mechanical, like a garbage truck or cement roller. It's ugly, one of the worst."

"Jesus, do you think it's an Italian job?" Tom is alluding to a spat of mafia style murders that took place in San Francisco. In the end they turned out to be Chinese mafia made to look like Italian. I never quite understood it, but I like Chinese food better than Italian.

"There have to be some really big Italians on the loose," I say getting back on track.

Tom grabs a donut from the box and nearly takes the whole thing in one bite. Sticky glazing gets caught in his moustache. Pieces fall out of his mouth and land back in the open box. I grimace. I think about the other cops that are going to dig into that box like it's the last food on earth.

"Look Tom, they're probably going to bring me in and run me up for a while, so I prefer to get things square at my office beforehand. Can you keep me in the loop?"

"Sure. Let me know if you need anything." He looks at my stocking feet.

I look down. My socks are red with clay. "Careful of the new girl, she's a climber," I say, scratching my face.

Ricketts nods in agreement as drool runs out of his mouth and drizzles down on to the remaining donuts.

"See you later," he mumbles as another donut occupies the entire space between his throat and his lips. Ricketts turns up the hill.

I've seen him gorge himself sick before and have written it off as an isolated incident, but now I am beginning to wonder if there are deeper issues at work here.

At the bottom of the hill, the two security guards that chased me into the woods last night are talking to the local police. They give me some really surly looks as I approach my truck. They're big and scary. I shoot back some looks that I think are even surlier. They counter with mock growls and barks. I shoot daggers, and they can only muster a leer and a scowl. The cops are getting a little edgy; one has his hand on his gun as if some type of *West Side Story* face-off is going to break out.

I jump into my truck to leave. I consider the body one more time. I rub my tired eyes until I see the psychedelics and the sheriff deputy who waves me out of the front seat. We have a small discussion about my driving my suburban before I settle into the passenger seat of his police cruiser. The cops offer to give me a lift back to the boat in Sausalito. Meanwhile, they'll also be taking my truck apart piece by piece at a local impound lot. I wouldn't be surprised if every tool in the back is bagged and tagged.

The drive back to the boat only takes fifteen minutes, but when nobody is talking, it seems like an eternity. As we round on to the southbound 101, I try an icebreaker.

"What gauge is that shotgun?" This is a great icebreaker when sitting in the front passenger seat of a moving police cruiser. You are guaranteed to get a rise out of the driver. Ask a few more questions about the make and model, maximum load capacity, then if you feel really confident, reach over and touch it. That's how I wound up in the back seat for the remainder of the trip. More room to spread out anyway.

Chapter Four

Charley is rubbing her jaw against my pants. She rolls all over them and barks. I wonder what she likes best; the smell of the scrub oak, or the odor of human remains. My money is on the funk of the human remains. I should also state that my pants are on the floor and not on my person.

"Charley! Knock it off," I say. Charley is short for Charlene. She has long blonde hair and four long legs, and she knows how to use them.

"Out, Charley. Out," I shout.

Charley grabs my pants and bolts playfully out of my cabin. I can hear her running around the main salon, then forward to the V-berth, then up the companionway to the deck. A quick glance out the transom porthole reveals the worst; Charley strides by on the dock dragging my chinos behind her.

I live on a sailboat and it isn't the weekender variety dry docked in some boatyard. The keel on this old girl has seen thousands of miles of ocean. It has beaten through a million waves and limped into as many ports. I just wasn't on it when it did. I bought it because it was seasoned. She is the *Suzanne*. I know not the origin of the name. It came with the boat.

I have sailed on many boats but the *Suzanne* is my boat, the first boat that I have ever owned. She is strong but nimble, stout but graceful. She has a very light helm and easily follows my direction. I keep her in a slip in the Schoonmaker Marina in Sausalito; it's my primary address right now.

I used to live with a beautiful marketing executive in Mill Valley. Theresa worked for a very successful internet company and used all her stock options to buy the not so big, but very expensive house on the hill. But all went tumbling down with the price of her stock, and I, of course, was quick to follow. It wasn't so much a tumble for me, but a forceful push - heave and a hoe. She dumped the house below market, packed her things in her car, and last I heard, went back to one of those states that don't have an ocean or mountains or even hills.

It's a relief to be living back on the water. I have a much greater sense of independence, tied to the dock with six lines and I can up and go whenever I want. The boat hasn't left the bay in two years, but it will soon. I'm in the planning stage of global transit. They say that sailing is eighty percent planning or ninety percent or…there is a lot of planning. The more you plan, the better prepared you are for the unexpected. If all goes well *Suzanne* will take me to where I'm most comfortable, the open ocean, distant lands and deserted islands. So now I plan and soon I'll throw the dock lines.

I stand in the steaming shower and try to scrape off the death that clings to every strand of hair and in every crevice. Eventually I pour an entire bottle of Listerine over my head. This seems to loosen the odor's grip. I adapted this stench removal technique from a Denver cabbie who explained to me the benefits of pouring Pine Sol in the wash: "It kills the lice and leaves you smelling pine fresh." I don't have any Pine Sol on the boat, so Listerine will have to do.

Fresh laundry is laid out on the settees in the main salon which encompasses the galley, the navigation station and a combined seating and dining area. It's where the crew would take their meals, exchange stories, and pass the time off watch.

A few cabin sole panels are up, exposing the water system below. The water pump hasn't been priming and I'm in the middle of replacing all of the hose clamps.

Pilot charts and cruising guides are spread out on the dinner table. I like the odd sounding names of South Pacific ports: Apia, Hiva Oa, Nuku Hiva. I like studying weather patterns until I am blue in the face. I especially like the images that are conjured up in my head; being barefoot for weeks on end, light warm breezes, and the rhythmic sound of folding waves chasing me across the deep blue Pacific.

I think about a thousand places I'd rather be. It keeps me in a constant state of detachment. I am not always here and I am not always there. It's like having one foot on the dock and one foot on the boat. It's bad luck.

I shake out a pair of jeans and I'm on my way to the office. I throw the board across the companionway and spin the combo lock. I rummage through a dockside basket full of my shoes and grab a pair.

Carl Sandburg's fog retreats to the Muir Woods and climbs the steep hills to the west of Sausalito. A stiff breeze kicks up white caps on Richardson Bay. At the end of the dock club rowers slide their sculls into the cold green water in advance of the thirty knot breeze that gets going in the afternoon. The pants that Charley stole this morning are hanging on the railing next to the rowers club, obviously rescued by one of the rowers. Charley split. If she needs me, she'll find me. I grab the pants off of the rail and toss them into the trash dumpster.

My boat is tied up in A-Basin; it's the big boat basin. They say you should always buy the cheapest house in the best neighborhood. That is exactly what I did. My boat is on the petite side, it barely makes fifty feet while there are two twenty-meter boats tied up on both sides of me.

Officially, A-Basin is not a live-aboard marina. It is illegal to live aboard any boat in Sausalito, but there are some who do. The harbormaster allows it, but only for four or five of us. We have to keep a low profile: no potted plants and no hanging laundry. Our boats must be able to leave the dock and return under power. We like to live on our boats because we're sailors and it is the cheapest rent in all of Sausalito. The harbormaster likes it because we're added security. If something breaks, we fix it. If something floats away, we grab it. If somebody creepy is poking around, we chase them off. It's a fair trade.

"Hello, Roy," I say to the man who lives at the end of the dock next to the scull launch.

"Jack." He returns the wave.

Roy lives on an old steel schooner with a cat named James. He is very formal with his cat, me and everyone else. I would guess that he is about fifty. He keeps his boat immaculate and always freshly painted. You would be hard pressed to find a single rust stain. Roy defies the live aboard stereotype. He is well groomed and always well dressed in khakis. He is also a ready hand to help me into my slip when the wind is ripping. The only thing I can say that is a little creepy about him is that he keeps to himself. He doesn't boat talk you to death. He doesn't actually leave his boat very often and he will never be seen lounging on deck. He's got a story and he's not sharing it with anybody.

I don't blame sailors for boat talking. We all live below sea level and some of us rarely interact with other humans. So when we do, it's like we've just come out of the desert after forty days and forty nights. People think we're all nuts because we are. Who else would live on a boat?

Roy lifts his coffee mug toward me. Now I'm not sure if he is keeping tabs on the entire basin or just me.

Chapter Five

It's a five minute walk to the office but I drive it anyway; a habit I picked up living in Los Angeles. You never know if you're going to need the car. I drive everywhere.

I usually arrive at the office in the beat up Chevy Suburban with its faded roof and rusted out wheel wells, but right now it's being towed to the impound lot out on the bay-fill in San Rafael. With the suburban gone I'll have to depend on the backup car, an Audi Q7. When you live on a boat nothing lasts and nothing stays nice. Everything on a sailboat gets a funk and everything gets dinged, scratched and worn out; but not my Q7. It is not a boat car; no sails, solvents or crap of any kind are allowed inside it. I don't even like to drink an iced tea in it, but I do, sometimes. The Audi was my only luxury purchase and I never would have been able to buy it without the stock Theresa touted me on. I bought low, sold high and bought the car. Theresa bought her stock low, sold lower and bought the farm.

I roll into the 7-11. I have to see about this itching on my face. I noticed it after the shower. It's hard to see what's itching in a fogged-up vanity mirror. I've walked into a San Francisco restaurant wearing a badly shaven, lopsided goatee on more than one occasion because of that mirror.

I check my rearview mirror. It's hard to get the big picture. My face feels like its growing. I move my face around but I still can't see it all at once. I'm fine. It's as if I don't owe the money until I slide the letter opener through the envelope and actually look at the bill.

The 7-11 has a small pharmaceutical section frequented mostly by the anchor-outs and the Laundromat crowd, but I find what I need in an anti-itch cream. I take the pink bottle to the counter. The price is shocking, and so is the look on the cashiers face.

"What happened to you?" The clerk is a weathered-faced, anchor-out with the perfect job and all the ninety-nine cent hot dogs he can eat.

"You wouldn't believe me if I told you." I try not to look him in the eye.

"What did you do, stick your head in an anthill?" He points to the trashcan lid-sized shoplifters' conscience hanging from the ceiling behind me.

"Holy..." My face is swelling with large red sores erupting everywhere.

"We've got a bigger size in the back." He is referring to the puny bottle in my hands. He does have a point; the small bottle looks ridiculous now. "There's no sense in dabbing."

I stare at him. "What should I do?"

I feel something weeping from my cheek, a drop of ooze lands on the counter.

"I'll get the bigger one in the back."

I nod.

The manager leaves the counter and heads for the back. There is a small rack of bandanas on the counter. I imagine myself wearing one like a Taliban. The salty dog clerk returns with a pint of the pink stuff.

I throw the bottle on the passenger seat and beat the two minutes of traffic upstream to the Marina Bagel shop. Two brothers from New York do a nice bagel and keep their elderly mother busy by making her fill small cream cheese containers. I don't like it when she licks the spoon, I go with the shmear. There's no sense in dabbing.

I turn onto Bridgeway toward the central district. This is the real Sausalito, not the tourist version. I pass Dunphey Park which straddles the spit of land between a small marina and the Sausalito Police trailer park. My office is on the third floor of an old, but not so historic converted apartment building on Caledonia Street in downtown. We're across the street from the Marin Movie Theatre and next door to Smitty's bar.

Beneath my office, I have three parking spots in a carport posted with "No Parking" signs. This still doesn't seem to deter the beach bozos from points Midwest and beyond from parking in my spot. This undesirable situation has led to a close and often illicit friendship with Dolly the meter maid. She has cited so many of these people that the towing company sent her to Hawaii last year for vacation. I have the post card on my wall to prove it. Two of the spaces are currently occupied; one with my assistant's new Mini convertible and the other with an unidentified Lexus.

I take each step to the third floor as if I were climbing the pyramids in the Yucatan. I poke my head around the corner and examine the office door. It's a standard door with a brass number six and a sliding nameplate. Today it reads Brubaker & Son Investigations. The door is open, a crack. I remove the nameplate and slip it into my back pocket. I turn the six upside down. Ellen Jacobs is going to have to do some detecting if she comes looking.

Enza, my little Italian firecracker of an assistant, waves me in. Enza is the real deal from North Beach via San Rafael. Family roots that go deeper than oak. Her family came in the 1800's and didn't leave the city until the white flight of the Seventies when inner cities became urban wastelands.

The waiting area, a.k.a. the living room, is empty except for Enza, who sits behind a vintage teal McDowell-Craig steel desk. The toilet flushes. Someone is in the bathroom. "Lawyer, client or potential client," I ask Enza.

"Jesus Christ, what is that all over your face?" Enza pushes her rolling desk chair away from me. "Is that contagious?"

"I think it's a spider bite. I spent the night in the hills above Tiburon. Is that a client in there?"

"It's got to be poison oak." She hands me a tissue. "Christine Flynn, know her?"

"No."

"You're oozing."

I dump the bagels on her desk and run into my office, which is really the bedroom of the apartment. It may seem weird, but I like to be seated in my desk chair before the client enters. I found the chair sitting at the curb on special trash pick-up night in the town of Ross.

Sometimes I get lucky; vis-à-vis my desk chair, and sometimes I wake up with dead bodies.

My company should be called Tangent Investigations except that I would never be in the office. The chair – right - I like to keep it formal, in the chair, behind the desk. I like to be in control at the onset because I end up losing the control in the long run, and I have to fight like hell to get it back.

Today is no different as the leather lets out a gasp when I land in my throne. I am not sure of the provenance of my chair before I pulled it out of the trash, but I can tell you it was one of the things that Theresa rolled off her balcony into the creek bed far below her "Great Room" on the night we had "The Talk."

Never break up with a girlfriend when she is having a low blood sugar attack.

Enza picks up her steno pad and walks in. Her ridiculously high heels creak beneath her. She hides her exposed belly with the steno pad.

"What happened with the Dutton case?" She leans a hip against the side of my desk. She is wearing the skinny jeans that are all the fashion.

"Which case?" I'm finding it difficult to stay focused.

"Dr. Dutton, the plastic surgeon. You were supposed to be documenting his bedside manner."

"It's still developing." I hear the bathroom door open and the prospective client pads across the lobby to the coffee table out of view. I hear her flip through some magazines.

"Why do you wear that blouse if you're just going to cover up your belly with the steno pad?" I say this staring out the window at the boats moving slowly up the main channel. I can see Enza's reflection in the glass.

"Why do you act like you have eyes in the back of your head when I can clearly see their reflection in the window?"

She's tiring of my little game.

"Where are they looking now?" I ask coyly.

Enza looks over her shoulder at the door and turns to leave.

"I ran into some trouble this morning on the Dutton case, but it didn't involve him. It involves someone else."

"What kind of trouble?"

Thank God not her kind of trouble. I'll take dead body trouble over Enza's kind of trouble any day.

"I ran into a dead guy. The sheriffs will probably call here, as well as the boys over at Tiburon P.D. They may drop by and take me away. They may just tear gas the place and burn it down after filling me full of bullet holes. Just put a call in to Frank and take the rest of the day off. Don't forget to lock up." I slide my drawer back and toss the nameplate into it. It lands among several others with numerous fictitious business names.

"Is there anything else, or should I wait for the IJ in the morning?" Enza doesn't scare easily, nor is she easily amused. She's talking about the *Marin Independent Journal*, a fairly decent paper with a dead-on horoscope.

"Pick up the newspaper in the morning," I say, without missing a beat.

Judging by Enza's expression and her posture: hands on hips, clearly waiting for me to expound, I know I can't escape with the movie trailer version of the events of this morning so I quickly recount the happenings on the hill. I throw in a few words about the chief and Ellen Jacobs.

"I noticed that you spent more time describing Jacobs than the dead body; very telling." she says with a smirk.

"Why, are you jealous?" I ask sheepishly.

"It just proves to me that your juvenile way of showing you like someone isn't just reserved for me." Enza rolls her eyes.

Awkwardness has walked into the office and is doing a jig on top of my desk. "I can go on and on about the mutilated body if that's what you want?"

"You know I'm not interested in that." Enza glares at me.

I squirm behind my desk.

"What about the photos of the Dutton case? You need to tell me so that I can close out that case and schedule a final meeting with the client." Enza says, letting me off the hook.

I even have an answer. "The camera's SD card is in the Marin County Sheriff's one week photo lab. There is a salt bagel with yellow mustard,"

Enza grimaces.

"... and an everything bagel with just a schmear of cream cheese, lightly toasted, in the bag on your desk."

She smiles.

"I'm going to apply some of this teen cream and see what happens.

Give me five minutes before you send in the boat payment and my bagel."

"Just a schmear?" She turns back toward me and gives me a smile that could melt the ice in Hillary Clinton's veins. She lowers the steno pad.

"Careful, I'm an old man." My eyes are clearly on her as she walks toward the door. It's too bad I'm fifteen years older than she is and I'm a close personal friend of her father; he's a civic leader and the owner of the local gravel quarry. I can only guess what's at the bottom of his slurry pond: guns, a blood soaked Oldsmobile, a courier from Chicago.

"What about the body from last night?"

"This isn't a 'finders keepers' situation. If you want it you've got to ask the sheriffs for it."

"Funny. What do you think?" She's becoming impatient.

"I think it didn't look human. It was bad. They also impounded my shoes."

She looks down at my feet.

"Not these shoes," I say, off her puzzled expression. I make for the bathroom. "I have to go make my face look like a pink birthday cake."

My office has its own bathroom. It's your basic toilet, tub and tile. There is a double sink with a mirror opposite a small window that looks out over Smitty's rooftop. The room is very institutional: plain white towels, first aid kit, no shiplap. This is my first close-up view of my face in the mirror. It's bad, but not nearly as bad as I thought. It looks like road rash, except that my face is oozing. I touch it with toilet paper. This is a problem because the toilet paper is now sticking to it in little clumps. I liberally apply the pink fluid. Now I look like the fry guy on prom night with a bad case of "dull razor cold water." At least it doesn't look contagious. I open the bathroom door to start the day.

"Your face looks like you dunked for apples in a tub of Pepto Bismol," Enza says, very proud of herself, standing in the doorway to my office.

"Mrs. Flynn, Mr. Brubaker will see you now." Enza turns on her heel and returns to her desk and the gambling website she is building. I never ask.

I leap into my chair, nearly falling over backwards.

Marin is a small place. Everybody either knows everybody or

knows of everybody. I don't know a Mrs. Flynn. I hear her get up from the leather sofa and drop whatever magazine she was staring at. I could put Sheep Shearing Monthly on the coffee table and no one would know the difference. The clients are more interested in hiding behind the pages rather than reading them.

Mrs. Flynn is the polar opposite of Enza; she has the seriousness that only maturity brings and a body to go with it. Mrs. Flynn is tall and elegant but obviously troubled. Her burgundy blouse is pressed, but her black skirt is wrinkled. She is wearing conservative heels, making her seem even taller. Thick, dark brown hair frames a beautiful tan face that is weighed down by the dark circles of sleeplessness. She is going through something, and it seems like she is going it alone.

"Did Enza offer you coffee, Mrs. Flynn?" She sits down in the solid chair directly in front of the desk and doesn't answer. She has a hard time looking at me; with my face I don't blame her. Her eyes survey the room quickly, glancing over the sailing photos and the aerial shot of Sausalito I pulled out of the Chamber of Commerce trash bin. She looks at my framed license and my bachelor's degree. I think clients examine it because they think it's going to be a PHD or an MBA, or something significant. They must think I'm crazy for hanging it. I'm going to frame a copy of my Diesel Mechanics certificate I earned at the Royal Yachting Association, we'll see what they think of that.

"Call me Christine. Everyone calls me Christine."

"What can I do for you, Christine?" I am putting on my serious face, be it pink and oozy.

"My husband disappeared while returning from a business trip to Peru. He never came home."

Her eyes are on me now, wide and pleading. I pull a box of Kleenex out of my right side drawer without disturbing my lightweight Glock; that's not short for glockenspiel…I don't think. I push the Kleenex across the old steel desk. Christine gingerly takes a tissue and lightly brushes beneath her eyes.

Peru? Does she realize that we are sitting two miles north of the Golden Gate Bridge? This is not Peru. But I'm listening.

"How did you get my name?"

"His mother wants to have a funeral. Can you believe that? It's only been a week." She's talking faster now. "The U.S. Embassy can't do anything until they either get a note or a body. What am I supposed to do? The company is supposedly putting their best people on it, but all they're saying is that we have to wait and see. Jesus Christ, wait and see? I want to go over there, but I am not stupid. I can't go alone."

"Down there," I say.

"Down there?" she looks perplexed.

"You said 'over there,' but it's really down there, it's in the southern hemisphere." I'm a real stickler for direction. "I am just making sure that we're on the same page."

"Over there, down there, what difference does it make?" Christine is crushing the box of tissue in her lap.

"Well, there is," I lean forward and turn my palms up. "I'm only saying."

Christine is staring at me, puzzled.

She doesn't seem like one to let despair in the door. And if she does, she doesn't let it stay the night. I like Christine even in her current state. She doesn't play helpless for anyone.

"The Company? Does he work for the CIA?" I ask. My face is starting to itch like mad, and I am trying not to touch it. I don't want to draw her attention to it.

She is gazing at me with an odd expression. Am I still oozing?

"Do you think?" She says putting down the Kleenex.

"Think what?" Here we go round the mulberry bush.

"Do you think he works for the CIA?" I can see her mind is really working now.

"I don't know. You said he worked for 'the Company.' In foreign countries the CIA is also known as 'The Company'. I thought you were saying that he works for the CIA, but I could have been wrong." More glares. "Okay, I am wrong. What company does he work for, Mrs. Flynn?" I should be in the extrication business because I manage to get myself out of the tightest spots, like a puppy yanked from a drain pipe.

"It's Christine. He works for a computer company called Evo Liquid in San Francisco, but they were in Peru installing some big government software package." Christine looks down at her watch.

I am staring blankly. She must be timing me. How long will it take for this idiot - meaning me - to get it?

"I see." But barely, because I think my eyes are starting to swell. "Why did you come here? Why me? Isn't there someone the government can recommend in Peru?"

"I am not in Peru, Mr...."

"Jack."

"I am not in Peru, Jack, and to be honest with you, I have never been there. People tell me that you have been everywhere and that you might be perfect for the case, but I am having my doubts."

"When was the last time you spoke with your husband, Mrs. Flynn?"

"He called from the Lima Airport just before his plane took off."

"Have you spoken to the airlines?"

"It was a charter. They weren't willing to turn over their passenger manifest to me."

Hmm. "How did you come upon my name?" This woman is on fire, and who can blame her.

"I got your name from a friend of mine who knows your brother. She worked with him on some cases in the city."

When it came time to choose a college major, my brother Frank took the low road and got a Law degree. I, on the other hand, studied literature and writing. I had the lofty belief that college was for the intellect and should not be employed as a trade school. My brother got a high paying job right out of college, while my career was peppered with sailboats, a brief stint in the film business in L.A, and the occasional investigation my dad threw my way. I became better at investigating and drifted away from my writing. My brother became better at law and moved into a bigger house.

Frank keeps me busy. The plastic surgeon case was one of his referrals. When business is slow I'll camp out at the DMV doing background stuff, and Frank will throw me a bone. He mostly works with the big corporate security types, but I guess my piece of the business gives him a taste of the seedy side. I have to admit his referrals are solid and always pay, maybe not always on time, but they pay.

Christine gathers herself together and is sitting straight in her chair, waiting for an answer or a game plan. In truth, I'm just waking up. The caffeine which I should be drinking is sitting in a pot in the other room. I had a rough night, and frankly, I'm a little distracted by the memory of this morning's corpse, which reminds me of a poorly prepared dragon roll at the Sushi Man. I need another minute to formulate a game plan, but she wants me to give her something right now.

"The U.S. government told me that they don't get involved with domestic disputes. Do I look like an abused wife to you? My husband is missing...."

"Hmm."

"Sorry, I must sound like a crazy person."

"No, not at all." Something very strange happens; the telephone rings. It rarely rings and can be quite disconcerting when it does. The callers often accuse me of operating a carpet cleaning business which is one telephone digit off. I never give the calls a second thought except for today.

The telephone rings again. Has the sheriff's office pinned the dead body on me? Do they think that I'm holed up in my office and not coming out? Is the hostage negotiator calling? Are they going to begin a barrage of amplified rabbit slaughtering noises and a bombardment of Celine Dion songs to shake my cage and rattle me loose?

Christine continues her story while I listen in on Enza's conversation outside the door. I'm getting that warm feeling in my stomach that gradually increases to a hot inferno of corrosive juices. It's my brother calling. I should feel relieved but strangely I'm not. I think my sixth sense is waking up. Lassie, go get help.

Enza puts Frank on hold while Christine digs deep into her bag, for what, I have no idea. Due to my intense powers of observation, this all happens in slow motion, like an action sequence in a John Woo movie. I stare at Christine's smooth hands, her thick brunette hair. I study the contour of the back of her knees directly above her sculpted calves. I begin to think about the body lying in the woods and its bare skin. I think of its hands torn apart. I remember the orange sky through the branches high overhead.

I am still fixated on the trees when I realize that Christine is talking to me in slow motion. She is pushing a document into my hands. The paper is covered in some scrawl I can't make out. This is the end. My brain is wasting. All the ground beef from all the burgers I've eaten in my life have finally turned into a massive blitz of mad cow. What once were words and letters on a page have turned into some mocking gibberish. I can't make sense of anything, the gibberish and Christine's facial expression. Suddenly, Enza is speaking to me through the intercom and growing ever more impatient.

It all rushes back into focus when Enza steps into the doorway and shouts, "Hey! Frank is on the phone."

At that very moment I look at Christine who looks at me. I look at the document which is obviously written in Arabic. Christine is about to say something when I turn and tell Enza, "I said I'd call him back."

"Next time say it out loud," she says, with one hand on her hip. And there is that steno pad again.

"I'll call him back."

Christine is staring at my license on the wall. Is she having second thoughts?

"You wanted me to call him, remember? He wants to hold."

"Hmm." It is obvious Christine is wondering what the hell she is doing in this idiot's office. "I'm sorry, Mrs. Flynn, I have to take this call. I can have someone look at this and I'll get back to you. Enza has a schedule of fees in her office, assuming of course we accept your case. Please excuse me." That's about as smooth as I get.

Christine stares at me as if I didn't say a word. She takes a deep breath while holding her blank stare.

"I don't know what to do." There are more tears and quiet whimpers. She drops her head.

I'm confounded. Here I think she is sincere in her grief, but then she puts on this act, complete with tears. Wait, are her eyes deceptively dry? Is she faking it? I take a bold step around my desk and reach over, gently lifting her chin. I look deep into her eyes and check carefully, because in a second I'm going to call her on the carpet and put an end to this B.S.

She looks up to me with her sad eyes running with tears, real tears. Crap. Now I have to say something and she's waiting for me to say it. "I have to take this call." That's not the voice of concern, but it's all I got.

"I'm not going anywhere until you help me." She again digs through her bag as I move toward the office door.

I think I'm being played. She has the look of someone who is unrehearsed, yet something isn't right. The "Christine had a little lamb" act can't last forever.

"Hmm." I look at Enza and she sort of gives Christine the 'You go, girl' expression. Enza glares at me as if I were the devil for trying to pull the eye bit back there. Clearly outnumbered, I excuse myself and take the call at Enza's desk.

I pick up the phone and watch as Enza and Christine begin their friendship. I have clearly lost a confidant and will be swimming against the current from here on out.

"Listen, Jack. Lucy didn't pick up her meds yesterday." My brother's deep impartial voice stirs up a bit of resentment in me like too many beers stirring up undigested pepperoni pizza. "Her money is sitting on my desk."

"I thought I was the one that called you?"

"Yeah, so what? Did you hear what I said?"

Lucy is our little sister. She is twenty-eight and she is supposed to have been the savior of our parent's marriage. Unfortunately she's become its biggest casualty. Lucy is now an outpatient at the Redwood Psychiatric Hospital in San Rafael and a current resident of the Redwood Counties Reintegration Facility.

I'm getting that sinking feeling. When she doesn't pick up her money, this means she didn't get her medication. She can't get her money without first picking up her medication so ordered by the court.

"I can't talk to you now. I have a client in my office, I found a dead body, and I have poison oak. I will have to call you back." My obstinate dog Charley has found her way to the office and now she is staring up at me.

"Lucy is in the wind. Call me back in five minutes." My brother hangs up without saying 'goodbye' because he knows he can't bill for it.

I look into my office. Enza is finally writing on the steno pad, and hopefully it's just a recipe for pecan pie. Christine hands Enza a business card and a cell phone. What else is she going to pull out of that bag?

"Cortisone." Christine closes a plastic tube into my hand. "You seem to be having some issues with your face."

"It's a little poison oak, that's all," I say with my back against the door frame. "It'll clear up in a few hours."

"It looks contagious," she says, staring at the area between my eyes and mouth.

"Poison oak," I say again.

"I've agreed to your terms and I gave Enza, who is very intelligent by the way and should be doing more than just answering phones, some pictures of my husband and a cell phone. Use it to call me or use it for anything related to my husband's case. I don't want to end up with a bunch of your incidental charges for which I have no recourse. Call me once you've figured out what this document is all about and let me know when you would like to leave for Peru. I'll make the arrangements. Thank you for your sympathy, but now I need your help."

I think I've just met Mrs. Hyde.

I look at Enza who is no help and has a huge smile on her face. Her arms are crossed with the steno pad pressed tightly beneath them. "I haven't decided that I am going to take your case, Mrs. Flynn." And I am on to you, I scream out loud in my head, and I have been to Peru and I don't need to go back.

"You're going to take it." Christine marches toward the door.

"How do you know?"

"Enza said so."

Christine disappears out the door as Enza pushes past me.

"What did you say to her?"

"I told her that you were the best man for the job and had actually worked abroad."

"Really?"

"No, not really, I told her you were desperate and needed the money. I'm going to lunch, then home." Enza grabs her purse and she too heads for the door.

Charley is sitting in the waiting area. She stares up at me.

Chapter Six

The funny thing is Enza is right. I do need the money. The boat needs to be hauled and painted, the bank owns most of my Audi SUV and the Suburban uses more fossil fuel than a small airline. I just have to figure a way to pay for it all.

So I work.

I like working, but I like not working more. I like getting up early and wandering into the office and reading the paper. I like going for a long lunch and having my one margarita. I like telling Enza I am cutting out early and then going to a movie to the old theatre across the street. I like tinkering endlessly on the boat, rebuilding water pumps and electric motors, cleaning the bilge, and polishing the stainless.

I don't call my brother back in five minutes or even ten. Charley and I walk down the street to the Good Neighbor hardware store for a cup of black tea and a newspaper.

Big Marty owns the Good Neighbor which is in an old historic schoolhouse kitty-corner to the city park. Big Marty drags out the trash barrels, aluminum ladders and redwood latticing from inside the store early every day regardless of the weather. He carefully arranges them in front of the windows across the width of the narrow store and then methodically sweeps the sidewalk. When the rains come down in sheets and the wind howls, Big Marty dons his rain gear and completes the drill by covering everything in heavy plastic. He never misses a day.

Inside the store the aisles are narrow and the shelves climb to the high open-beamed ceiling. Library ladders slide along the shelves among the stacks of open boxes which hold everything from nails to pipe fittings and electrical fixtures. The back wall is dedicated to marine supplies; encompassing varnishes, resins and all the necessities required to apply them. I have been known to stare at the wall for ten minutes at a time caught in a varnish induced stupor. I usually walk out of the store missing one crucial item which forces me to either return to the store or scrap the job and leave it for another day.

The central fixture in the store is the check-out counter shaped like a square bar, open in the center with two lift up sections. There are two registers on opposite corners. Marty still handwrites the receipts on the winding receipt machines and adds them on a calculator screwed to the counter. The registers are surrounded by flashlights, pens, screwdrivers, key fobs and a variety of candy bars. The countertops have been screwed, pounded, chipped, cracked, doodled, sanded, filled and varnished.

Next to the storeroom door a stained Mr. Coffee pumps out a daily ration of thick and often bitter construction-grade coffee. An assortment of personal mugs lines a shelf above the makeshift kitchen. A polished paint can filled with teabags shares a small counter with a microwave and a tiny sink.

I grab my ceramic sailor's head mug from the shelf, fill it with water and slip it into the microwave for a couple of minutes. Through the store's plate glass window I can see people stop to pet Charley. She acts like she cares more for perfect strangers. Sometimes I get the sense that she is using me.

The Good Neighbor is the unofficial coffee house for the real locals; the hill people and the boat people who live and work in Sausalito. This is where the people come down from the mountains and up from the sea. This is the proverbial longhouse of Sausalito. At the Good Neighbor the tea is always free, for me anyway. I tried to pay for it the first few times, but eventually I gave up. It took me a while to figure out my tea was free because of my father.

The few Saturdays I remember spending with my father we would come to the Good Neighbor with projects back at home always hanging in the balance between just started and never to be finished. We came here for a box of nails, wedges to keep the loose hammer head from sliding down the handle or a new ladder. My father was a sucker for a shiny new aluminum ladder. He had seven or eight ladders leaning against the side of the house.

My father rescued abandoned wood benches and old rowboats and dumped them next to piles of bicycles waiting for a new tube, seat or chain. He was good at building fences out of scrap lumber to cover up the eyesores around our yard. It wasn't long after Dad stopped building fences that he stopped coming home. His junk pile was cleared unceremoniously by a group of laborers when my mother sold the house.

I barely tolerated him. We fought on the dock and we fought on the water. It was all I could do to not work for him. He was on a case more often than not helping a perfect stranger. He spent every morning at the Good Neighbor. Don Brubaker traveled to crazy places and told elaborate tales. Don was the greatest liar that ever lived and he divorced my mother. I resented the neighbors waving to him. He saved big Marty more times than I can recall, so the tea is free.

I pull a barstool up to the counter and open whatever newspaper might be lying on there. A few customers wander about the store followed by Marty's minions, a couple of high school kids trained to answer questions and find solutions. While Marty's store is small compared to the big box stores in San Rafael, he has just about everything you would ever need. If he doesn't have what you are looking for, the minions are there to figure out how to make something else work in its place.

If you want to know what is happening in Sausalito, sit at this counter and in one morning you will know everything.

"You gonna put something on your face or do I have to put up some caution tape?" Big Marty's belly moves up and down when he laughs.

"I'm working on it," I say, frustrated by my appearance. I bury my face in my mug. The steam offers relief from the itch.

Big Marty has the widest and squarest shoulders of any man that I have ever met. He is not overly tall or overweight; just big. He has a short neck, a square mouth and a bald head. He is a pretty strange looking guy. He drinks a lot of coffee and eats donuts like a chain smoker smokes cigarettes.

Big Marty was always around when I was a kid. He was at my Holy Communion, my confirmation and every other Catholic excuse to serve cold cuts and drink from a rented keg. Whenever he saw the Brubaker kids he gave us his mother's mass card with a fresh folded twenty dollar bill paper-clipped to it. He still hands them out thirty years later.

"What are you working on? Anything exciting?" He speaks in a low grumble punctuated by the occasional rise in pitch, to make a point. He traces over the few drops of spilled tea with a thick bar towel.

"Actually, I have a few things going on; domestic infidelity, missing person, identity theft and a recently discovered dead body." I put down my paper, thinking he is going to let me talk a little shop.

"Same old, same old, some things never change, eh, Jack?" Big Marty lifts the countertop and sidles through before dropping it. "Watch your fingers and toes, kids." Marty walks to the front door and blocks it with his huge frame.

I never know what he is thinking as he watches the cars go by. I'd be thinking about the new big box stores in San Rafael, the lack of parking on Caledonia Street and Marty's nickel and dime size sales.

"So what is it, Marty?" I ask, after a long drag from Davey.

"I'm thinking how lucky cormorants are." Marty turns to face me, his silhouette casting a shadow on the open barrels of assorted nails.

"How's that?" How is it that Marty thinks about cormorants?

"They can fly for miles yet they can also swim under water for long periods of time and catch fish. That's pretty damn amazing. I don't know any master fishermen who can fly and stay under water for long periods of time."

"I never thought of it that way." Never, ever.

"It just proves that we can master more than one discipline, like you, for instance. Watch your fingers and toes." Marty lifts the countertop and sidles back into his fort.

I grab a chocolate cruller from the pink box. It's a knee jerk reaction when the spotlight shines on me. "What do you mean?" I do eat other things besides donuts and bagels, by the way.

"Not only are you a private investigator, you're a pretty damned competent sailor, too." Marty is flipping through index cards in a shoebox. He never looks me in the eye. He carries on an entire conversation while doing something else.

"I'm not that great a private detective. If I was, I wouldn't be sitting here right now. And I'm definitely not that good a sailor, you know that."

"You're as good a detective as you want to be, and sometimes you seem to want to be very good. As for sailing, shit happens, even to the best."

"Whatever you say, Marty." Through the front window, between the ladders and garbage cans, I can see the black Shar-Pei dog that sits in the open door of the frame shop across the street. His owner is inside cutting sheets of glass, adding the staples and fixing the wire. The Shar-Pei was bred to guard, and that's all they know. They sit and wait for the day they will be called up. Marty stands guard next to his ladders. He keeps his eyes open year in and year out and waits for the moment when he will be called to action, his role as guardian. My role is finding people, or at least, putting their seekers at peace.

I'm not sure what the body in the woods was here to do. He might have been put here to make someone a murderer. I am not yet sure why I found him and I may never know.

"Tell me about the body if you can, Jack." Marty is looking deep into his coffee, stirring in a spoonful of dry creamer.

"Sure, Marty."

This I can do. I like discussing some cases out loud. It helps me see things that I might have missed. Often times I see everything, I just store the observations deep in my subconscious. I watch the scene pass through my mind again, but with the dust knocked off the sounds are clear and the smells more distinct. I'm good at seeing things and places and describing them to a "T". I get into trouble when I have to look a little deeper, beneath the surface. I have trouble seeing people for who they really are.

The store is empty except for the minions. I keep some details to myself rather than start a run of rumors. I tell Marty how I found the body. I don't tell him that I was on the tennis player's property or about the dabbling nip and tuck doctor. Those are details that can get me in trouble. Marin is a small place, too small to be dropping names.

I tell him in detail about the terrain: the trees and rolling hills, the canyon and the creek at the bottom. I think about the possible entrances to the canyon where one might carry a badly mangled body. I think about the possibility that the person walked back there with the killer and then was murdered. This I put out of my mind because of the severity of the disfigurement. I tell Marty about Ellen Jacobs and Tom Ricketts. He has followed some of Jacob's cases in the papers and he isn't impressed and he never approved of Tom when we were kids but that was before Tom became a pilot and a cop.

Marty listens intently while sorting the drill bit display. I tell him about the Tiburon police and the county sheriffs. I scan the shop looking at the possible tools one might use to twist a human body. There are lengths of rope, sledge hammers and reciprocating saws. There are rolls of plastic, chainsaws, come-alongs and barrels of chain.

"How would you do it, Marty?" I finish the last few sips of tea.

"I'd use my goddamned bare hands." He shoots a look to the minions who are listening a little too closely. "Get back to work."

The pimply teens scramble.

"That's where I'm at. No signs of tools, footprints, or a sign of struggle. The body was dumped, but it lacked the usual trappings one might find: plastic, duct tape, tarps and blood."

"It was also dumped far from a road," Marty adds.

"Exactly. Most bodies are dumped a few feet from where one might open the trunk of a car or drop the tailgate of a pickup truck. Once I determine how the body got there, the floodgates are going to open up."

"You sound like you're a cop assigned to the case."

"It's plain curiosity."

"If I were them, I'd bring you in on the Q.T." Marty sees someone looking at the oak barrel planters on the sidewalk.

Oh, they'll bring me in all right, into the gas chamber. I can see the small room at the end of a red carpet getting closer as I wave to the witnesses.

The cell phone vibrates itself across the counter. Frank is calling.

Chapter Seven

"Lucy is missing again," Frank barks into my ear.

I take the phone outside and meet Charley. I feed her the rest of my donut as we walk along Caledonia Avenue. Frank has done some checking already. He called the hospitals in Marin and Petaluma, as well as the police departments. They know Lucy but they haven't seen her recently.

"What about Mom?" I ask, knowing that it's a stretch. Our mother was last seen in the arms of an Army veteran named Vic, driving off in a huge Winnebago with a license plate frame that says, 'Back off, Jack off!'

"I called her in Mobile on her mobile."

"That's funny. I think you said something funny, Frank. I am not sure you meant it, but it was funny."

"It just turned out that way. Vic and Mom are visiting some of Vic's kids down there in Alabama. They haven't heard from Lucy in ages."

"Lucy's done this before, Frank. I am a bit more concerned about my own predicament right now."

"Maybe I can help you with your situation so that you can help Lucy."

I explain my situation to Frank, beginning with the photos of the plastic surgeon and his concubine, the security detail that chased me through the woods and the murder of crows. Frank listens hard without interrupting.

One of Frank's best traits is listening. He hears and remembers every word. He swallows them, digests them and then spits out apt legal strategies. In this case his only concern is that I not meet with the county investigators without an attorney present. He gives me the number of a stand-up guy in San Rafael. But I know that Frank will be the man pulling the ropes from behind the big curtain.

He and I have always been at odds with regard to Lucy. He is of the mindset that we should catch her when she falls, while I believe we should only be there to pick her up. He wants me to watch her more closely, believing that my relaxed schedule allows me more chances to get away. He blames his schedule on his inability to make the round-trip to San Rafael. There's a thick forest of guilt surrounding Lucy, and the bottom line is, she's missing.

Lucy has a few haunts that I know about through contacts at the hospital and the local police. She usually runs with the same crowd. The police can't do much more than keep an eye out for her on the streets, so it's up to me to dig a little deeper. The last time she went missing we found her spending the weekend in a friend's yurt in the Mendocino Mountains. She was not happy when she learned that we had mounted a search for her when she wasn't really missing at all. At the time, Lucy was just getting away from San Rafael, which can be a dangerous place for people who live on the fringe.

Recently, Lucy's been living in a halfway house. We thought she was safe there. Frank and I agree that I need to go up to the valley north of the city to take a look around, turn over a few rocks and kick in a few doors (not really…but maybe).

~ * ~

I'm back in the Audi. I put the two cell phones on the seat next to me. Charley is comfortable in the back on a plush dog bed. I drive through town and pass more docks to my left and a couple of popular hotels on my right. The hotels climb several stories up the steep hillside and remind me of Amalfi or Positano, Italy, but without the charm among other things. Tourist traffic creeps along as I enter the shopping district. This place loads up with the lunch crowd which steps off the ferry and walks the few steps to the ice cream shops and gift shops crowded with discounted fleece and ornamental blown glass.

The road opens up as we follow the waterfront passed Ondine restaurant with its unobstructed view of the Belvedere, Angel Island and the city. Small businesses give way to a motley group of houses.

I park illegally in front of Santa's house, a small cottage built into the hillside. The words "Santa's House" are painted on the roof in white letters five feet tall.

Santa's real name is Dolliver and Dolliver is real nuts. He struts around town with his signature goosestep and wears an open white trimmed Santa's coat. Dolliver's lived in this tiny little bungalow across the street from the bay for thirty years or more. He retired from the Navy and is spending his retirement writing for military trade journals. For the past ten years he's been the perennial shorts-wearing Santa of Sausalito.

I'm not sure how a person can go from a disciplined government lifestyle to wearing a Santa suit in the middle of summer, but this is how it happened.

Dolliver bought into an all-night poker game in the backroom of Smitty's bar and couldn't meet his mark. Rather than get slapped around by the local heavies, Dolliver was shamed into wearing a Santa suit for the annual boat parade.

Nobody else would do it. It was a ridiculous job that was hard to fill. One year they offered to clear the volunteer's unpaid parking tickets as an incentive. That year Santa was a twenty-year-old community college student.

In Dolliver's reign he was surrounded by a crew of ten dwarfs dressed as elves on a little sailboat that cruised down the main channel. Leading an armada of sailboats, motor yachts and kayaks all draped in Christmas lights, Dolliver, drunk on Gordon's gin, stood on the bow and waved to the crowd lining the waterfront. A short-statured dwarf named Hal was at the helm. Hal couldn't see over the eight tiny plastic reindeer lashed to the lifelines, let alone see over Dolliver teetering on the bow.

When it happened, it happened fast. The boat slammed into a channel marker. Dolliver was launched overboard like a barrel from the deck of the Orca. Nine dwarves rushed to his aid but couldn't hoist him out of the water. Somebody who wasn't drinking all day got a line to him, and for more than five minutes a bunch of little hands was locked on to his arms but they just couldn't get him out of the water. It was a frightful sight, seeing all those little people in pointy shoes and floppy hats waving for help. I thought it was all part of an act, a little oompah-loompah dance number. The hard driving beat of the Bee Gees pumping out over loudspeakers didn't help either. The little elfin cries for help got lost in Barry Gibb's high notes.

Everyone raced toward him in dinghies and sailboats as Dolliver just bobbed up and down, waiting to die. Finally, a local crab fisherman came by, hooked a line around his chest and hoisted him out, depositing him on his boat's slimy aft deck.

To this day, Dolliver credits the Santa coat for heading off hypothermia and saving his life, but I credit the crab fisherman and Dolliver's point two-seven blood alcohol content. The coat is a little worn now, but he still wears it proudly. He still marches around town and he still waves to all the tourists. The dwarves were never asked back.

I peer in Dolliver's window and pound on the door long enough for any normal human to get from one end of a thousand square foot house to the other.

I figure he is out seeing who is being naughty or nice. I remove Christine Flynn's letter from my pocket and add a quick note about translation and Santa's friends down in the military. I also include a short list of what I want for Christmas....not really.

I stuff the envelope into the mail slot in the front door. I knock once more.

"Put your hands out where I can see 'em and step away from the door."

The reflection in the Dutch front door reveals an utter horror. It's not Santa in his furry red coat with yellowed lining and juniper breath standing behind me, it's his ex-girlfriend Shirley, the Sausalito Man-Hater. I do as I'm told because she's boat people and boat people pack the heat: well-oiled Smith and Wessons, Glocks, and Colt forty-fives.

"Come on now, Shirley?" Shirley's got the crazy-eyed thing going with just a hint of matted hair and running mascara. "Where's your gun?"

"The man's got it up at county but I don't need it." She pushes harder.

"I can see that."

"Listen, you ugly queer." She quickly looks over her shoulder for the 'Man,' who took her firearm away per her latest restraining order, "I'm not screwing around anymore. You took my Dolliver away and turned him into a gay Santa."

"Whoa, whoa, whoa," I protest, waving my hands.

"I bet you that's what he says when you're sticking your…"

"That's enough, Shirley. Watch the language." She quickly looks away and back again, allowing me just enough time to grab the oar and push it with the full force of my two hundred and ten pounds into her chest. She goes down. Her head smacks the pavement pretty hard. For a brief moment I feel bad. I don't like it when people get hurt, even when it's a whacked-out delusional.

Shirley looks up at me in disbelief. "You are a son of a bitch." She sits up.

I've still got the oar. A crowd of tourists are looking at me from the walking path across the street. People start shouting for the police. I stand here with the weapon in my hands as a do-gooder pulls out his cell phone and begins to dial. He'll never get a signal.

"Are you okay, young lady?" A pale-legged behemoth wearing a yellow "Golden Gate" fleece vest with the sales tag still on it makes his way across the street.

I keep my cool. I know Shirley and this guy doesn't.

Shirley gets to her feet while rubbing the back of her head. Spit trickles down from the corners of her mouth. I keep the oar pointed at her as she steps back.

"Put the oar down, buddy. Is this man hurting you, ma'am?" This guy is obviously not from around here. The Samaritan has left his wife on the opposite curb and marched over thinking he is going to help a 'little lady' in trouble.

"This is none of your business, big bird!" She says pointing at his wife, "Go back to your fat inbred sister and have your man sex, you perverted freaks."

I knew she couldn't resist. This is why we call her the Sausalito Man-Hater.

This decent, ruddy-faced, God-fearing man clearly shifts his confused expression toward me and looks for some sort of explanation.

I give him a shrug.

She turns to the slightly bloated and flummoxed man. "You

molested me." Now she is shouting, "Molester! Molester! You molested me!"

The man tries to calm her while his wife takes off down the street covering her ears. As if in slow motion, he slowly places his hand on Shirley's shoulder.

"I wouldn't touch her if I were you," I say, dropping the oar to my side.

There are no words to describe the look on this guy's face when he realizes that he has just been sucked into, what will probably be, the worst vacation memory of his life; one that he will carry to his grave.

The kicks come fast and furious. She lays into his pasty white legs just below the cuffs of his shorts.

"He tried to have ugly man sex with me," she shouts with her hands on her hips, as she tries to kick the crap out of him. It's as if he got too close to one of the River dancers in a blind rage.

She maintains the insults at the top of her lungs and lets one more kick go just a little higher, just high enough to ruin a man's week. Just high enough to make an old hernia scar open up like pita bread at a Lebanese restaurant. Without so much as a breath, without so much as a sneer, she waves her fist over the fallen hero and then moves off into the parting crowd and disappears, leaving a cloud of mutterings and curses hanging in the air.

The man looks up to me as if I were party to his attack; as if this is some street performance and he's expected to toss a dollar into an open guitar case.

I have nothing to say. I extend the oar and the man grabs it and pulls himself up to his feet. Dumbfounded, he turns toward his wife who is heading down the street and hobbles after her tossing out "honeys" and "dears". She keeps going.

The crowd turns away and all is well again on the waterfront. Charley never gives it another thought. I, on the other hand, am shocked to hear Dolliver's door open.

"Is she gone?" With his fluffy Santa hat askew, Dolliver is standing in the doorway holding my envelope.

Chapter Eight

"Why didn't you let me in?" I lean the oar against the door.

"How do you think I feel? I've been stuck in here all morning." Dolliver studies the envelope as he follows me in. "Why don't you go upstairs. I'll get you some tea."

"No thanks on the tea. I stopped at Big Marty's." I look around the room and things haven't changed a bit since the last time I was here, save for another neat stack of magazines.

"Big Marty's father was a Mussolini henchman. You know that?" Dolliver shakes his head as if I should know better.

The walls are lined with bookshelves. Every corner has a stack of magazines or videos. A few sailing paintings are on the walls, as well as the usual brass gauges, clocks, and candlesticks one would expect to see in this nautical town. "I think we're pretty safe with Big Marty." I say.

"He's just waiting in the wings."

"Where's the telescope?"

"Upstairs," he says, scratching at his beard while he pours hot water into a stainless coffee mug.

I climb the narrow spiral staircase to a small room with a wall of French doors facing the water…and a telescope. Missing are the stacks of periodicals and dusty lamps shades. This room has a desk and a sofa that both face the water. A flat screen monitor and keyboard are the only items on the desk. Behind it, against the back wall, a credenza holds several banks of CPUs, a police radio and a printer/FAX/scanner.

I'm drawn to the telescope. It takes only a moment for me to have my right eye pressed against the eyepiece. I swing the long brass instrument around. A narrow band of Angel Island crosses the lens. I skip over the turn of the century immigration buildings, the battered remains of a pier and barely visible dirt road cut into the hillside. I pass over the rough waters of the Raccoon Straits and land on the distant Tiburon hillside. A helicopter hovers high above the hill. A group of windshields reflect the sunlight back into my eye.

"See any clues?" Dolliver asks, rubbing his chin. He has a gravelly voice. He keeps his white hair short, but not buzzed. His cheeks are rosy with gin blossoms.

"I don't know what you're talking about."

"I wasn't born yesterday." Dolliver points to the police radio.

"The investigation is ongoing," I say as I return the cover to the eyepiece.

"How's the love life, Bru?"

"Come on, Dolliver." He knows that I don't talk about that, but he asks every time without fail.

"It's a roller coaster, ain't it?" Dolliver puts his hands out in front of him like he's holding the safety bar. "Clack. Clack. Clack. You're going up that hill and looking forward to a wild ride." He jerks his head back. "Clack. Clack. Clack. Then you realize the first hill is a lot steeper than you thought. Crap. You're scared. What did you get yourself into? You want to turn around but then you're being seduced into this ride and you kind of like it." Dolliver is leaning back, looking up at the ceiling. "Then you reach the top and you start over it, but because there are so many cars behind you, you jerk slowly over the crest. Clack...Clack... You have all the time in the world to study your freefall into the abyss. You're at the top and there doesn't seem to be anything new. Hell, you got the girl already, but what do you do now?" Dolliver is leaning over and looking at the floor. "Clack, then whoosh. You're free, and you're racing down so fast and steep, your eyes are open but you can't see anything. You're blind, man. All you can think about is what makes you happy, and she isn't it." Dolliver's arms reach for the ceiling, and he hoots wildly. "Here comes a turn and another hill. Finally, all you want to do is get off this crazy thing. Then you shit your pants." Dolliver collapses in his chair. "That's love my friend. It's a goddamned roller coaster." Dolliver waits for me to say something. "An E-ticket ride."

"Gotcha," I say, nodding toward the computer.

"Right." Dolliver is already pounding the keys with his gnarled arthritic hands. Band-aids wrap a few fingers while scabs cover others. He pulls the letter out of the envelope that I carefully placed it in earlier. He takes a quick glance and then spins around in his chair and places the Arabic letter onto the flatbed scanner. With another press of a key, the laser scans the document.

"Whoa, aren't you a little cavalier about losing possible DNA evidence?" I say as he flattens the letter out on his desk.

"Yeah right," he says. With a big bloodshot eye behind a magnifying glass, he scans the fibers, the tiny wrinkles and microscopic valleys. He removes a pair of tweezers from his desk drawer to prod a little closer; pick up a little hair or an eyelash maybe.

"A hair," Dolliver says, studying it against a small desk light.

"Really?" I move behind the desk and peer ever closer. He turns it slowly beneath the glass. The hair is grey and long with a slight curl at its end. "Interesting."

I don't know what to say. Who is the guy? Was Christine's husband graying? Could this be the hair of the victim or the perpetrator?

"Whose could it be?" I say, leaning over his shoulder now.

"It's mine. It fell out of my nose. Sure as hell is long, isn't it?"

Nice.

Dolliver zeros in on the letter. "It's like searching for a needle in a haystack."

"How's that?"

"This probably has prints all over it, but nobody to match them to. It has more DNA evidence than the inside of a White Ford Bronco. The document was recently printed and then roughed with clean hands. It's as if the creator was going to throw it away and began to ball it up, but stopped. Do you know where this letter came from, Bru?" Now he turns to the computer screen where the image of the letter is criss-crossed with lines. English words in red hover over every other Arabic word.

"A woman named Christine Flynn. She said it belonged to her husband, who has since gone missing." I twist my wristwatch.

"Nervous?"

"Anxious."

Through the open doors, I watch a sailboat racing away from the city. Wind from Hurricane Gulch rushes down the canyons here and attempts to blow the struggling crew back to San Francisco. "I've never met her before today. She said she had heard of me through my brother. It's a friend of a friend thing. She'll check out."

"This letter doesn't. I'm running it through my basic translator but it's having a little trouble with some of the more technical language. There is a new version of this translator sitting in the military's computer at the International Language Institute in Monterey, but I can't get at it until later tonight." Dolliver gives me a big smile. He likes to act like a dangerous criminal, when point of fact he is only involved in high-tech mail fraud.

"What does check out?" I lean over his shoulder and stare at his flat screen.

"It's Arabic, contemporary, almost western in wording, almost. I'm not trained for this stuff. If it was about guns, bombs and the *Intifada,* there'd be no problem, but it's some sort of business document."

"Is there anything there?"

"Probably, but you've got to call me tonight after the library closes."

"Library?"

"International Institute."

"Right." I hand him my business card with my cell phone number. He must have tens of my cards by now. I look out toward Tiburon and the helicopter is gone.

Dolliver walks me to his door and scans the front walk for Shirley.

"If you want my advice, Jack, I'd forget the letter and go right to the source. The wife probably threw him in the bay. Follow the wife. Hell, I paid your Dad to follow all of mine."

Chapter Nine

I left the letter with Dolliver for "further examination", as he put it. I'm not counting on the letter to solve the issue of the missing husband, but it may give us a few clues or at least lend a new perspective to the investigation.

I believe everything happens for a reason and that there is no such thing as coincidence. I believe that the cosmos all around us is willing and able to help us if we were only able to tap into it. And I believe that the cosmos sometimes taps into us. The tapping starts when Charley and I pass through San Rafael on the way to Lucy's last known whereabouts. The cell phone rings. It's Detective Jacobs.

"Where are you?"

"Doesn't anyone in your line of work begin a conversation with 'Hello, how are you?'? You all act like this is the first death in the county's history."

"It's the first human mutilation in the county's history and it's not the first time you've been found with a dead body, is it?"

She seems to know more about me than I know about her. Note to self: never start a fight with someone you've never seen in battle before. "What do you want, Jacobs?"

"We need you to come in."

"When? Today?" I pass the county seat on the hillside to the east of the 101. It's the only county office in the country designed by Frank Lloyd Wright. It was designed to disappear into the hillside of rolling oak, but the bright blue tile roof gives it away. It's like the government wanted a stealth building from which they could watch over their taxpayers. I think Frank was pretty adamant about the blue roof. I don't think he was fond of a camouflage system of government.

"Now," she says.

"I've got my dog." I clench the steering wheel with white knuckles. The urge to scratch my face is overwhelming.

"Find a sitter."

I think Jacobs has a cruel side. "For how long?"

"It depends on what you tell us. Where are you? We can send a driver."

A driver? What a polite way of saying, 'we'll send the SWAT team out to break down your door, drag you out from under your bed and parade you across your neighbor's lawn in your underwear'.

"Will I be under arrest?" I move into the fast lane and pick up the pace.

"Not by definition."

"That's because I am not in your custody, but the moment I am, will I be under arrest?" She pushes, I push back.

"No. You are wanted for questioning. Why don't you come in?"

"And if I don't?"

"You'll become a person of interest."

"Aren't you being a little forward?"

"How's this for forward, we'll get a warrant."

"Then wake up the judge."

"It's three o'clock."

"It's an expression." Click. That's me ending the call. I have some things to do before I go work pro bono for the government.

The traffic thickens on the 101. Charley and I creep along in a sea of cars. It's like a million horizontal elevators with all the passengers staring straight ahead. I exit the 101 in Novato. I thought about what Ellen said about Charley. I have a feeling that I better drop her off at my brother's house. If they stop me I'm not sure what they would do with her.

My brother and his family live at the end of a cul-de-sac in an oak shaded neighborhood just outside of town. Their house is modeled after an old California bungalow, except the term bungalow is an understatement. It has a rolling lawn, a swing, and a multi-car garage.

Luckily, no one is home. I'm not prepared to make small talk or answer direct questions from the nephews and nieces.

My brother's wife, Pepper, is doing the soccer mom circuit. I leave

Charley on the front porch with a full water bowl. I tell her to stay, and that's where she'll be until someone comes home. She knows the routine.

I spin the car around and I head back to San Rafael. Rolling oak covered hills rise up around the suburban towns as an ever widening freeway covers the level landscape. I exit near the Terra Linda section of town. From here I will head down a narrow highway to the outskirts, where they put the halfway houses.

I think about Christine. I think about the body in the woods. I keep trying to do the math, but I can't figure out what killed the person. I think about how my quiet life turned into a circus in a matter of hours. I wake up next to a mystery, I meet a beautiful distraught woman, a scary detective, and my sister disappears.

Not far from the highway is the Redwood Counties Reintegratio n Facility. Lucy has lived here on and off over the last year since her latest arrest for possession.

Lucy suffers from multiple personality disorder; she refers to herself as crazy. Lucy used drugs in an effort to quiet the voices, but the drugs created all new ones. Frank and I bailed her out of jail more than once. We even put shoes on her feet, only for her to sell them the very next day. She is troubled.

The house itself is a converted farmhouse set back on several acres. A gravel driveway leads up to the house which is fronted by a large porch. Several of the residents are sitting on benches, no doubt counting the beer trucks that pass by on the highway.

I'm met in a sterile living area by the house mother, Glenda. She is tall and intimidating. I follow her to her small windowless office.

"Lucy was really doing well. We were very surprised when she didn't come home." On the wall behind Glenda there is a large poster of two kittens hanging on a clothesline and captioned, "Hang in there". "She was never late, never broke curfew. She was improving," she says in a motherly deep voice.

In the end, I haven't done a thing for Lucy. She has done it all herself and I have merely been a reluctant witness. I can't make Lucy do anything she doesn't want to do. I can only try to prove to her that she is not alone.

"Did she have a job?" Most facilities like this are tied into state work-release programs.

"She was working at the Mexican restaurant in Novato, but then she took a job at a similar place in San Rafael. It's a lot closer."

"How did she get to work every day?"

"The bus line stops at the corner every morning and evening. Lucy had the lunch shift and the start of the dinner shift. She was back every night before ten."

"Would Lucy have had an opportunity to leave the premises other than for the purpose of work?"

"On our residents' days off we arrange a van to the mall in Terra Linda or the factory outlet stores in Petaluma. We encourage our residents to learn how to spend and budget. It will eventually help them when they leave here. We also arrange trips to the beach and a favorite horse ranch nearby. My boys and girls are not in prison, Mr. Brubaker. They are recovering from poor life management."

"Do you remember Lucy's state of mind the day she disappeared?"

"As I said, she was doing very well. She kept to her meds schedule and seemed generally happy. She was slogging through this and was determined to complete her time here."

"That is good to hear. May I see Lucy's room?"

"No, I'm sorry. We've already filled the room." Glenda looks at her watch.

The guise of caring has rubbed off to reveal just another hotel stay without the honor bar.

"Did Lucy leave anything behind?"

"There's a small box of personal items in a storage locker in the garage. I can have someone go with you."

"I would appreciate it."

"Mr. Brubaker, I can't let you take anything. Those are her personal effects and must be kept here until she either returns or sends for them. Please, look but don't take."

"Glenda, when did you realize she was missing?"

"Saturday night. She missed her curfew."

"When was the last time you saw her?"

"Saturday morning. She had brewed an ice tea and had a large muffin. She liked the cranberry ones. Lucy was going to work."

"You have a good memory."

"For the useless things, I guess. I honestly couldn't tell you the state capitol of Montana."

"Helena."

"It's Glenda." She snaps and glares at me as if I were the biggest jackass in her office.

"I was saying that Helena is the capitol of Montana. Sorry." Glenda has found me out and now she thinks I am a jerk. She re-aims her steady glare with much more intensity.

"I am sorry to pester you, but I have a couple more questions."

"Don't worry about it."

"Do you remember what Lucy was wearing when she left?"

"No idea, except that she always wore the house sweatshirt, maybe jeans. I think that's all she had."

"Did she leave any clothes behind? If she did, we might be able to deduce exactly what she was wearing when she left."

"I'm sorry, Mr. Brubaker, but as I said, she only left behind a small box of personal items."

"So, do you remember her leaving with a tea, a muffin and possibly a large duffel bag of clothes?"

"I am not an idiot, Mr. Brubaker. I do not know what she did with her clothes. She may have given them away. She may have been wearing every piece. I simply do not know."

"I apologize, ma'am. I am not accusing you or this institution of any impropriety. I am merely trying to determine her mental state when she left and what she was wearing. The fact that her clothes are not here suggest that her departure might have been planned." And that, Glenda - I do not know your last name - is good news to me because it reduces the chances that she might have met with an untimely fate.

Glenda pushes her chair back from her desk. She pushes a few buttons on the telephone and then speaks into the receiver, "Arnie, I need you to take someone to the garage." The intercom echoes through the halls.

"Did Lucy have a man she was seeing?"

"Not that I know of. There were a few men here, but not for her. She was a lot higher caliber than the dirt bag assholes that stay here. We wouldn't allow it anyway."

"Thank you again." Men are definitely a tricky subject with Glenda.

"I just hope little Lucy is doing okay."

Arnie, maybe in his early twenties, drags his right side into the office. It is obvious that he was a victim of a paralyzing malady.

"Arnie, this is Mr. Brubaker. He will need to see Lucy's stuff." Arnie turns and leaves when I stand up to follow.

I lean into Glenda. "What happened to Arnie?"

"He's on a very slow recovery from a stork."

"You mean stroke?"

"No, I mean stork. He was attacked by a migrating sand hill crane. They can reach five feet in height and have very sharp beaks. Damn near killed him." She nods her head, somewhat stork like.

"Glenda, there is one last thing. Why didn't you call me last week when Lucy didn't return?"

"It's very simple. You're not on the list. Good luck, Mr. Brubaker." Glenda has something on the tip of her tongue, but she lets it go.

"May I ask who is?"

"I am not at liberty to say, but maybe if you have asked me the same question months ago, we wouldn't be talking right now."

I nod. Lucy had been in a good place, albeit a cold, corporate one.

Chapter Ten

I follow Arnie, very slowly, down the sterile hall. I'm in one of those classic situations where you want to pass someone, but you can't. I am practically breathing down his neck, but he refuses to pick up the pace. This could drag on forever, literally.

Before we ever reach the back door I think about my conversation with Glenda. Lucy was fine when she left and not under duress. She didn't leave any clothes behind unless, of course, Glenda was wearing them right there in front of me, but I have a feeling she was telling the truth. Sometimes it is easier to forget about something than try to figure it out. I think Glenda may have asked the clothes question herself, but let it go after not finding a simple solution.

I'm hoping that this was a planned getaway, but I'm also wondering why I wasn't on the list. Frank was on the list, but I wasn't on the list. Dolliver was probably on the list.

Arnie opens the garage door. The old nag of a garage with a sagging roof has been turned into the lost and found department. Several aisles of steel shelves hold cardboard boxes, hairdryers, stereos, and piles of books. Each aisle is marked alphabetically. I find Lucy's small cardboard box in the first row. I take the box outside and sit down on a bench next to the driveway.

Arnie drags his right foot in the gravel making shapes that resemble crop circles. He hasn't looked up from the ground since I met him in Glenda's office.

I remove the lid and find the contents are disorganized. There are several small beanie baby-type plush toys that I remove and place on the bench next to me. Lucy was never one to play with dolls. More often than not she chased after her older brothers on the baseball field or in the hills behind our house. I imagine that she might have earned these in a reward program in one of the many facilities in which she lived. I understand why she might want something soft and gentle in this sterile world.

There are several Polaroid pictures of people I don't recognize, but judging by the backgrounds, they're probably of friends she met here. I make a mental note of their faces. They're old and young, and male and female. Glenda was right about the men; complete dirt bags. I hope Lucy didn't take off with any of them.

There are plastic leis and several strings of Mardi Gras beads. In addition there are several books, including a Nancy Drew mystery.

I turn to Arnie, who is very involved with his circles. "Arnie, can you help me for a moment?"

Arnie sidles over to me. He's nods. Arnie is holding his hands close to his stomach. His pants are baggy and his t-shirt is too small.

"Arnie, do you know any of these people?" I show him the photos. He nods at all of them. "Are any of these people still staying here?"

"They're all gone a long time ago." Arnie says clearly, without any delay.

"When did they leave?" I ask.

"Well, some left maybe a year ago and a couple died here."

"How?" I am caught off guard by his candor. Could the facility be responsible for Lucy's death?

"They killed themselves!"

Crap, I think to myself. "What about Lucy? Did you know Lucy? Where did she go?"

"I liked Lucy. She was nice to me. She didn't belong here."

"What happened to Lucy, Arnie?" Arnie was drooling now. He probably isn't used to talking. He has a half smile on his face as if he was remembering Lucy right now.

"She left Saturday. She's not coming back."

"How do you know, Arnie?"

"Because she said so."

"Do you know where she went?"

"She didn't say."

"Does she have a boyfriend?"

"I was her boyfriend." A smile grows across Arnie's face as he returns to his crop circles.

"Did she leave with anyone?"

"No."

I look again at the Nancy Drew book she left behind.

Before Lucy became a teenager, before things became confusing, she would wedge her little body on the narrow shelf in the bay window of her bedroom and read Nancy Drew from start to finish. She was happy and normal then. She was small and boney, but strong and feisty. Lucy used to grab my arm to drag me off somewhere. When I resisted, she would bare her teeth and growl. I always relented.

On those rainy days when I had read everything in the house and had nothing left - no cereal boxes or TV guides - I read Lucy's Nancy Drew's.

A last look reveals several more books of little significance and a few folded magazine clippings. I move them aside and find a bundle of letters tied together with ribbon.

I unfold the magazine clippings. There are about ten full pages of travel photos of the South Pacific with turquoise water, palm trees and corals reefs. The pages resemble every person's dream of an escape to a deserted island. The clippings may have been taped to her wall in her dormitory, providing the only beauty in her life. I fold them and return them to the box.

I remove the letters. The first letter I open is from my father. A short note tells of family events and is signed, "Love Daddy". I look through the remaining letters and find them all to be from my father. They're all dated, with the final one being right before his death. The first letter was optimistic. Dad held out for her intended return to a normal life. The postmarks were from Mexico, Hawaii and everywhere else he traveled for work. I never knew that my father wrote letters. I never knew he cared so much for Lucy.

While Arnie concentrates on the ground in front of him, I transfer the small bundle to my jacket pocket. I look at Arnie with his hunched posture and his intense concentration on the ground beneath him. Using his lame right foot, he has created a dramatic gravel circle ten feet across with an incredibly straight line that intersects several smaller perfect circles. It resembles something from a Japanese Zen garden.

I return the box to the shelf. Arnie brings down the garage door.

"Thank you, Arnie. I'll show myself out."

Arnie nods and drags his right foot across the gravel, destroying his elaborate design, and returns to the house. I follow the driveway out to my car. I remove the letters from my pocket and put them on the passenger seat next to me. I can only hope that there might be some clue to my sister's disappearance hidden somewhere in the letters.

Chapter Eleven

I drive the five miles through the rolling ranches and the patchwork of fence lines that surround Marin's western flank back to San Rafael, where Lucy held her last job. The trees that line downtown San Rafael are leafed out in brilliant green, and the people seem to wander from shop to shop, never noticing the beauty above their heads.

I park my car at the center of town where I begin my search. I consider the letters one more time before putting them in the glove compartment.

San Rafael is the small urban center of Marin community. The town's make-up has changed over the years, from fishermen, to hippies and yuppies, to techies from the city. A small group of buildings include the usual bank and post office, a real estate office, and the restaurant where Lucy worked. Nearby are several restored historic homes occupied by a small market, antique stores and a bar or two.

The restaurant is open but empty. A young waitress responds to the bell that rings when I open the door. She grabs a menu from the end of the counter and offers, "You can sit anywhere."

I think about eating. I'm hungry but I want to keep moving forward.

"Actually, I'm not here to eat. I'm looking for someone."

The waitress has the expression on her face that one gets when they aren't doing anything, but might feel obliged to do something. The cook peers at me through the service window of the kitchen. I have stirred up a bit of suspicion.

"There's nobody here but us. Look around."

"I can see that. I'm looking for Lucy Brubaker."

"We don't talk to cops," she puts her hands on her ample hips.

"I'm her brother." I look over to the kitchen, but the cook is no longer there.

"How do I know? Got any I.D.? Otherwise, man, take off."

The cook comes through the kitchen door, wringing his hands in a dish towel. "Who's this guy, Rayleen?"

"He's says he's Lucy's brother."

"I'm just looking for Lucy." I show my business card to the hard-faced waitress. She takes it in her hand. I notice a tattoo on the skin between her thumb and her index finger. It's an ugly prison tattoo.

"Is he for real?" The cook takes my card from Rayleen.

"Looks like it. Go back to the soup, Kevin. You got to get it done."

"Whatever." Kevin turns to the door in slow motion. He moves like he's got all day or all year.

"It would be great if you could answer a few questions about her."

"I don't have much time. I'm getting ready for the dinner rush."

I think Rayleen might be delusional. There aren't enough people in town to fill the restaurant, let alone create a wait list.

"I tell you this…she never showed up on her last shift. I had to handle the whole place by myself. I never heard from her either way. She just up and left."

"Do you remember when that was? What day?" I knew I had to develop a timeline.

"Maybe it was Tuesday or Wednesday. Who the hell knows?"

"Do you know if Kevin knows?"

"Kevin would be lucky to know his own name." She turns to look at Kevin, who is staring into a red hot heat lamp.

I can smell marijuana smoke escaping from the kitchen.

"Damn it, Kevin, you're supposed to wait for me," she calls out to the kitchen.

"Did she tell you anything; like where she might be going or if she was planning a vacation or trip?"

"Junkies like her don't go on vacation. They just disappear."

It is all I can do to keep from leaping on the slacker chick and ringing her neck. "My sister was not a junkie."

"Whatever." Rayleen turns the last of her attention to me. "Go ask Manny down at the Crushing Season. He probably saw her last. Go find Manny. I gotta go."

"Call the number on the card if she turns up. I'll make it worth your while." I can't stand to be in the presence of this woman any longer.

Rayleen stuffs my card into a jar of business cards on the counter and shoots me a dirty look.

With that, the bell rings again as I walk out the door.

The Crushing Season is a bar just down the road. It never seemed to make it with the well-heeled crowd and has settled for the wage earners and a few of the nefarious locals. It's a decent place to find a dirt bag, if that's what you are looking for and I guess this Manny guy fits the bill.

Weekdays, the Crushing Season is filled with the degenerates who drink all day, pass out and get into trouble at night. They beat their wives, fall down in the street, and crash their buddy's cars.

It's almost impossible to see inside on a sunny day. The contrast in light is so extreme that they make you for a cop or a Narc the moment you open the door. Most of the patrons sit with their heads hanging down over their drinks. I don't blame them. There is nothing more depressing than drinking in the middle of a weekday in a small town where change comes along once in a long while.

As I split the saloon doors open, I still can't see anything as my eyes struggle to adjust. I accidentally bump a few heads with my elbow as I walk down the narrow aisle between the bar and a row of tables. I know I hit somebody pretty hard, but the guy doesn't say a word. He's either on parole, doesn't want to start anything or just doesn't feel it yet. I walk straight to the back of the bar, where I pull out a dart from a Donald Trump dartboard and place it behind my ear.

"I'm looking for someone," I say to the bartender, like he's never heard that before.

The bartender is clipping his nails over the ice box. "Aren't we all?" He has a tattoo on his arm that spells "Edie."

"When was the last time you saw Lucy Brubaker?" I show him a recent picture. "Do you know her, Edie?"

He gestures and points at his tattoo. "It's Eddie, duh. Are you going to buy a drink, or what?" he says, pulling a glass off the shelf behind him.

"Beer in a bottle," I answer. I always order a bottle in a bar like this. It's like getting a free deadly weapon with every purchase. "Have you seen her or not, Eddie?"

"Easy, man. I haven't seen her, but her friend Manny tried to use her EBT card in here a couple of nights ago." The bartender puts the beer down in front of me.

"Who's Manny?"

"He's your basic alcoholic, co-dependent junkie."

The usual dirt bag one might meet in rehab. I scan the rest of the bar. A guy sits at the serving station at the end of the bar. Two laborers sit in a table opposite the bar, and three ne'er do wells sit at tables with their backs to the bar. These are the idiots I must have hit in the head on the way in. The jukebox is quietly playing a Mexican polka. Beer logo mirrors and neon signs hang on the opposite wall. The place is dark and dingy and smells like bilge water.

"How do you know it was Lucy's EBT card?"

"It had her mark on it. She wrote 'LB' on it."

"For someone who isn't legally allowed to accept them, you seem like a pro."

"Listen, buddy, I don't have to take this. Drink up and get out of here"

"What's your cut for accepting them, Eddie? Ten bucks?"

"None of your goddamned business."

"Hmm." I lean in closely and show him a twenty dollar bill. After scanning the room, he takes it in his hand and leans in close. You would think he was ratting out the mob.

"Manny sells bulk tube socks at the swap meet on the weekends," he whispers.

Eddie is proud of this useless info, thinking that it was worth the twenty. I stare into his eyes. I nod then smile. I grab his shirt collar and pull his scrawny shell over the bar and onto the sticky floor.

I've got my knee on his head, pinned to the floor, and both of his wrists in one of my hands. I use my free hand to recover my twenty. Nobody in the bar even flinches. Nobody gives a crap. I remove the dart from behind my ear and put it directly in front of his eye.

"Manny has been staying in an abandoned house down on Deervale Street in San Geronimo. You can't miss it." The dam breaks and a river of information flows forth. Amazing what a little pressure will do. Now he won't shut up. He talks about Manny's predilection for wearing women's shoes, about Manny's rap sheet and his lazy eye. He talks about his own troubles with Manny. He talks about an ex-girlfriend in Windsor. He talks about his mother in Topeka.

"Shut up Edie, you're boring me!" That's right, I called him Edie. Well Edie starts to go nuts. As he squirms and struggles, profanities flow forth from his stinky mouth. He spouts some really shocking language that is only spoken in the dark recesses of our state penal system.

I jam the dart through his right nostril into the wood floor. He is instantly quiet, but he continues to pant like a dog.

"Thanks for the info, Edie." I let his hand loose and stand up. I place my foot on the tail of the dart. "I'm sure you won't be calling to warn your buddy Manny, right?"

"What about my nose?" Eddie was still snorting and spitting.

"Put a ring in it."

Chapter Twelve

The sun is setting as I turn down a gravel road. The road is lined with grass filled culverts. I spot the house. It's a small clapboard house, leaning to the left. The windows are boarded up and its front door hangs on its hinge. There's no driveway and no area designated as a lawn, just dirt and a battered metal swing set. The garage door lies on the ground inside the garage.

I do a quick scan of the neighborhood. No one is outside. There are no barking dogs, no playing children. There is only the sound of the highway. I remove my Mossberg shotgun from beneath the seat in the back of the Audi Q7. I slam the hatch. The sound of the door slamming seems to come and go so fast it's like it never happened. The neighbors probably stopped hearing things long ago when this house was invaded by the bottom feeders.

Over the distant hills which block much of the ocean air during the day, the sun light fades. It is as if the cold Pacific waits for sunset before it exhales its chilly breath over the valley and forces the warm air to flee inland. I pull the collar up on my jacket. It's not going to be any warmer inside.

A line of crows settles on a nearby telephone line, their wings in close and their tail feathers rigid. They're pointed directly toward the west, into the breeze.

The heavy door of the house offers some resistance. I push against it with the barrel of the shotgun. The door opens only a couple of feet before I have to put my shoulder into it. It gives the rest of the way. Once inside, I bang the door a few times with the barrel of the weapon. I don't detect any movement in the house. I tentatively step over the sill plate into what used to be the living room. Trash and debris are piled up in the corners: beer cans, nasty blankets, needles and burned aluminum foil. Numerous

"Pup and Taco" bags lay on the kitchen counter. "Pup and Taco" is a fast food joint in Larkspur.

I poke through the food bags. They smell fresh, as fresh as grade 'C' beef can get. Whoever was here eats at "Pup and Taco"…a lot.

I keep an eye out for anything that would put Lucy in this place. I hope to find a lead on her whereabouts, but then it would be a double-edged sword if I found it here. I swing the barrel around and into every corner in the half light.

The family that once lived here took everything with them. They left this place so bare that it had no protection against thieves and drug addicts, the hated and the forgotten, the lowest forms of human life.

There is a sound coming from the back of the house. The hated and the forgotten might still be here.

"This is the police! Who's there?"

There is nothing, no more movement, no sound. Not smart and not professional. I am not the police. I am an idiot, and whoever moved in the back bedroom knows this now. It could be Manny or it could be my sister.

My heart is beating faster, and the sun is failing me. I try to settle myself. I don't want to be here when the sun retreats completely. Numerous doors line both sides of the hall. I can only imagine they lead to bedrooms and bathrooms, and to whoever is making a heavy shuffling noise.

I pump the shotgun. It is a sound that everyone understands; it's the international sound for 'who dat?' With the Mossberg pointed squarely at its center, I begin to move through the narrow hallway. There isn't much that can escape its deadly spray.

I lean against a graffiti covered wall opposite the first door. A small amount of yellow light leaks from beneath the door. I level the gun at the door and kick it in. The frame parts from the wall as the door explodes open. In a flash, I see someone outside run by through the gaps in the boarded up window. It might have been Lucy. She would have been medium height and blond and happy. She would have bright eyes and she would give me long hugs where she sort of just hangs on me like a child. I want it to be Lucy. I quickly lower the gun and move to the next door, which is already open. Again, through a window, I see someone move outside.

I hurry to the back of the house and swing open the third door. There is no window, only darkness and a two-by-four Douglas fir stud swinging out from it. I feel my nose crack and the warmth of my own blood as it empties out of my face. I stagger up against the opposite wall. I blast one of the 12-gauge shells out of its chamber before taking another shot of timber full in the face.

This must be Manny. His face appears out of the darkness and his dirty hands grip the length of wood. With this last shot to my face, the redwoods and the cedars I saw this morning appear out of the fog. I can see the cloudy sky and the long broad cedar limbs green with moss sway in the wind overhead. Something is falling from high above the trees. Something is falling through the smoke of discharged black powder. It is slowed by the branches and tears off sections of moss and needles. It comes ever closer, tumbling in the limbs. It's the two-by-four.

Chapter Thirteen

The darkness and cold are back. This feels like a bad joke. I half expect to wake up in the woods next to another body. I feel the pain in my head and face. I prop myself up and sit against the wasted drywall and exposed studs. The open closet where Manny gave me his best shot is directly across from me. To my right is the hallway that leads to an open door at the back of the house. To my left is the living room. Bands of light dance across the ceiling. I quickly reach for the shotgun that I always swore would have to be pried from my cold dead hands, but it's not there.

There is the light again. Damn the dark, and screw you, whoever you are. Just toss me the flashlight and go away.

"Brubaker?" someone shouts from outside.

Who in the hell?

"It's Tom!" a voice calls from just outside.

"Yeah," I barely get it out after a few coughs. The taste of dried blood on my lips hints that I might have more damage than I expected from two decent swings of a two-by-four. I run my tongue across my teeth. They're all there, maybe a little loose, but they're there. I guess it could be worse. Then I hear her voice.

"Brubaker, come on out. We're going to help you."

It's Jacobs.

They must think that I've barricaded myself in here. The next step would be the teargas followed by the battering ram.

"I'm all right. I'll be right out. I just need to freshen up a bit."

"Stop screwing around, it's just us, Bru." Tom is standing next to me. He crept up and I didn't even know it. He's a good cop with military training.

"What time is it?" I ask, with Tom's light blasting me in the face.

"After eleven."

"What day?"

"It's still Tuesday."

"Damn, my doctor is golfing tomorrow."

"You don't look that bad. Can you walk?" Jacobs asks with a hint of selflessness.

"Why wouldn't I be able to walk?" I grip my legs. They feel okay.

"Because your shoes are gone," she says.

Damn, second pair today. I'm starting to run out of shoes, and the week isn't half over.

"Detective Jacobs." We're still not on pleasant terms as she wants to incarcerate me. "Can you get me a pair of sandals out of the Audi?"

"No." She is standing right in front me now.

She's a real piece of work.

"Your car isn't here," she says with a grimace.

I assume that my poison oak is no longer a factor in her expression.

"The same person who took your shoes took your car," Tom says as we walk through the minefield of syringes.

"…And my shotgun," I add.

"Nice." Ellen sweeps the floor with her shoes.

"Do you need EMS?" Tom guides me outside into the swarm of emergency vehicles.

"Maybe just a touch-up. How did you find me?"

Several deputies enter the house behind us.

"One of the neighbors heard the shot and called the Sheriff's office. She took down your license plate number as the car drove away."

"What took you so long?"

"The lady didn't actually call it in until after her husband got off the internet. It was about three hours later. We got here as soon as we could."

"She's got dial up?"

"Why didn't the San Rafael police roust me?" I'm again confused by who responds to what and where.

"It came over the radio. I called Tom Ricketts. I didn't know what kind of condition you were in. The locals had the house surrounded while I drove up from San Rafael." Ellen grips my arm as she walks me over to her sedan.

"I'm glad they didn't wake me."

Ellen sits me in the front seat of her car and gently buckles me in. I smell her hair when it brushes against my face. I feel like I am ten years old again and sitting in the nurse's office after a decent scrap.

"Frank tried to reach you earlier, but Manny answered your phone. He's got your car." Tom leans against the car.

"Frank has my car?"

"No, Manny does." Tom says.

"How do you know it was Manny?" I ask.

"He answered, 'This is Manny. How can I help you?'"

"Right."

I pat my hip. I still have Christine's cell phone. I had grabbed it before entering the house.

"We want you to leave your phone on for a couple of days. When we do find Manny, there might be some good leads in your phone's call log." Ellen closes the door. "They might lead you to your missing sister." Ellen says, as she gets in to the sedan next to me.

"Am I being arrested? Because if I am, I want Tom to do it. I think it's his turn."

"No, I'm taking you in to fill out a police report and answer a few of my questions about the guy in the woods."

"I hope it doesn't take all night, because it's league night."

Ellen looks at Tom through the open window. He shakes his head.

"Try to stay out of trouble, Bru." Tom slaps the roof of the car, and Ellen pulls out of the driveway.

Chapter Fourteen

I didn't talk much on the way to the station. I kept a bag of ice pressed against my battered face. Ellen spent the trip on the telephone. She reported the Audi Q7 as stolen while I called Enza. Enza didn't answer and I wasn't about to leave a message. I'm not sure that she could understand my new swollen lipped accent anyway.

We reach the county building in what seemed like only a couple of minutes and park in a small parking lot meant for county officials and police detectives. I strain to get out of the car.

We take the east side elevator to the third floor. It's where they book the deadbeat dads, potheads and animal sacrificers. What does that make me? Ellen leaves me in the hands of a young booking officer so that she can check in with her superiors. The officer leads me to a strange half-room with three solid walls and one made entirely of chain link. It's like an old storage closest that was emptied out just before I got here.

After what seems like an eternity or enough time to plot out a prison break, Ellen returns, sauntering down the hall.

"You want fries with that shake?" I ask, at a volume that only my elementary school cafeteria lady could hear.

"I'm sorry, did you say something?" She stops in her tracks.

I shake my head, afraid to speak.

"Do you need anything?" she asks.

"Freedom?"

"Soon. Sorry but they're booking in a bunch of Hell's Angels on a meth sting. Bad timing I guess. We had nowhere to put you."

"How about the Starbucks across the street? Just call me when you're ready."

"I wish I could."

She looks tired, but her white shirt is still impeccably white and her curves are still very curvy. Her pants are muddied and torn from her earlier altercation with the tree branch. She hands me a few wet paper towels and a plastic bag filled with fresh ice.

"This place feels like a storage closet," I say, as I take a look around.

"It is a storage closet."

"Damn, I'm good."

"It's the earthquake retrofit thing, I think. They're working on the cells."

"Is this the before or the after."

She smiles.

I sure am having a good time for someone who may spend the rest of his life in a closet half this size at Pelican Bay.

"I'd hate to think what happens when they run out of storage closets," I wonder out loud.

"We all have to take a suspect home with us."

"What are you waiting for?" I ask.

"Funny, but not really. Your lawyer is upstairs. We're waiting for an interview room."

"You didn't come down here to tell me that. You could have made me sit here all night. What's going on?"

"There is nothing going on. I'm just being polite."

"Your good cop routine is quickly turning into an inconsiderate cop routine."

"Excuse me?" Ellen folds her arms beneath her. "Screw you. I was just trying to be nice with all that you've been through in the last twenty four hours. And do you know what?"

I lean into the fence, close enough to smell her perfume. Close enough to see a hint of affection in her eyes.

"What?" I answer.

Ellen grabs a handful of the chain link and pulls it back and then lets it go. The links snap back into my face and send me reeling. I sit on my ass and look up at a very happy Ellen Jacobs.

"You don't think I did the killing in the woods, do you? Unless, of course, you have a thing for murderers," I say, pushing the ice against my face.

With a widening smile, she turns away. "Is that a confession?" She heads for the hallway door. "Someone will be down for you soon. Hang in there."

"Hang in there? Is that some macabre jail cell joke?"

"Ha, Ha, Ha," The door slams behind her.

It is about twenty minutes before two deputies come down to fetch me. They lead me up some stairs and down a long hallway. With the ceiling arches overhead and windows lining one wall of the hall, it is institutional architecture for the masses.

Through the tall windows I can see the speeding traffic of the 101 racing northward. That's where I should be going. I should be looking for my sister. I should be tracking down Manny. I rub my wrist where my watch should be, but the deputies took it.

The boys lead me past a bench load of greasy, wild-eyed bikers and into an interrogation room. My lawyer is waiting for me as is…

"Detective Jacobs," I say, extending my hand to Ellen. "Counselor," I add, turning to a small anxious man.

"Harry Gaines." He grabs my hand and shakes it vigorously. He must owe my brother a lot. "May I have a few minutes with my client before you begin?"

"Sure, I'll go…"

"Get a pot of tea?" I say with a smile.

"I have to recommend that you not say anything, Mr. Brubaker." The hunched over lawyer with a weight problem is probably wondering what he'll bill for that piece of advice. I wonder if there is standardized pricing for jailhouse clichés.

"Coffee," she says, as she leaves the room.

"What happened to your face, Mr. Brubaker?" Gaines quickly opens his briefcase and removes a digital camera and takes a picture of the grid-shaped redness across my bruised face. "Did they do this to you? Did she do this to you?"

"Easy, Perry Mason, let's just get down to business. What did they tell you?"

"They told me you were involved in the investigation of the murder of an unidentified person found early this morning in Tiburon." Gaines returns the camera to his briefcase and begins to remove a folder.

"What else did they tell you?" I'm sitting in a steel chair across from the lawyer. His hairline has receded past the point of his most recent wave of hair plugs and has left them stranded out in the open like palm trees on a deserted island. He rubs his eyes behind thick glasses and loosens the knot of his tie.

"Nothing. Which leads me to believe that they don't have anything."

"Did they happen to tell you that I was the one who found the body? Did they tell you I was the one that called it in?"

"No, they did not." He looks at his empty notepad.

"This leads me to believe…"

"That they're simply trying to shake you down for information. They think you are related to this murder – correction – death - in some respect and are simply following every lead." That rolled off his tongue like a true professional. As much as you can't like a guy who gets paid to get real criminals set free, I am beginning to like this guy.

"Did they read you your rights?"

"No."

"Then you're merely a witness to an investigation."

"Then let's walk out of here."

"Can't do that. You'd be impeding the investigation. That gives them cause to lock you up."

"So what are you here for?"

"You called me."

"Right."

"Did you do him?"

"Who, the guy in the woods? No way, he was already dead, and I'm not into the dead ones."

"All right then. Answer all of their questions to the best of your ability and call me when they give you an orange jumpsuit."

"Where are you going?"

"Bed. If what you said is true, I don't need to be here."

I look down at my jeans as Jacobs walks in with coffee and a bad cop, a buzz-cut brute named Bill Stevens, a real bone cracker.

"Goodnight." Gaines shakes my hand and exits the room.

I lean over the table to Bill. "Can we talk?"

"Nice face, wise-ass. Just shut up and listen." Bill seems like he is in a bad mood.

"How do you guys get so thick? Your arms are like a second baseman's, your neck is like a lineman's, and your head is like a third grader's."

I guess it's the baseball reference that pisses him off, because he bats the cup of coffee at me before I can dodge it.

"Shut up and listen. I'm not going to say it again."

"I asked for tea." I was soaked but it was worth it.

"Detective Jacobs…" Stevens gets up from the table and exhales dramatically at the one-way glass.

"That's enough, Brubaker. We need your help. Are you happy now?"

"I'm still here, so I'm not happy. But I'll do my best. All you had to do was ask."

"Asshole," Stevens mutters under his breath.

"You can't help it, Bill." I'm beaming and I am in charge.

"Finish it up, Jacobs." Stevens slams the door behind him.

Jacobs is facing me with her head slightly down. She has a broad smile and is stifling a laugh. She is avoiding the cameras that must be rolling. Stevens, by now, is probably eating a burrito behind the glass. Jacobs is definitely tired, as I can see her smile fading. I look beyond her at the acoustic ceiling tiles. The thousands of little holes remind me of the stars passing over head this morning. Or was that yesterday morning?

"How did the person die?" I ask, to seemingly deaf ears.

"I did some checking on your sister." Ellen takes a packet of ibuprofen out of her pocket and slides it toward me. "I couldn't find anything on her. I ran her through the DMV, and she is clear."

"She doesn't have a driver's license." I place the pills on my tongue and swallow them dry.

"Not according to the DMV. She got it two years ago and it's up for renewal in three more. She's got a clean record. What's the matter?"

With my bottom lip sitting on the floor, I must look like a dope.

"I'm surprised, that's all. Lucy doesn't own a car."

"I think you have to dig a little deeper. There's probably a lot you don't know about her. Once you start looking for a missing person instead of your sister, you might have more success."

"Yeah." The scope and size of her case just got a lot bigger. I think about the Lucy that I know, and I wonder who she really is. So far I've been searching for a little girl that I'll never find. I need to look for a grown woman.

"Now I need your help. Tell me why you were in the canyon last night?" Ellen is back on message.

"I told you and the chief this morning."

"Humor me, please. You need to tell the glass," she says, pointing behind her.

"I was working an infidelity case. I was taking some photos from a highpoint above the infidel's house. The local goon squad chased me into the forest, where I fell asleep."

"Security guards?"

"Apparently some of the homeowners have a private security detail. I woke up next to the body just before dawn. I backed out and called Tom Ricketts."

"You have some interesting sleeping habits, Mr. Brubaker. But we're looking for more than that." She sits on the edge of the table opposite me. The last thing she wants is to be on my level. Jacobs reaches into her jacket pocket and pulls out a package of photos and sets them down in front of me.

"You're a good photographer, maybe a little too good." She fans out the photos.

I take a quick gander. These are the shots I took last night, "I was kind of hoping for that burnt edge wedding frame look. Did you get doubles?"

"Shut up, Brubaker. If we find out this girl with the doctor is under eighteen, we're going to bring you in for child porn and statutory rape."

"You can't do that." I feign shock.

"Try me." Jacobs finally sits down across from me. "Do you think your subject had anything to do with the man in the woods?" Back to the

Q and A.

"I don't know. The guy I'm working on is a plastic surgeon who moonlights at the aging center. He has a line on unlimited Viagra and picks up his girls at Sam's waterfront bar in Tiburon. As far as I can tell, the only charge you could bring on him is using a shop vac in a purpose other than what was intended. If you hand me those photos, his case will be closed and off my desk."

"We might be able to arrange for you to get the memory chip back if you continue to be forthcoming. What were you doing in San Geronimo tonight? Does it have anything to do with the John Doe in Tiburon?"

"I already told you."

"It's not for me," she says, as she motions to the glass.

"I was following up on a lead. My sister is missing, and I'm investigating her disappearance. It seems the last person who might have seen her was a junkie named Manny. I believe that Manny is responsible for my missing car and my broken nose."

"We're sorry about your sister and hope that you locate her. Unfortunately, we have to revisit the body in the woods."

She takes another long look at one of the photos on the table.

I take a sip of Steven's coffee he left behind. "Can you tell me anything about the scene in the woods that you might have discovered after I left?"

"You know I can't."

"What's going on?"

"Tell me everything again. Everything," she says, as she settles into her chair.

I want to tell her that she looks beautiful and how great those pants look on her, but I don't think that was what she meant. I go over the sequence of events of the previous evening that led me to wake up next to the dead body. During my re-telling I think about anything that might have been overlooked, but nothing comes to mind.

"I don't remember the smell when I went to sleep. It was damp, and I was breathing hard. The ground was soft and as absorbent as a roll of paper towels, but what I can't figure out is why I didn't smell it until the following morning."

"We're waiting on a time of death and the autopsy. This information should shed light on the subject."

"Any cause of death?"

Ellen rubs her eyes. "Not yet." She tosses my Suburban keys on the desk. "It's in the lot downstairs. Get some sleep. We'll talk again."

I pick up the keys. "Thanks for dragging me out of that house." I look back as I walk out the door. Ellen nods. She looks exhausted.

Ellen used the term "John Doe" in the interview room on purpose. She's too smart to let go of a bit of information like that. It was a small gift. It doesn't mean much right now, but it's the only thing she could give me. She is showing me that she isn't all that bad. Or she could have just let it slip.

The victim was male.

Chapter Fifteen

By the look of my reflection in the stateroom head's vanity, I probably should have taken them up on the EMS offer. My eye is swollen and purple. My cheek is swollen and purple. My lips are swollen and purple and my forehead is butterflied together. I open the medicine cabinet to a myriad of expired pharmaceuticals, all bearing the name Theresa. Among the brown plastic bottles is one marked hydrocodone, a generic a la vicodin. I think of a quote from an old cruising guide: 'It is imperative to have a good stock of pharmaceuticals for any long voyage.'

Right now, I don't care about the man in the woods and I don't care about my car. I only want to go to my happy place and the big 'V' will take me there.

I settle into the aft cabin beneath the low overhead. After tossing two Vicodins down the hatch, I finish off a bottle of water. I pull the heavy comforter over my head. In fewer than fifteen minutes the deck of the sailboat is no longer there. I can see straight up the mast into the billowing clouds and a handful of stars. The rigging shakes with the midnight breeze. The sea lions make a ruckus by the fisherman's dock and an occasional heron floats above in a heavy cross breeze.

I smile to myself as a thought passes through my head, which seems to be detaching itself from my body. Serial killers don't kill adult males. This thought will leave my mind along with all the pain, all the itching, all the disappointment and all shortfalls that make up my life. I can hear the rhythmic slapping of the wind-driven waves against the hull. The taut lines creak with every gust.

"I know you don't like the dark, but I do." Lucy is leaning against the tall mast, her long arms around it. She is looking straight up into the sky. Her curly blonde hair sweeps across her face. She brushes it away and beams at the stars.

I look up at the same sky as clouds race overhead. I lose my balance and stagger toward the boom to regain it.

"Where have you been?" I ask, while rubbing my face. "We've been searching all over for you?"

"Around," she laughs.

"Around? You're killing me, Lucy. Frank is worried sick, and my face may never be the same."

Lucy glances at me and then back at the sky. "Do you know why I like night-time?"

"Does it have anything to do with the great number of hiding places?" I can feel the cold. The vicodin puts everything into slow motion.

"You're going to freeze to death. Come inside." I open my arms, hoping to corral her to the cabin below.

"During the day, when the sky is bright blue and without a cloud, it's like a big bottomless ocean. The only solid thing is the ground beneath me. What's to keep me from falling off the earth? At night, if I fall, I always have a place to land." Lucy points up at the stars.

I look up once more, bracing myself against the sail covered boom. The broken clouds move ever faster, sweeping away the stars. The sky changes from black to deep purple, to deep blue.

Light fills the cabin. The curtain on the deadlight is drawn open and someone is sitting beneath it. Peace came with the vicodin, but it was fleeting.

"Good morning, Jack."

"Lucy?" The light blasting through the deadlight behind her is reminiscent of a UFO landing.

"It's Enza." Enza takes a few steps across the cabin and bends over me. "How do you feel?" She places her hand on my forehead.

"Did you see Lucy?" I ask.

"Was she here?" Enza is humoring the injured guy with the head trauma.

I realize Lucy's visit was nothing more than a dream. "I guess not. How are you?" I ask.

"I am pretty good. I'm not the one who woke up in the woods next to a dead body, got my ass kicked with a piece of lumber and then ended up unconscious in a crack house." She walks out of the cabin and disappears into the galley.

I drag my feet over the side of my double bunk and press them down on the cabin sole. The cabin sole is a lofty name for the floor. It's all varnished teak and covered in soothing blue carpet. "What's the date and time, Enza?" I am getting too used to asking what day it is. If this keeps up, I'll forget my name and begin eating my meals from a small glass jar with a picture of a baby on it.

"It's Wednesday, noon." She hands me a bag of ice. "You're going to need the ice. Take these." Enza hands me four white pills.

"What are they?"

"Anti-inflammatories. They'll bring down the swelling. Can you walk?"

"Why wouldn't I be able to?"

"I don't know. In most beatings they usually break the legs." She smiles.

"Who are they?"

"Forget it. I made you breakfast: eggs, bacon and toast. I brought the newspaper."

"You're kidding?"

"I am. I brought take-out from the Lighthouse cafe. The police came by the office today, but apparently Jack Brubaker, Spiritual Advisor to the Stars, wasn't in," She places the ice gently against my forehead.

I remember slipping that sign into the slot on my door. I have my memory. What a relief. The fuzziness is going away.

"Who was it?" I stand up, using the grab bars in the overhead to steady myself.

"There was one woman detective in a county car."

"Ellen. She was probably just dropping by to say 'Hi'. Where were you?"

"I was watching from behind the stacks at the bookstore across the street. I bought a book about international tax shelters."

"I don't want to know. I'm going to take a long shower and wait for Ellen to show up. Can you go back to the office and find out everything you can about Christine's husband? Get a complete resume: where he went to school, the background of the companies he worked for, his current company and what he does for them, who he works with. Find out where the Flynns' live and for how long, and who they play bridge with."

"Google him?"

"Google him!"

"Can I ask you a question?"

"What's that?"

"What is bridge?" Enza has her hands on her hips.

"I have no idea. I want to know everything about them. It is time we earned a little money. Let's find this dude."

"Let's?" Enza turns on her toe and makes for the companionway stairs.

"Enza," I stop her, "thank you."

"Anytime, boss. Feel better and keep your face out of hot water. Use the ice."

"I will."

Enza turns and climbs the few steps to the deck above.

I flip over the newspaper on the table. The body made the corner south of the fold. It reads, "Body Found in Tiburon". That's all you need.

Chapter Sixteen

The shower spray roars in my ears and the stream pummels the back of my head. I feel like a piece of tile in a tile cutter, like a piece of metal on a lathe, like a tooth getting drilled. I feel like a…well, it doesn't matter. The water leaves me shaking when I step out of the shower. The pain is sharp and pounding. I wonder if my head actually split wide open and exposed my brain. I look in the unreliable mirror just in case.

The purple is fading, thank God, but I wonder how long I have to live with the black and yellow.

"This is where you live?"

Did I just say that out loud or is Ellen Jacobs standing in front of me while I gently dry my hair with the towel; the towel that is not currently wrapped around my waist, the same towel that is blocking my vision. To be safe, I turn away from the sound I just heard and firmly wrap the towel around my waist.

"Either angle is fine," Ellen says, leaning against the opposite side of the cabin.

"Damn it, Jacobs. No consideration. I'm going to file a complaint." Now I am hopping on one leg trying to get a pant leg on.

"Are you sure? I might have to testify." Her arms are crossed. "It'll be a short testimony."

Not if she wears that get up: tight grey pants with an open red shirt over a black t-shirt. The shoes look like Doc Martens.

"I guess the first thing she did when she left the valley was hit the mall and burn the wranglers."

"I still have them," she says smiling.

"Did I say that out loud?"

She nods her head, yes.

"All of it?"

"I don't know, maybe."

"Can you give me a second?" I ask politely.

Now we've turned our conversation into a staring contest. I'm actually glaring at her. "Make yourself useful and pour us a cup of coffee."

Ellen grins, nods and exits to the galley. "Cream or sugar?" She asks while making a racket in the galley.

"Neither." I answer. I finally get my chinos on and a blue button down over a t-shirt. I join her in the main cabin. I quickly scan the place for any contraband that might provide a clue to my true character. There's just a stack of sailing mags and a pile of laundry.

"You've got a great place here. Doesn't it get a little cramped?" She hands me a mug.

"Not when I'm alone."

"That doesn't sound fun."

"Weren't you just interrogating me last night? And if my memory serves me correctly, I was this close to avoiding prosecution by fleeing to France."

"My bosses were watching. I had to give them something. It wasn't much of a show."

"I guess you should have blackened my other eye."

Ellen takes notice of the Eastern Pacific chart on the table. I fold it up and move my laundry off the settee. Ellen joins me at the table. "Going somewhere?"

"Maybe, but not any time soon. I have a lot of work to do before I can take off." I unroll the chart for the North Bay. I place the Styrofoam container that holds my first real meal in twenty four-hours on the chart. I dig in. There is a moment of silence. The thick sourdough toast is tough to get my swollen mouth around, but not impossible. The bacon is thick and wiggly, and the eggs are eggs.

"I'm sorry, did you want some breakfast?" I ask with four inches of bacon dangling out from my mouth.

She pulls back and shakes her head.

"Vegetarian?" I ask, as the bacon flaps around like Gene Simmons' tongue.

"After that display, I'm thinking about it."

I finish the rest of the food with a few more bites. The vicodin is taking a while to clear out of my head.

We set our mugs on both ends of the chart to keep it from rolling up.

"The North Bay chart includes the entrance to San Francisco Bay as well as Richardson Bay, which is bordered by Angel Island, Sausalito, Mill Valley and Tiburon. Raccoon Straits is between Angel Island and the Tiburon Peninsula. It's like a big six-way intersection with boats instead of cars, and churning tides and currents instead of asphalt. Parts of the East Bay and San Pablo Bay are also visible."

I can't help but notice Ellen's beautiful hands.

"Which is water and which is land?" Jacobs asks from behind her coffee mug.

I shake my head.

"Kidding, just kidding. I know how to read a chart...well, kind of." She immediately places her finger directly on the spot where I found the body.

"I'm impressed."

"I used to ski on the delta. My dad had charts on his boat."

I drag my finger along the creek from where it enters the bay to Ellen's. "It's hard to believe anyone would dump a body this far from the road."

"Or the water. He had to be killed there." Ellen sweeps her fingers along the visible roadways and the waterline.

"I don't think so." I lean back and look up at the overhead hatch which is peppered with rain drops, like so many jigsaw pieces waiting to be pressed together. "But, let us suppose the person was killed there. What was he killed with?" I look into her eyes. "This is the part where you divulge the early findings of the autopsy; by accident."

"So I just let it slip? I have fifteen years of experience bagging bodies and you expect me to let the crucial facts of an autopsy slip?"

"Maybe."

"Not to a seedy private detective living on a worm ridden sailboat, loosely tied to a collapsing dock in a run-down marina filled with ne'er-do-wells and losers."

"Wow. Come on now, the boat is in beautiful shape and you'd be hard pressed to find a collapsing dock in Sausalito."

"Seedy?"

"I'll give you that one, but I am not a loser."

"Fine, but 'ne'er-do-well' has not yet been determined."

We catch each other's eyes and we don't know what to say. We're caught in a pregnant pause. We both look down at the chart.

Ellen breaks the silence. "You have to swear to me on your mother's life that you won't tell a soul. I could lose my job."

"And end up back in the Central Valley, it's tempting."

She shoots me a look that just misses me and bounces around the small cabin before coming to rest in my laundry.

"Okay, I swear."

"Our decedent is a John Doe between thirty-five and forty-five years of age, blue eyes and brown hair."

I offer, "Did I mention that you look especially great today?"

"Tone it down, will you?"

"Cause of death?"

"Not yet. Stevens and I were in there last night. He had trauma all over him. It's very bizarre. Animal attack keeps coming up, but it doesn't make any sense. No bite wounds, no claw marks."

"So this forty-year old schmuck wanders into the woods, doesn't leave any footprints, ends up in a canyon far from the road, and winds up getting mutilated. There is no sign of any heavy machinery working in the area, no steam roller parked next to the body. And the California Grizzly has been extinct for over a hundred years. Am I doing the math right? It's not adding up."

"It's new math. We must have missed something. Let's go out there and take another look." Ellen puts her mug on the counter behind her.

"I was hoping you would say that." I watch her for just a little too long.

She stares back at me, probably feeling a little uncomfortable, and looks around the boat. I'm sure she's trying to figure out who I am. She's not going to find out by staring at my Halloween themed boxer shorts, or is she?

"Were you trying to read my mind? I heard somewhere that you were a spiritual advisor." She is holding my door plaque.

"You've been by the office."

Chapter Seventeen

The sky is pushing the clouds down on us.

I follow Detective Jacobs' sedan onto the wet freeway, going north toward Tiburon. I use the time to check my messages with Christine's phone. There is a message from Christine who asks about the status of her case. She sounds sincere and sweet, but then she ends it with a directive for me to call her. The second message is from a very excited Dolliver. Apparently he got word back from his friends at the language institute. And just like Dolliver, he won't be specific over the telephone since he is under the impression that every piece of communication equipment he uses is wire-tapped. I'll call him later. The last message is from my brother Frank. He says Lucy missed a court date. He wants a status report on Lucy, and so do I.

We pass over the causeway that lets highway traffic flow north and south over a bite in the bay. The tide pushes seawater beneath the causeway and into Mill Valley on my left.

I call Tom Ricketts and leave a message at his desk concerning my sister, my car, my shotgun, and Manny. I get off the freeway and merge toward Tiburon. I follow Tiburon Boulevard for several miles as it parallels the waterline of Richardson Bay. Through the rain I can see Sausalito pressed beneath the clouds across the bay. Ellen Jacobs' sedan continues to speed through town. Ellen is trying to lure me into a speeding ticket, so I back way off. She passes the Tiburon P.D. as if she has a "Get out of Jail Free" card. She is a sadist.

We pass Belvedere Island, Old Tiburon and the ferry dock. With Angel Island dead ahead we turn up into the hills. The narrow streets lead past some of the more historic houses. Mansions hidden behind hedges and electric gates dominate the higher altitudes. Here the poop rolls downhill from the twenty million dollar mansions, to the ten million dollar ones.

We find the construction site where the police had set up their base camp yesterday. There is nothing left except for a rented fence to keep people from parking. We park alongside the fence.

"No guards? No police tape?" I say pulling on my heavy rain coat.

"No evidence," Ellen responds.

After ten minutes we arrive at the crime scene. There is something to this I can't pin down. I know there are clues all over the place, but they aren't immediately evident. Sometimes you have to let the snow filter through the rocks. It's in the stream that your answers become apparent. I'm sounding like the Dalai Lama.

I return my focus to the scene. Nothing is the same. The leaves and debris from the forest floor have been removed. Small bushes and fallen branches have disappeared. The crows are gone and the rain seems to have washed everything away. The floor was scraped clean like a fresh wound left bare to heal.

I push my hands deep into my coat pockets and roll my shoulders forward. I stare down at the ground. A few heavy drops make it through the forest cover above. A few more hit the ground.

Ellen is doing her own assessment. She scans the surrounding tree trunks and surface root systems. She breathes deeply. She probably smells the wet ground, fresh cedar needles and light chimney smoke spilling into the canyon. I can smell Ellen. She's wearing something gentle.

"I don't remember him wearing any shoes. Did you find any shoes?" I ask.

"No. There was only one sock remaining. We searched both trails but found nothing."

"He didn't walk in, and he wasn't carried." Ellen and I are finally on the same page. She's picking up what I'm putting down.

Big chunky drops begin to fall all around us. I watch a leaf dip and spring back under the impact of a rain drop.

"We know why you didn't smell anything." Ellen is biting her upper lip.

"Is this going to be another slip?"

"Muy grande," she says hesitantly, still deciding. "The John Doe might have been frozen, but more likely very cold. The M.E. got a body temperature in the fifties when he arrived on the scene. He was very cold when you fell asleep next to him."

"It was cold the night before, but that doesn't explain the odor the next morning."

"The M.E. thinks that the crows opened up the DB's stomach and exposed its contents."

"Nice."

I look up at the rain and study a single drop as it falls from high up in the canopy. Several drops hit branches and a few make it through. "Well, what did he have for dinner?" I ask Ellen.

"You've got more than enough information already Brubaker. Hell, you're still on the short list of suspects. You shouldn't even be here. I could lose everything." Ellen's frustration is evident. The rain is pelting her rain gear. Water runs down the brim of her hood.

"Just asking," I say as I pull my hood back and stare up at the trees overhead. "What took me so long?" Sometimes I have to get hit over the head before I get it. "You'd better get somebody up in those trees to look for his shoes.

Ellen pulls her hood back and looks into the trees. A smile lights up her face. "I'll get Bill on with the FAA and find out who has been flying over Tiburon during the past week." Ellen lets out a hoot and throws her arms around me.

It's in that moment that we realize we are standing directly on the spot where the John Doe came to rest. We separate and climb slowly and silently out of the canyon. Ellen has her cell-phone in her hand and watches for a signal. Her mind, no doubt, focused on her next course of action.

I think about the body falling from an airplane high above the small forest. Was there a struggle? Was he already dead and just dumped? Falling through the canopy probably tore him apart, ripped off his shoes and separated the skin from his fingers and the clothes from his back. The murder investigation is underway.

As she bounds down the slope toward our cars, Ellen is already talking on the phone. I lag behind, thinking about my next move, when Ellen drops out of sight. I come upon her sitting in a murky puddle at the base of the trail. She is still talking on the telephone even as she drips with mud. She puts out her hand and I help her up.

Ellen stops me before I reach the Suburban. "We have an I.D. on the John Doe." Her hand covers the cell phone, "Some communications software Guru…"

"Let me guess. Colin Flynn?"

"How'd you know?" Ellen closes her phone.

"It's been that kind of week. How did they I.D. him?"

"He had a credit card receipt in his coat pocket. It was pretty damaged; no name, just a few numbers remaining. They ran a program that guesses the last four digits among twenty three thousand credit card holders with the first digits."

"You found all this out in that quick call?"

"Not necessarily."

"Huh." I offer a confused kind of 'huh' with a bit of 'what does that mean?' mixed in.

Chapter Eighteen

The idea of my sister being found dead in the woods crosses my mind as quickly as it takes for me to kick it out. She's probably wandering around The Haight digesting several grams of mushrooms in her stomach. This thought keeps me focused on the positive, Lucy is definitely somewhere.

There are lots of reasons Lucy might be missing. Skipping a court date is probably one of them. There's nothing worse than having to go to court to pay a fine or serve a night in jail. I don't blame her. I imagine the stress she is under. She doesn't have the money, and she can't think rationally when she withdraws from her meds.

I'm a little relieved that the court element is involved. It gives her another reason to take off, instead of just disappearing under duress. I have to attack things as they present themselves. I can't worry about something that hasn't happened yet.

I don't think that anything happens in the blink of an eye. I believe everything becomes apparent. My perception of Christine Flynn's husband and marriage was that things were not great, but they were going as well as could be expected. Then something bad like an explosion happens, or a car bomb goes off, or a building falls down. It was as if the bomb had been blowing up and the building had been falling down all morning. The wheels were in motion long before we arrived. We just ignored it. I'm losing this ugly little war against perception, and that's not good.

I'm spinning my wheels.

When Ellen and I arrive at Christine's house, Stevens and the usual local police are in the driveway. The craftsman style house with its white-framed windows and dark stained shingles is now part of the crime scene. Police cars block the driveway and are double-parked in the street.

Neighbors line the curb. You can hear them talking in hushed tones. The case has already been decided here on the sidewalks of Larkspur.

The garage door is open, revealing an older GMC Tahoe parked next to Christine's Lexus. There is a laundry area and some neatly stacked boxes. There is no sign of a workbench or even a set of household tools. Colin doesn't seem to have been a do-it-yourselfer.

There is a "Support Your Local Police" sticker on the bumper and a strange symbol in the rear window. The symbol looks like a small dog sitting and howling at the moon, its body is criss-crossed with lines. All I can figure is that it is something Native American. The Flynn's are not the type of people who have propellers on the tow hitch receiver.

Tom Ricketts pulls into the driveway and rolls down his window. "Hey, Ellen, you'd better get that garage door closed. You never know what can grow legs and walk away."

"That garage is out of your jurisdiction, Ricketts!" Ellen snaps back. She has a lot on her mind.

I'm sure that Ellen will have the car inspected and the room searched at some point. I'm a little surprised to see Tom. He's not the kind of guy who follows the company line. He's more of a rogue, barely staying out of trouble; a good officer in a small department that tends to ignore certain things to protect the bottom line. I'm wondering if he's succumbed to the pressures of being paid too little to protect the assets of the super wealthy.

He motions me over to his car. "I heard that you're out of a job," he says, while he sits next to a passenger seat full of empty fast food bags and burger containers.

"Word travels fast."

"Never underestimate the power of the radio."

"I thought it was the pen."

"Huh?"

"What brings you down here?" I ask, still mystified as to how he stays in shape after eating all those super combo meals.

"We've got some guy in Sausalito with a carload of stolen radios. I'm following up on a related case."

"Right," I say, my mind drifting to Christine inside the house. "We'll talk soon, eh, Tom?"

"Yeah...Hey, Jack. You're probably off the hook with that Flynn guy. I wouldn't worry about it. His wife probably did it. Case closed, huh?"

Tom lets out a laugh, as he jerks his car out of the driveway and knocks over a trashcan. That isn't the first time that Tom has made me feel uncomfortable. The closer he gets to his twenty years in the business, the more easily bitterness forces its greasy film to the surface.

I watch Ellen make the necessary overtures to get me inside the house. Christine and Colin's home is a perfect beachy looking place with bleached floors and whitewashed walls. You could eat off the floor, and that's exactly what Christine seems to have been doing since her husband disappeared. There are open bags of ready-made salad spread out on the dining room floor. Some have forks and the dressing still in them. A few leaky containers of Tommy Wok Chinese food form a line up against the wall opposite the kitchen. I think the spicy orange chicken did it.

Christine is a mess. It looks like the news hit her like a hard slap in the face. She is gaunt, her thoughts somewhere else, as Stevens, the burly detective, tries to talk to her. Christine's eyes catch mine from where she is sitting on the sofa. I would expect her to concede with this latest turn of events, but she seems resolute. Stevens' thick hands are wrapped around a police notebook and a pen, and he seems to be going over the case in his head. The writing is secondary. Stevens sees me and shoots Ellen a look, the "I hope you know what you are doing" look.

Christine clutches a tissue in her hands and leans forward with her elbows braced on her knees. She looks ready to get up and walk out the door. She leaves Stevens at the sofa and walks toward me. She puts her arms around me and presses up against me. I look over her shoulder at Ellen and Stevens who both stare right back at me. It is a very thorny moment.

Christine steps back and realizes the same. The tears come. I guide her to a chair and hold her shoulder. Ellen marches past me, grabs my arm and drags me into the kitchen. Stevens is hot on her heels. Within seconds, Stevens has his hands on my chest and shoves me against a very nice set of custom kitchen cabinets.

"You and the wife in there killed him, didn't you? I ought to kill you and the broad and save the county courts a shitload of money." Bill clamps down harder.

"You've got a lot of penned up frustration, Bill."

I look at Ellen. She seethes with anger. "What's going on, Jack?"

I can't speak until Stevens releases my throat. Suddenly, he throws me across the room, and I slide across the floor. I slam into the equally nice breakfast table. A uniformed officer sticks his head in the door. Stevens nearly tears it off just by looking at him. The young officer has seen enough and ducks out.

Ellen is calm. This is why she is a good cop. "What is your relationship with Mrs. Flynn, Brubaker?"

I could use one of those spa treatments right now. "Mrs. Flynn hired me to find her husband...yesterday." I rub my neck.

"That's convenient." Stevens is moving toward me again, but Ellen raises her hand and stops him in his tracks.

"It's a lot of bad luck which I seem to have a lot of lately."

"How long have you known the Flynn's?"

"Can I get up?"

"Stay down." Stevens clenches his fists.

"Answer the question." Ellen adds.

"I met her yesterday, and I have never met Mr. Flynn...alive."

There is a brief respite, a pause. Ellen is thinking hard now. "Can you give me your exact whereabouts, with witness corroborations, for the last three to five nights?"

"I can." I don't know if I really can, but if it keeps me from flying through the bay window, I can.

"Get him up, Bill."

Bill seems reluctant, but then he almost rips my arm off as he drags me to my feet.

"How did you meet? When and where?"

I look at Bill and he doesn't seem satisfied because I have no broken limbs. "Christine Flynn came to my office yesterday. She asked me to find her husband. She said he never came home from a trip to Peru. I told her I wouldn't take the case."

"This was after you woke up with him in the woods." Ellen is doing the timeline.

"Correct. I returned to my boat, cleaned up and I went to the office. She was there. She made no appointment."

Ellen ponders the new information, "Why didn't you tell me before?"

"I don't normally solve cases before I get them. I didn't know it was Flynn in the woods until you said so."

Ellen ponders the situation again. "We have work to do. A lot of that work has to do with connecting you to this murder. You had better get lost, Jack." Ellen nods toward the door.

"That's all I want to do. Call me," I say, making the international hand gesture for telephone.

"You've got to be kidding. Can I kill him, Ellen?" Bill is pressing the barrel of his handgun against my chest.

"Get out of here, Jack. That's it."

Stevens pushes me back into the living room and Ellen follows.

Mrs. Flynn moves toward us. "What do I do, Mr. Brubaker?"

"Get a lawyer." I want nothing more than to make a beeline for the front door.

"Mrs. Flynn, I have to take a look around your home. Is that all right?" Ellen takes out a police notebook from inside her blazer.

"You don't have to let her, Mrs. Flynn," I add, before attempting what seems like a daylight jail break. "Unless there is an immediate and imminent danger, they have to issue a warrant." I am going to make sure that they don't get it that easily after the hockey match in the kitchen.

"One way or another, Mrs. Flynn, we have to search your home," remarks the ever sensitive Bill Stevens.

Christine thinks about it for a moment. "I have nothing to hide. Please go ahead and look around. Jack, if you could go with her."

"We would appreciate it, in everyone's best interest, if Mr. Brubaker would be excused." Ellen has returned to the impersonal detective-type.

"As I do not yet have a lawyer and I am extending a courtesy to you, Detective, it is in my best interest that Mr. Brubaker accompanies you on your inspection."

The hockey game in the kitchen could turn out to be the warm-up. When these two women lock horns, only then will the bell sound for the main event.

"Yeah," I say with a nod. This isn't the right moment to express my condolences to Christine, and I am sure she understands this.

Stevens backs down first. For a brief instant, we see eye-to-eye. Ellen briefly holds her ground and then relents.

"Please wait here, Mrs. Flynn. Brubaker, follow me." Ellen turns toward the stairs.

"And don't touch a goddamned thing." These are pleasant words from warm and caring Bill Stevens.

"Did you ever think about writing for Hallmark?"

"I'll be with Mrs. Flynn. Feel free to shoot Brubaker if he tries anything." Stevens says.

Even Stevens seems to understand the gravity of the situation.

"Right." Ellen never stops moving up the stairs. "Let's not talk, Jack. Let's get through this, all right? Don't touch anything, don't open anything and don't move anything."

"Wouldn't that be included under touching?"

"Do you want to have another discussion with Stevens?"

"How about we all get together for a barbecue?" I add.

Ellen ignores me.

We take the stairs up to the second floor. Through a window I can see several deputies fielding questions from the neighbors on the front lawn. Christine's private life has been taken away today. Detectives are walking through her home. Her neighbors are learning everything they can. Nothing belongs to her anymore: the house, her husband, even her own face. Everything will be drawn into the mind of the public and perverted into something it isn't.

Ellen and I silently concentrate on the task at hand. We start with the bedroom at the top of the stairs. It is a plain guest bedroom with windows facing the woodsy backyard of overgrown grass and clumsily strewn patio furniture. Ellen opens a closet. Linens are organized on a shelf above a rack of women's clothes. We find nothing unusual here or in the bathroom.

The next room down the hall is being used as an office, with a small desk against the window and a sofa facing a TV on the opposite wall. Ellen looks in the trash can and opens a few drawers and peers into the closet.

Pictures of exotic places cover the walls: the Pyramids of Giza, Machu Picchu, and the Great Wall of China. Most of them show a young Colin Flynn wearing a backpack or holding it at his feet. Again, nothing here seems unusual.

The last room at the end of the hall is the master suite. This room doesn't even resemble the tidiness of the previous spaces. Clothes are tossed in corner of the room. The bed is unmade. Drawers are left half open; some are empty, others crammed with clothes. There is a laundry basket with neatly folded clothes sitting on the bed. Ellen finds two pieces of luggage in the closet.

"Do you think there is a piece missing here?" I ask.

"Maybe." Ellen takes both pieces out and checks the tags.

"Most people buy sets of luggage. Colin was a bit of a traveler, and I am sure he would have a matching set of three or four bags," I say, hinting at my own travel experience.

She doesn't seem to care.

"I like to go on hikes in the woods. I enjoy clubs but I am not afraid to spend a quiet evening at home in front of the TV with a good bottle of wine. I am a movie fanatic and I like to rollerblade."

I am giving Detective Jacobs every opportunity to figure out my sense of humor. She ignores me again.

"He probably has a three or four piece set," she says. "He was supposed to have been on his most recent trip for less than a week. You're a man, so which bag would you have taken for a week?"

Ellen's demeanor has changed drastically from this morning on the boat. If I could read chakras, I'd say hers were blocked right now.

"First of all, I want to thank you for confirming what I've thought all along; I am a man."

Ellen gives me the "please get on with it" look.

"I would take a larger bag because I tend to over pack. I like to be ready for anything."

"Right."

"But then again, I don't like to check a bag either. It's easier just to carry on for international travel."

"Right."

"But he wasn't flying commercial so it doesn't even matter."

Ellen is already in the bathroom. I follow her there. As she has in each of the previous rooms, she carefully picks through the waste basket. She opens the cabinets with a latex gloved hand.

"Did you find a man's travel kit with a razor in it?"

"That's what I am looking for, if you would just let me do my job." She shoots me a look in the mirror.

I shoot her a smile. Ellen brushes by me. No travel kit. I open the medicine cabinet; again, nothing unusual. These were very healthy people with nary a prescription.

I look around the bedroom one more time. I feel uncomfortable about my intrusion into Christine's private life. I think about my home and the secrets I hide. I'm sure that there are two hundred million other people in this country who are ashamed about some things in their life that they would be mortified if anyone was ever to discover them.

Light bursts into the room when I open the curtains to the view of redwoods in the backyard. The light bounces off the stark walls, instantaneously warming the room.

"I told you not to touch anything," Ellen says from the doorway to the room.

"Sorry." I close my eyes and feel the warmth. I think about the folding whitecaps rising up and giving me chase across the South Pacific. It is the purest white I have ever seen. It is made up of a billion small air bubbles fizzing away into oblivion, but the purity is suspect. I really don't know what makes up the content of the deep ocean, but I am sure it isn't pure.

Christine's life isn't pure either, but I don't think Christine has anything to be ashamed of. She is a strong person and resolute. I want to believe that Christine did not kill her husband.

The exhaustion from the past two days; running in the forest, scratching poison oak and getting my face smashed in is starting to take hold.

"Let's go, Brubaker."

"Yeah." I follow Ellen down the stairs into the living room.

Christine is back on the sofa but now she is resting on a pillow she pulled onto her lap. Ellen removes a pad and pen from her pocket to begin her questioning. Stevens is in the kitchen opening and closing cupboards.

"One quick question, Christine?"

"I don't think so buddy." Stevens points a pen at me like a poison dart.

I shake my head, "Christine, what kind of bag did he take with him?"

"Let her answer, Bill."

"I guess he took a tan Coach carry-on, why?"

"I'll be looking for that too. We'll be in touch."

"Thanks."

"We'll be contacting you, Brubaker." Ellen gives me the "Get lost" glance.

"You know how to find me." I raise my hand to make the international gesture for telephone.

"I got it, Brubaker." Ellen finishes the gesture.

I slip outside.

Several police cars are parked in front of the house. Neighbors are still congregating on the sidewalk. The garage door is still open and unguarded. I decide to take a look.

The garage is the downhill part of the house where everything not tied down usually ends up. There's an odd collection of moving boxes on shelves. Most of the boxes have been labeled and crossed out, suggesting several moves; a few apartments or a condo before Christine and Colin settled into the big house.

The SUV is unlocked. I use a shop towel to lift the handle and open the door. I climb in and shut the door. Immediately I recognize the smell of stale cigarettes. It's not strong, but it's there and partially masked by the green pine tree deodorizer hanging from the rearview mirror. Colin might have been a closet smoker. If Christine was a smoker she would have been puffing like my Grandmother sitting in front of a slot machine in Vegas. Does Christine know that her husband was a smoker? What else was he hiding? Was Colin unknowingly complicit in his own death?

There is some change in the drink holder. I open the central glove box with the towel. There is a vehicle manual, insurance and registration, nothing out of the ordinary. I look straight ahead. The windshield is clean, but there is a small parking stub beneath the wiper blade. I didn't notice it from outside because it was just below the level of the hood. The backseat is empty. I have to get out of the car to check the trunk area.

I open the door again and remove the parking stub from the wiper blade. It's a basic ticket with the parking rules on the back. I turn it over to reveal a stamp; its blue ink is smudged beyond legibility. I consider it a moment before pocketing it.

I don't find anything interesting in the trunk area. I toss the towel on a stack of boxes and leave the garage.

Chapter Nineteen

A missing person case has been solved, but a murder case has just been opened. I put in a call to my brother, Frank. His secretary takes the message, "No new news." I think about calling my own lawyer to describe the recent events at Christine's house, but I figure, what's the point. I didn't do it. She may have done it, and she may figure out a way to pin it on me. I'm not yet an official suspect, but the sooner I find out who killed Colin Flynn the better.

I call Tom to ask him about the possibility that Flynn was dumped from a plane or a helicopter. Tom flew warthogs in the Gulf War. After that he was an M.P. in the reserves and managed to solve a pretty high profile murder case.

He remains an active pilot and knows more about flying than anyone I know. Tom answers but he can't talk; he says something about struggling with a suspect and hangs up.

My growling stomach reminds me of the front seat of Tom's car and the numerous Pup and Taco bags at the house in San Geronimo.

I try to kill two birds with one stone by stopping at the Pup and Taco. The Cup O' Hot Dog with chili and a burrito will satiate my dark cravings for poor quality fast food, and a few well-placed questions may provide me with additional information about Manny. By the looks of the house in San Geronimo, Manny ate at Pup and Taco religiously. But who could blame him; two tacos and a drink for three bucks is the best deal in Marin.

~ * ~

I walk up to the small window in the red roofed A-frame.
A young girl with a headset takes my order.

"Is it possible to get mad cow from eating a hot dog or would I get mad dog?" I ask. My famished sense of humor can't even crack a smile with the teen so I continue with my barrage.

"Do you know a guy named Manny?" I ask her as she puts her hand up.

"That's four tacos, two burritos and a super soda, sir." Her gum smacking is beginning to annoy me.

"I asked for a Cup O' Hot Dog and a burrito!" There is nothing worse than getting burned at the fast food place by someone whose sole job is to take your order and put it in a bag.

"I am not talking to you!" She says to me as she clicks on and off her belt mounted radio. "Pull up to the window for your food and your total." She spins on her heel and steps across the narrow A-Frame where she takes the cash from a scrawny guy in a blue Audi Q7.

I recognize the car. Great car, fast and reliable, and it's mine.

"Hey!" I shout.

"Wait your turn!" the girl screams back at me as she hands Manny the food.

I run around the front of the small A-frame hot dog stand. I see the rear of a blue Audi Q7 SUV pulling way. "Damn it."

The pimply faced punk girl sticks her head completely out of window number two and drops my bag of food on the pavement, "Hang on for your super sipper soda sir."

"No thanks," I say, as I grab the bag off the ground and make for the Suburban.

I jump into the front seat. I start it, throw it into gear and stomp on the gas in one motion. I bounce over a parking bumper, cross the sidewalk and jump the curb into traffic. My food momentarily leaves my lap and floats up to the ceiling. For an instant, I know what it is like to be in outer space. The Cup O' Hot Dog and the burrito separate themselves from the bag and return to my lap.

The chase is on and Manny doesn't even know it. I make a few lane changes until I'm only a few cars behind. I have the horrifying realization that Manny has food in the car. Tacos are not good drive-thru food, they're horrible drive-thru food. So help me if he eats a taco in my car, I'll kill him, but either way I'm going to kill him.

Manny pulls away from the light. I can't follow him too closely. If he catches on, he could turn up the speed and that'll be it; shredded cheese everywhere. I cut off a few cars and slip in behind him. I take a moment to quiet my stomach and force the burrito into my mouth. I think strategy as I wolf down the beans and rice concoction. If I pull up next to him and he recognizes me, he'll run. I can follow him until he stops, but then if I lose him, I've lost him.

I see Manny's profile as he turns to eat a taco. Better judgment says corner him, stop him, drag him out of the car, and beat him until he's senseless.

But I lose my cool. I lay it on the horn. Manny crushes the taco in his hand and sprays the interior with lettuce, cheese and grade C ground beef.

Manny blasts through a changing light. I am right behind him. We make a hard left onto the 101, right in front of a trailer park. We mix with the bridge traffic before getting immediately off the freeway and onto Sir Francis Drake Boulevard. Manny throws a left and blasts toward the town of Ross. We follow the road past high-dollar private schools, the county hospital and the community college. Manny is kept in check by several other SUVs. He is jumping around in the driver's seat like a hopped up meth freak. He jerks the wheel left and right. He dives on the brakes and jams on the gas.

My blood is beginning to boil. Manny slows down as he approaches a red light. I come up next to him and I lay on the horn. Manny doesn't move. This guy is out of his mind. He stares straight ahead as if I wasn't even there. I can't decide whether to continue this chase or get out and pummel him. The left turn light changes to green and Manny jumps on it. He cuts off the car next to him and darts down a side street. I give chase.

This street leads directly into the Marin County Park. I'll just run him down at the dead end. I'll take the door off my own car. When he gets out I'll back over him. I'll put my rear tire on top of him and I'll do a burn out.

I cringe when Manny swerves toward some garbage cans. You've got to be kidding. I lay on the horn again to dissuade him, but it's of no use.

He piles through the cans sending garbage flying. Trash rains down on my hood. The Suburban's windshield is covered with empty bags of organic potato chips and magazines. A vegan magazine open to a wheat grass colonics article attaches itself to the windshield and blocks my view. I notice the length of garden hose in the picture. Now I know what I am going to do with Manny when I get my hands on him. I turn on the wiper and the windshield is scraped clean. Manny is already stopped ahead and is out of the vehicle and running across the grass. I slam on my brakes and jump from the truck. We're in Marin County Park.

Manny is a junkie, so how fast can he possibly run? I take off down the same slope and follow him through the middle of a girls' softball game. The hitting team wasn't ready for Manny but they're lined up for me. Along with countless obscenities, a few well-timed base hits zing by my head and several balls rain down around me as I cut across the playing field. I feel like a sheet metal duck at the Circus Circus casino. These girls are serious about their game.

Manny bounds a low fence.

You're not supposed to concentrate on the leap, you're supposed to concentrate on the landing, but of those landing images I conjure up, all but one, ends in castration. So I stop, and step over the fence as several more balls sail in.

Manny races into a grove of thick woods. I bound over a few logs, my face lashed by switches and my shoes muddied. I glance down at the dark soil covering my feet. I see his prints next to my own. Those are my shoes, the ones he stole the other night. This gives me the will to dig a little deeper. I push on. I can hear traffic now, lots of it. Enough is enough. I force myself through the last thicket and collapse in a pile on the sidewalk. I'm on Sir Francis Drake Boulevard, and Manny is getting on a bus. I leap to my feet and race to the door, but it closes. I slap hard on the glass. The pony-tailed, white-haired, hippie bus driver flashes me a look of sheer terror. The look one would have when faced with the black and blue swollen face of a frustrated detective.

As I jog alongside the bus, Manny walks down the center aisle to the back. I'm finally face to face with the weasel. This jerk may have done something to my sister and it kills me that I can't do anything about it. He is scrawny, acne-faced and unshaven. He has a lot of nerve to smile at me. The bus picks up speed and there is nothing I can do to keep up. Manny sits in a window seat closest to me. He leans toward the glass.

"Where's Lucy?" I shout, while pounding on the window.

Manny leans closer. He presses his mouth up against the glass as if he was going to say something. Instead, he just blows into the glass inflating his cheeks like a puffer fish. He drags his nose back and forth along the glass, giving him a pig-like appearance. Then he turns away. I memorize the back of his head because that is what I will be looking at the next time I see him; he'll be face down in a pool of his own blood.

Chapter Twenty

"Freeze! Get down! Lay Down! Get away from the car! Put your hands where we can see them."

This sounds all too familiar.

"Right," I say, stepping away from my car as I gently lay down in the grass with my arms spread out. I relish the feel and smell of the fresh cut grass. It reminds me of my fatherless childhood. Actually, it wasn't so much fatherless as it was...father-light.

I used to play dead, lying face down on the family lawn until my father came home from work. Sometimes, I was there for hours. What I remember most is the smell of marathon sod.

"Help him up." Tom Ricketts shoes are inches from my nose. He's wearing new white socks, very bright white socks. Tom buys bushels of them at Costco. Several years ago, while I was on a ride–along, I watched him load the trunk of his cruiser in the Costco parking lot with recycled boxes stuffed with frozen goods, DVDs, bestsellers and bundles of socks. We were supposed to be on the beat. Tom once put a 24-pack of paper towels in the back seat with a juvenile suspect. The kid was scared to death. He told the kid that we were going to make him clean up his own blood.

Note to self: To instill fear in a youth offender, make him or her hold the implied instruments of his own demise; blue tarps, ropes, a bag of lime. It's like making them dig their own grave. They'll tell you everything you need to know.

One of the police officers extends his hand and pulls me to my feet. Tom is already rooting around in the back of my Audi SUV.

"You're letting Manny get away." I say, still sucking a little wind from the chase.

Tom pulls his head out of my car, "What are you saying?"

I quickly explain the car chase and the bus. I give him the bus number.

"Are you going to stop the busses? How about a helicopter?" I say, hoping that this lucky lead stays warm.

"Jack," Tom grabs me by the shoulder and walks me toward the front of the wagon, "I know you want Manny to lead you directly to your sister, but you and I both know that isn't going to happen. Manny is a small-time thief and a junkie. He isn't a kidnapper and he isn't a murderer. If he was, he would have killed you back in San Geronimo."

Tom is not telling me anything I don't already know. He is simply pulling me back to reality. I was hoping. "I know what you're saying, Tom. It's just that I need something to happen. I need a break. I've got nothing on Lucy except that Manny may have been the last one to see her. I want to know what state she was in. I want to know what she was wearing. I want to know if she said anything to him."

"We've been friends our whole lives Jack. We're going to find her, but we can't waste our time on Manny. There isn't going to be a bus chase and there isn't going be a helicopter. Manny is a moron and can't help but turn up again. And when he does, we'll be there, and we'll come down hard on him."

"I want to be there."

"You'll be there. Is any of this stuff yours?" Tom is pointing at large empty glass aquarium and one of those fisherman's nets on a pole.

"I've never seen them before."

"It's obvious that the perp's slimy prints are all over these items. Get a picture of this fish tank." Tom Ricketts motions to one of the other officers standing by. The officer goes to Tom's car and grabs the digital camera off the seat. He takes a few pictures. The cargo area is fairly clean except for the foreign items and some fish scales.

"I'm a little confused by these tanks." Tom rubs his chin.

I look at the tanks. No sand or pumps, just empty tanks. "You think he's stealing fish now?" I ask.

"Probably. There's a lot of money in Koi fish. I once heard about a frat boy killing and grilling one at Santa Cruz. The tree huggers were up in arms and practically lynched him."

"Bizarre."

"Nothing is bizarre anymore."

I look at Tom and his perfect white tube socks and his Kirkland golf shirt and I disagree.

I see a runner in the distance round the bases on the baseball diamond. That person could have easily been Lucy, forcing herself on the team, getting picked last but never failing to get on base.

I turn toward the front seat of the Audi thinking that I might be able to grab the letters in the glove box but I'm instantly repulsed by the burger bedlam in the front seat.

"Is that blood? Camera now!" Tom Ricketts shouts to his lackeys, as he peers over my shoulder.

"Ketchup. He went through the Pup and Taco," I say.

"Chill on the digital, boys. This guy was a pig."

There are burger wrappers everywhere. Broken taco shells fill the seats, ketchup packets are mashed into the carpet. Every cup holder has a super sipper cup in it.

I pop open the glove box and find it empty. "Damn it." No letters.

"'What's up?"

"Manny took something that belonged to Lucy."

"Your insurance will replace it."

"Not quite." My mind returns to the bus and the image of Manny blowing against the bus window. I am going to eviscerate him.

"If I were your insurance company I would total the car for this alone," Tom remarks, referring to the half hotdog jammed into the ashtray.

"I'll kill him," I say, with very little irony.

"Easy, big guy, you're not off the hook yet."

"What's that supposed to mean?"

"Remember the dead guy in the woods?" In a hushed voice, Tom turns the conversation on a dime. "They can still try to build a case around you, so be careful. Every cop in town wants to solve that thing. I heard the wife was your client. You're already guilty by association. Now all they need is motive. You don't have motive, do you Jack?"

"I barely have association. I've only met the woman once." The burrito grease in my stomach is getting stirred up.

"Twice." Tom lingers on the word. He is waiting for a reaction.

I don't react even though I should. I've been asked to help find a missing husband and now there is a bear of suspicion chasing me.

"Did you hear anything more about Flynn?" I try to redirect him to the investigation.

"Nothing official. Did Jacobs let you in on the course they're following with regard to Mr. Flynn in the woods?" Tom Ricketts asks right back.

"No, just that they identified him. They don't have any leads or a cause of death other than what we kind of figured out on our own."

"You found him. How do you think he died?"

"It looked like he fell out of the sky. That's the best that I can deduce by the wounds and the placement of the body."

"Wow. Sounds a little crazy, don't you think? Not many people are falling out of the sky these days." Tom looks to the sky just to be sure it's clear.

"It just makes the most sense, that's all. Stevens was going to check with the FAA for any leads. That's where we left it."

We ponder the fast-food wreckage another moment while the other officers hover close by.

"I doubt he'll find anything. It's a needle in the haystack." Tom is not the eternal optimist.

"You must have contacts up at Marin Airport. I don't want to put you in an awkward position but maybe you could ask around."

"It's a little premature if they don't have a cause of death, don't you think? Besides, no judge would issue a warrant on speculation alone."

"You're probably right, but I was just thinking that if Ellen Jacobs' office is going under the assumption of death by fall, it wouldn't hurt. Maybe you could get to the info, right or wrong, before they do. You've got a much better rep around here."

Tom runs his hand through his hair and glances at the two officers working the recovered vehicle; my Audi Q7. "I'll see what I can do."

"Tom, if you were to happen on any information you would let me know, right? I just want to get cleared as you said."

"If I hear anything that will benefit you, I'll let you know."

"I would appreciate it."

"Hey we're old friends, right?"

"Of course."

"I've got some advice for you. Now that you've solved your own missing person case the same day you got it, you can move on and concentrate on other things, like your sister." Tom seems antsy, as if I am keeping him from his kid's soccer game that he just remembered. "When you get burned out you go sailing like the old days."

To my dismay a tow truck pulls up to the front of the Audi Q7.

"Sorry, Jack. We've got to tow it. It was probably used during the commission of a crime." The officers direct the tow truck to the front of the car.

"If you hear anything about Manny, you'll let me know?"

"You'll be the first one to hear."

"Thanks, Tom."

"Save your time and energy, forget about the Flynn case. Go find your sister." Tom turns to his underlings and orders, "Not a scratch. Get this to the yard ASAP. I want pictures and prints and detail it when you're done."

Tom carries on with the work, tagging and bagging the junk in the back. I remove the last of the garbage can debris off the hood of the Suburban and climb in. In the rearview mirror as I drive away, I watch the front of my Audi jerk up into the sling of the tow truck. The Q7 will never be the same.

Chapter Twenty-one

I resolve to understand the dog sticker in the back window of Flynn's car. The easiest way for most people to check out the meaning of a symbol or logo would be to log on, use a search engine, whatever that is, and get its origin, but not me. I'm a sailor and the best place for sailors to learn about symbols is in a tattoo parlor.

Victor's Waterfront Tattoo rests atop pilings in the San Rafael canal on the east side of town. It used to be a barber shop before a parolee, with a passion for ink, bought it. Kasai, an Angolan transplant pronounced Casey by his clients, runs the place. He studied art in San Quentin, received his bachelor's and was on his way to a master's degree when the parole board deemed him safe enough to re-enter society. That decision saved the taxpayers thousands.

Kasai is sitting in a barber's chair set in the back of the small shop.

"Finally signing up for some ink, Jack?" Kasai puts down a copy of Ink magazine.

"Not today, Kasai." The thought of him coming after me with a needle is terrifying.

"You might want to put some Maori war paint over that shipwrecked face of yours."

"Thanks for the suggestion, but I'll heal."

"You'd better hope so."

"I'm looking for a match on a dog logo I saw in the back of a car window."

"Like a sticker or what?"

"Yeah, a sticker." My eyes are drawn to the walls covered in tattoo designs. Kasai has everything you could think of; from cartoon characters to company logos and a million different kinds of lettering in a bunch of different languages.

"It looks like a sitting dog howling at the moon?"

"It's probably native American. I've been doing a bunch of them lately." Kasai gets up and moves his huge African frame to a bookshelf filled with large black binders. He pulls one from the stacks and opens it on the counter. After paging through it, he finds a section on Native American symbols. He turns a page revealing the same howling dog.

"That's it."

"It's the Coyote. I just did a bunch of them on some flighty white women. They kept asking for the dog, but it's a coyote."

"Do you know who these women were?"

"Sure. They're a bunch of bored ex-wives who live up on the hill in a Mill Valley commune. They're putting them on their ankles. It's got to be a cult."

"Do you know where it is?"

"Sure, they gave me a flyer for Pilates or something. Do you think I need Pilates, Jack?"

I look at his huge muscles bursting from his shirt. "Can't hurt."

Kasai hands me the flyer. "Be careful, there are a lot of very impressionable women up there."

"Right." I look down at the flyer and there is the coyote howling back at me. "Pilates, Yoga and tantric pottery classes offered daily in a wooded environment."

This is the same coyote that I found on Flynn's SUV.

Chapter Twenty-two

Back behind the wheel of the Suburban, I call Enza to get the latest information and she has plenty.

Enza answers her cell phone right away. "I'm at the office putting the final touches on the Flynn file. Got any leads on Lucy?" she says.

I'm starting to sound like a broken record. "Nope. Any Messages?"

"Nope."

"Why don't you meet me at the café in Mill Valley? We'll go over it."

"I'll be there in fifteen."

"Perfect." I hang up the phone. That gives her a few minutes to get there. It's a good starting point for my trip up the hill to the commune. I take the alternate route through the hills of rolling oaks and million dollar mini mansions. As I drive by the tidy lawns and rope swings, Lucy presses heavily on my mind.

Lucy is doing a good job of rallying the troops whether she knows it or not. I'm beginning to think that searching for her might be irrelevant. When I do find her she'll want to know why I was looking. She doesn't like us interfering in her life; she's never interfered in mine, except for times like this.

I pass a lawn full of kids playing four-way catch exactly as my brother and sister had done so many autumns ago. The only thing on our minds was the game of catch. There was nothing else to worry about. I could use a game of catch today.

I was not around when Lucy began her downslide. At that time I was too concerned about trying to find myself and my purpose in life. I was among fellow backpackers and in youth hostels, bars and discos, tromping around the world. I wasn't around when Lucy let herself go; when she stopped throwing things away, when her apartment turned into a storage locker piled with boxes and trash. I wasn't around when she was evicted. I wasn't there when she left the grid.

I'm beginning to think that my father was not so bad, or at least not as bad as me.

I call my brother's office in the city. I hold for five minutes before he takes the call. He's the only law firm in town that uses country hold music. Frank never seemed the country type, but here it is. I sometimes wonder if he dresses up like a cowboy when no one is looking.

"Anything new?" Frank doesn't even say hello.

"I had a run in with Manny, the junkie who rearranged my face last night. There was a car chase and a foot pursuit that ended in his getting away. So far he is the only lead I have."

"What about the halfway house?"

"I investigated it pretty thoroughly, but they've got a new tenant in her room and they're moving on. The personal items she left behind didn't have anything to offer. The manager of the house wasn't much help either." I think about the call list at the halfway house Glenda wouldn't allow me access, but I don't want to bring it up. Nothing will be achieved by getting into an argument with Frank.

"The restaurant where she worked didn't have anything to go on either."

"What about a boyfriend?" It sounds like Frank is reading something else at the same time, multi-tasking.

"Nothing points to her having one. Until I get a break or she checks in, the case seems pretty cold."

"Manny may be our best bet." I'm not a fan of Frank using the term "our," but I let it go.

"When Manny surfaces, I'll be there."

"What about the high-tech dead guy, Colin Flynn, in the woods?"

"How do you know it was Flynn?"

"I have friends in high places too."

"I found him. I'm off the case. Did your friends tell you that the sheriff would be off mine?"

"You'll be fine, if you don't do anything stupid," Frank says in a fatherly tone.

"Find Lucy." Frank clicks off.

Soon I'm driving down the narrow streets deep into Mill Valley. It's a hiding place for San Francisco. What can't be hidden in plain sight in neighborhoods like the Haight and the Castro is forced to move out over the Golden Gate to Mill Valley. The Valley is a conservative community guised in a faux liberalism. Its environmental stance is really a form of nimbyism (not in my back yard). There is the hot tub community, the cocaine community for affluent adults and the crystal meth community for their children. We can't forget the environmental action groups: Save the Slugs, Heal the Seals and Free the Trees. Then there's voodoo, Santeria, shamanism, and square dancers, free love, pay for love and the swingers, and they're all hiding among the redwoods beneath Mt. Tamalpais.

It's the perfect place for people like my sister to grow up and totally spin out of control with nothing but a moth-eaten, threadbare safety net that is held up loosely by a bunch of so-called adults who've forgotten the parental responsibility they never had in the first place.

The deeper you go into the Valley the denser the trees and the tighter the hold becomes on privacy. The closer you get to Mt. Tam the taller the fences and the thicker the hedges. The same mountain that provides the watershed and the town's chilling afternoon shade guards its citizens and their dirty laundry like an unyielding sentry.

The small village spills out into wetlands where there are two roads leading into town from the highway, one from the south and the other from the north. There is access to the beach communities of Stinson and Bolinas through a series of dangerous twists and turns, where more than one disenchanted house wife has tried to off herself by driving her German SUV over the edge.

I settle down into an outdoor table in a café at the intersection of several shop-lined streets. A few skateboarders and hacky-sackers waste their afternoon kicking, tripping and sometimes falling. Families with their purebred retrievers and purebred children gather and glide from store to store.

Enza parks her Mini Cooper illegally in a red zone directly in front of the patio. She tosses a thick manila folder on the table and then takes a long hard look at my face.

"Turn your head to the right," she says, placing her long slender fingers on my cheek. "It's going away, but…"

"But what?" I ask, expecting to hear her use the term "permanent scarring."

"I don't know. It looks like it is turning green."

"Green?"

"Green."

Enza puts her hand on my shoulder and draws me closer. She is wearing high heels and a tight athletic sweat suit with the words 'Hey Now' stenciled across her butt cheeks. Sensing all other eyes upon us, I feel uncomfortable. This is a faux-liberal family town.

Enza licks her finger and wipes my face, "It's coming off."

"All of it?"

"Just the green."

I remember being face down in the park. "They must be grass stains," I say. "I was in a foot pursuit with Manny in the park that ended with my face in the grass and a cop's boot on my head." I use a slight exaggeration with regard to the boot. Sometimes you have to spice it up a little with Enza or you lose her attention.

"What happened to Manny?"

"Lost him to the Golden Gate Transit Authority, but Ricketts assured me that he'll get him and I'd be the first one to know." Opposite the coffee store, my gaze lands on a woman in a long, flowing robe who is attempting to panhandle, albeit very subtly. There is something weird about her.

"Whenever you're ready?" Enza opens the file in front of me.

"Right."

Enza printed a lot of material off the internet. She compiled press releases from Flynn's company, the Flynn's resumes and their credit reports. Enza cross-referenced the company with news services on the Web and came up with numerous articles regarding the company's ventures and global successes. Their business seems to have a lot to do with the hardware that connects companies to the internet. They have commercial switching stations for high speed communication. There is a lot of technical speak. I let it go for now.

I take a long look at both Christine and Colin's resumes. A lot about a person can be gleaned from these simple sheets that everyone in business is required to have. We all make them up and we usually include every detail about our public lives as well as some of our personal details.

"Do you want to buy a girl a cup of coffee?" Enza rubs my shin with her toe.

"Sorry, sure," I say, tossing a five on the table.

Enza stares at the five. "Is there something wrong?" I ask, half expecting to be railroaded into a scheme.

"You know I can't just have a cup of coffee. I'll crave a cookie and there will be no end to it."

I pull another five out of my pocket. "There never will be."

"Do you want anything boss?"

"No."

"Sure?"

"Yep," I say.

"Thanks for all this," I motion to the documents that she carefully assembled.

"Just doing my job." Enza turns on her heel and makes for the counter. I return to the file.

Colin Flynn studied at the University of Michigan and graduated with a degree in Finance. He was in a fraternity and a member of several finance and banking clubs. No sports reported. He worked at a commercial bank in St. Louis for a couple years after college before he was transferred to the San Francisco office. He was there a very short time before changing jobs again to become a communications engineer with the high-tech company Evo Liquid.

Everything seemed fairly ordinary for a young man on the fast track to a six figure salary, except for one thing; along with his company change came a drastic change to his job description as well. One does not go from banking to engineering overnight. I decide that this bit of info will need more investigating.

I scan his frequent flier miles account. It lists numerous trips to Peru and one to the Central American banking capital of Panama. I make note of them and move on to Christine's resume.

She is the creative mind of the family. She got a Liberal Arts degree at the same university that her husband attended. She graduated a year behind Colin's MBA. She felt content with art history. She doesn't have anything filling the slot between Michigan and San Francisco. She may have been in St. Louis with Colin but her resume doesn't mention it. Her background is Sacramento, California.

As part of our normal routine, Enza included a bio of all the parents involved. I'm a strict believer that an apple doesn't fall far from the tree. Sometimes the skeletons in your parents' closet make nice housewarming gifts for the kids. In this situation, Colin looks pretty clean. His parents were suburban types who held normal jobs that didn't hint at anything sinister. Christine's father was a little more suspect.

So after a year off, Christine followed her college sweetheart to San Francisco to get married and be closer to her family. She comes from a family of rice growers in the Sacramento River delta, as a matter of fact, the biggest rice growers in California.

Her daddy is a pretty active guy. He's on an advisory committee to the World Trade Organization for Agriculture and he travels globally on a regular basis.

"When politics are involved I am always a little suspect," I said.

"Do you want a bite?" Enza returns and waves a cookie under my nose.

"No thanks, I'm almost finished. You did great work here." I quickly scan their credit information: credit cards, a couple car loans, but no mortgage.

"You know what's not in there?" Enza asks, while wiping a whipped cream mustache off her face.

"What's that," I say, closing the file in front of me.

"What's not in there is what my Daddy told me yesterday when he dropped off some lasagna at my place."

"I thought you lived at home."

"I live in the carriage house."

"Right." I forgot that the middle class calls them guesthouses while the rich call them what they are: carriage houses, gate houses, spare houses, cabanas, etc. "You know I don't like it when you ask your dad for information."

"He doesn't mind."

"I know he doesn't mind but that puts me in an uncomfortable position; Indebtedness."

"Don't worry about it, it's just a favor."

I feel a heavy pressure on my chest and a constriction in my throat.

"I asked Daddy if he had heard of Evo Liquid, and he said Uncle Benny told him about it."

"Uncle Benny?" My feet are beginning to feel heavy as if sitting in hardening cement.

"Uncle Benny is Daddy's stockbroker. Benny said that Evo Liquid is owned by a prominent South American who is looking to legitimize his transactions in this country."

"It's a front," I say, with a resounding bell ringing over my head.

"Exactly. Let's just say that agriculture is a global enterprise that often nets cash profits and these profits need to be reinvested."

"So you are saying that Evo Liquid is the outcome of truckloads of money that never make it back over the border."

"I'm not saying anything." Enza digs into her cookie, staring at me over the white topping. Her Daddy trained her well. Don't answer questions without a lawyer present.

I'll answer the question for her. "What no one is saying is that tons of cocaine is sold here in exchange for truckloads of cash. Rather than pay for securing its return through numerous third world countries, the cash is used to develop a corporate environment here. The corporations then reinvest overseas by wire transfer," I say, doing the math while speaking aloud.

"Money laundering made simple." Enza smiles.

"And I bet that Colin is just a pawn. He got his job through his young wife, who may have knowingly or even unknowingly dragged him in. It's her father who travels the world and meets agricultural leaders. Maybe he was looking to grow rice in South America."

"So he meets a Colombian farmer, the notorious Pedro Guerrero, who introduces him to other farming people." Enza is getting excited.

"The baseball player?" I ask, remembering the L.A. Dodgers in their Eighties heyday.

"Different Pedro."

"So either way, there is a connection. Evo Liquid may be the link in Colin's death."

"We've got to dig a little deeper." Enza throws her feet up on the chair next to me and crosses her legs. She's proud of herself.

A man at the next table can't take his eyes off her. If he only knew who her father was. Enza winks at the guy who is dressed in Patagonia fleece from head to toe.

"Enza, we don't have to dig any deeper. We just have to look a little higher." I notice, out of the corner of my eye, that two good-looking couples with identical golden retrievers collide and their leashes become entangled. Confusion ensues while they try to identify their own dogs. Dog names are called but the playful and capricious animals dart in all directions. Finally, the women in the group remove small bar code readers from their Marc Jacobs bags and aim them at the dogs' heads. The dogs are quickly sorted by microchip and returned to their rightful owners. Everyone has a laugh except me.

"I've got a spa treatment in ten, so if you don't mind." Enza gets my attention.

"Thanks again. You did great work. The only missing element is that Arabic letter and, of course, the question of Christine Flynn's complicity."

"Whatever." Enza's moved on.

"Uncle Benny isn't your real uncle, is he?"

"Don't be silly." Enza gets in her car and drives off.

Chapter Twenty-three

I'm probably on the short list of suspects for Colin Flynn's murder and I have no idea what Christine Flynn might be telling the police. Christine can implicate me in her own scheme or perhaps she and Colin have stumbled into something at Evo Liquid that would put them both in danger.

I toss the folder onto the front seat of the suburban. The cell phone Christine gave me rings. I check the number. I don't recognize it. I'm not in the mood to talk to Christine nor do I want to be interrogated when the police begin rifling through her telephone records. A warrant is probably already in the works. The phone rings again. But it could be Frank or Enza or Tom or even Lucy. I reach over to answer it but the call went to voice mail.

I press the retrieve message button. It asks for a password and I enter the phone's last four digits. It's Ellen Jacobs checking on my whereabouts. She apologizes for Bill Stevens' behavior but is adamant that I not go anywhere and that I not talk to Christine. I make a mental note to call Ellen.

I remember the flyer for Pilates I picked up at Kasai's as I drive through the narrow streets to the commune in the hills. There is nothing more relaxing than Tantric pottery classes to clear my head.

I recognize the street listed on the flyer and find it easily amongst the tall trees. I come upon the address and park in a turn out a few hundred yards beyond the unmarked entrance. The street is quiet. Most of the homes are either built above the street or cascade down beneath it. There is a wrought iron coyote logo mounted to a high wooden fence and a driveway disappears beneath a wide rolling gate.

I grab a length of rope from the back of the Suburban and study the fence for a possible climb. The fence is about eight feet high and has very few handholds. Without the rope, I'd be scratching at the fence like a mouse against aquarium glass. I toss the line around a limb of a cedar tree behind the fence and whip the tail of the line back toward me.

I hear a car coming up the street. I have nowhere to hide so I drop the rope and begin walking toward my car. Just as I reach the gate the car stops next to me. I can't help but look over at the car. A woman in a flowing robe gets out. It's the same woman I saw in town only a few minutes ago.

"Interested in signing up?" She asks as her ride pulls away.

Her beautiful eyes pierce right through me. "Signing up?" Her eyes are the deepest blue, like the ocean on a sunny day. They keep getting bluer and bluer. My pre-planned script has leaked out of my skull and on to the driveway.

She points at the flyer in my hand. Her hair is in pig tails and there is a large crystal dangling from her neck.

I try to put letters together to make a word and words together to make a sentence.

"Yes. I'm here to check out the classes." I'm back in the scene, carry on everyone.

"Come inside," she says as she opens a narrow gate next to a driveway. "Don't forget your rope," she says.

"That's not my rope."

She looks at me like I am an idiot. I leave the rope anyway.

The gate rolls open revealing a narrow pathway that twists and turns its way through the grove of giant trees.

"Are you coming?" She asks, looking down at the flyer in my hand.

"Sure." We start down the path.

After a moment of uncomfortable silence, and me staring at the bottom of her swaying robe just above her shapely calves, I speak.

"My name is Jack." And I speak like a twelve year old boy meeting a girl for the very first time.

"It's nice to meet you, Jack." She glances back at me then continues down the path.

"I didn't get your name." She doesn't turn back to me, not a glance.

This could be it. I may never be seen again. I might be walking into a trap. 'Flyer' might be some hypnosis code word to sign my entire estate over to whoever these people are. "Who runs this place? Is it a church or something like that?" Nonchalant.

"It's a community run by Red Fish." She says it like he is world renown.

"Really," I have no idea what on earth she is talking about. Maybe it has something to do with her diet. "You mean Red Snapper?"

"Red Fish is a spiritual leader. He is a remarkable man. He is not the fresh fish of the day."

The young woman looks directly into my eyes, "Red Fish has changed my life. He is the enlightened one."

"*The* enlightened one?"

"Red Fish lives on a completely different level." The path continues through the wood, alongside a driveway.

"Where did you meet?"

"I met him in the Nevada desert at the Burning Man festival. It's a really a great story." This nameless girl is looking back at me now, her face animated with excitement. It's as if she were in love.

"To make a long story short, while I was experiencing LSD for the very first time, I crashed my golf cart into a Teriyaki chicken cart. The revelers thought we were burning the man so they started tossing wood and accelerants on my golf cart. Some nice people dragged me out of the inferno, he was one of them. Red Fish saved my life. I smelled like the kitchen at Benihanas Restaurant. Then he drove me to Mill Valley and put me up in this house."

"Benihanas doesn't have a kitchen; they cook the food at the table." I say.

"Whatever."

Chapter Twenty-four

We reach a parking area next to a low fence that contains a compound made up of several buildings. The coyote is engraved on the fence post. I can see that it's same coyote in the windows of the cars in the parking lot, on the gate and probably on the ankles of flighty white women. The nameless girl is wearing bright white cotton gym socks.

The fog rolls overhead, creating a small eddy of open air surrounding the house and grounds. "It's as if Red Fish's powers are holding back the fog," the girl says smiling. She goes on to describe the buildings as the home, temple and offices where Red Fish runs a Web based spiritual awareness company.

"Are you okay?" I ask, with a forced hint of concern in my voice.

"I'm just getting excited," the girl says, hopping from foot to foot like a Somali tribal dancer.

She bounces up and down with her back rigid and her arms straight at her sides. This behavior is symptomatic of mental illness. She hops up and down for a long time. She still thinks she's at Burning Man.

I stand there watching her; as she goes up, my comfort level goes down.

A small pack of yapping dogs attack us. The girl immediately lies down on the ground and rolls around, letting them lick her face.

"Maybe I should come back at another time." When I can sneak in and not have to deal with this wacko.

She jumps up to her feet. "You have to meet Red Fish. I'm sure that he can help you decide on an appropriate Pilates course."

"Tantric Pottery." Never change the script in the middle of a snoop. She may be playing me, trying to find me out. "I'm interested in pottery."

"I'm sorry, pottery."

This could be a big mistake. I was never much for believing in commercial shamanism. I figure the outcome is always going to be biased by the amount of money you donate.

"Just meet him. You'll thank me." She tilts her head to one side and smiles.

The pack of dogs encircles us. She says the pack is led by a Lhasa Apso named Dalai. That's a bit much.

We go through a small fenced enclosure surrounding a group of well-tended Japanese rock gardens and continue through a breezeway between two buildings.

"These are the cleansing facilities." The girl wipes her face with a make believe bar of soap. Creepy.

"It says 'restrooms' on the door."

"You have to see the deeper meaning, Jack."

We continue walking within the odd circle of small houses and buildings.

"Red Fish built the compound based on an atoll with a central lagoon. The houses are fanned out around the central garden at imperfect angles. The houses are like islands, and the space between, like passes in the reef." Her dialogue sounds studied.

What is her name for God's sake?

We meander down a narrow path in the central garden overflowing with flowering rhododendrons, tree ferns, holly and juniper. Fountains and small streams bubble and babble in all directions. I hear voices but can't place their origin.

"We offer day and evening classes. Our curriculum includes several types of Yoga, Pilates and of course, the arts. We offer classes to the general public, as well as to those who prefer to live in the lifestyle here on the reservation."

Reservation?

"I don't believe that I ever caught your name?"

"My name is Maizy." Maizy gives me her hand as we walk through the gardens. "Red Fish gave me this name."

"I can't believe your name is not butter," I say deadpan.

"What's that?"

"Your name, I can't believe...Parkay?" I can tell by her expression that she doesn't get it. I let it go. "It was a corny joke." Maizy gives me the same blank look.

Lucy would have probably said the same thing to me. She was never patient when it came to my sense of humor, but I don't expect to find Lucy here. She's troubled, but not so much that she would cash it all in for a place like this. She isn't one for being told what to do. She would have filleted Red Fish if he even suggested she give up her name. I think again about my conversation last night with Ellen Jacobs. Is Lucy the same person after all? Have the years of institutional living changed her completely? Could she actually wind up in a place like this? I can't rule it out.

"I have to give it to this guy, Red Fish. He has a pretty serene operation going here." I get back on message.

The fountains continue to babble as beautiful Koi gasp at the water's surface. We watch the fish for a moment. The huge carp are practically climbing on top of one another.

"Some of these fish cost in the thousands." Maizy taps a couple on their heads. She coos to them like little pets.

I look at her eyes as she studies the tussling fish.

"Several were stolen...I mean, disappeared recently."

"Stolen or disappeared?" Something is beginning to smell very fishy, fishy like the aquariums in the back of the Q7.

"Crazy, isn't it?" Her stare cuts right through me. "Red Fish doesn't like to use words that pertain to criminality. It's bad Karma. He thinks it just better that we not attach negative terminology to things that go unexplained."

"Right."

"Are you a policeman? Is that why you are here? To help with the missing fish?"

"No, actually, I'm just checking into the pottery classes. I noticed your logo, the coyote."

"It's not a logo, it's a totem." Maizy reaches down and pulls down her sock, exposing a small tattoo. "It's to protect us. We're here."

We're standing outside a small cabin. A large bed is opposite the door. There is a small armoire and no other furniture. The tidy room is lit only with candles.

"Change into the robe that you'll find in the cabin. It will make you feel more comfortable."

"I was hoping to talk to Red Fish about the classes."

"Change into the robe, you'll see." Maizy touches my arm.

"I don't think that's necessary at all. I'm only here to talk to Red Fish about the pottery. Wait a minute, who says I have to wear the robe anyway?"

"I want you to." Maizy smiles and turns toward the pond.

Damn. I calmly remove my clothes and hang them in the armoire. I put on the robe embroidered with the totem. I think back to my youthful days as an Indian guide, a sort of cub scouts group but with Indians; very eighties. I remember the monthly meetings that included a seminar on tribes and their history. I remember the punch and cookies and I remember the stiff drinks all the fathers drank. We planned field trips and sleepovers, camp outs and sailing trips. And we also studied the symbolism of North American mammals in the Native American belief system. I remember the coyote clearly and he was the Trickster.

I turn to the doorway. Maizy is waiting for me. She may have seen me change. It doesn't seem to bother her.

"Let's go to the great room to meet Red Fish." She announces.

"Do I need to bring my wallet?"

Maizy giggles.

We follow a pathway through thick vegetation. I have now lost my bearings completely and am dying for a compass. In less than a minute we arrive at a great room. A set of open French doors lead into an open space. Roughhewn beams are overhead, floor to ceiling windows and large fireplaces are at opposite ends of the room. There are yoga mats laid out on the floor. Music seeps in from overhead. Maizy and I sit in the front row.

"I don't like sitting in the front row," I say in a whisper. "I don't want to be called on."

"You've already been called on, or you wouldn't be here. Assume the lotus."

Cute. Maizy crosses her legs as I tumble forward, my face pressed against the floor. I push myself up and settle for crossed legs and a rigid back. My face is dented from the impact.

She winces at my countenance. "Let's just relax and think about nothing. Just let everything come to you, not from you."

I do as I am told. I focus on nothing. I go to my happy place, but I come back because there's too much going on.

"Where's Red Fish? Is the pottery studio air conditioned?" Stay on message.

Maizy doesn't answer. Her eyes are closed and her palms are up. Goodnight.

I close my eyes. I can only think about Lucy and Colin and Christine. Lucy disappeared into thin air. It's like we all do from time to time. I wonder how many people can re-trace my steps when I drop off the radar. I wonder if this is the place where my screen will go blank.

I think back to the fish conversation. Expensive fish have gone missing and Manny had aquariums in my car. There can't be that many fish abductions in Marin. He must have been here as recent as last night. Red Fish must know Manny.

When I open my eyes, Maizy and I are surrounded by a large group of followers. A surfer-type guy is sitting directly in front of me, facing the group. Next to him is a sinister-looking guy with white hair and sunglasses. The surfer type is Red Fish, he has an odd smile on his face, like he is either trapped in meditative bliss, or stoned out of his mind. He rings a large Tibetan bell as the group stands and stretches. Red Fish looks vaguely familiar. A few followers talk softly. I wonder if they're talking about me.

"Meditation is over," Maizy announces and bounds outside.

I finally place the face or fish as it were. Red Fish is Gabe the Grifter; a confidence man I used for information before he dropped off the radar. I met him while he was doing a stint at San Quentin.

Sometimes I think in movie scenes: establishing a shot, San Quentin flashes into my head, surrounded by crumbling walls and rusting fence, it's a prison looming on the San Francisco bay. It is the Gulag of the California penal system. Gabe the Grifter walks the lonely walk to freedom in a tan suit and fedora.

I guess Gabe the Grifter is back, and so am I.

He recognizes me caught out in a lie. "Bru, how in the hell are you?

Damn, it's good to see you." Red Fish throws his arms around me and doesn't seem to want to let go. The microphone headset he is wearing presses up against my head.

Red Fish, aka Gabe the Grifter, aka the Shaman, aka Lose Weight Now Ask Me How is speaking into his headset. "Listen, everyone. I have found my friend and he is beautiful." He says this into the microphone. I notice that everyone is wearing headsets.

"You look well, Brubaker." His words contradict his facial expression. It must be the discoloration of my face that gives him pause.

"So do you...Gabe?"

"It's Red Fish, brother. I have finally found my true self."

"This seems a big departure from renting boards at Stinson." Gabe had once set up a small rental operation at Stinson Beach using stolen surfboards. It was short-lived.

Gabe's eyes widen. "I'm not sure what you are talking about, but I can tell you this: I recently learned that my grandfather was a Native American shaman and he handed down his spiritual abilities to me. Using some of the profits from "Lose Weight Now Ask Me How," I was able to lobby the Bureau of Indian Affairs in Washington to re-establish my tribe here in Mill Valley. We are an offshoot of the Miwok. Originally we only numbered about twenty back in the day."

"Back in the day?"

"Yeah, sometime in the 1700s. We have a historian running around here if you need the numbers. Anyway, I found that we could get some land and re-establish our place on Mother Earth. We picked up this estate at auction. Now we're heading toward true self-realization here. We're inviting everyone aboard to boost the numbers. We get a better deal on health care benefits," he says softly.

"Sounds like you've got it all figured out, Gabe."

"Red Fish."

"Sorry, Red Fish."

"Look, we've got a lot going on here and I want you to be part of it. We've got the meditation and, listen to this; we've got a Peruvian guy, just came in from Peru with enough ayahuasca for the entire tribe to experience the birth of mankind."

"I can't stay."

"Not even for the birth of mankind? Working on a case, eh Jack?"

"A couple. But bearing witness to the birth of mankind sounds very tempting."

"I'll tell you what. Stick around, have dinner, meet some of the squaws. We'll try a little of this Peruvian crap and see if that opens any doors for you, man."

This guy is a salesman first and a shaman second.

"You can learn a lot in an altered state. And if that doesn't do it for you, we've got yoga and Pilates."

"I don't know, Red Fish."

"Think about it." Red Fish has begun the same hopping dance that I witnessed earlier. His followers join in unison. The entire group is pogoing up and down except for the Peruvian...and me.

"I do have some questions regarding the stolen fish," I say, my head nodding up and down trying to keep pace with Red Fish's rising and falling.

"Okay. Save the questions for later. I'm real busy right now. What do you say?"

"I don't know. It's been a while since I've done anything like this. Actually, I really am busy, a couple active cases on my plate. You know the deal. Maybe another time."

"I'll waive the fee."

"Okay then." Twist my arm. "Sounds good."

The group eases out of the dance. They shake their arms and legs like they just finished a marathon.

Red Fish gestures for hug. And I lean in. "Whoa, Whoa," he says, "please don't squeeze the shaman." He turns to his followers, evoking an awkward group laugh. "Like the toilet paper...Charmin?" He explains as if I were already on the Peruvian herb.

"Right." I say. I wouldn't be surprised if everyone I meet from now on wears purple Nikes.

Maizy grabs my arm and pulls me aside. "I was watching you earlier. You didn't move in the meditation for at least forty minutes."

"You're kidding right?"

"It's called meditation."

"Really, because I was beginning to think that you slipped me a mickey."

Maizy has that confused look on her face like so many young people when I mention an era specific reference.

"Let's go relax in the hot tub." Red Fish makes a pronouncement.

Hot tub? "Relax?" I ask. "Do these people do anything but?"

"Meditating is not relaxing. Now, we're really going to chill out." Red Fish motions for me to follow.

Maizy grabs my butt. "Great stuff, eh Jack?"

"Yeah." The sun is gone and I'm surrounded by a bunch of people in long, flowing robes. I don't know whether they're angels or ghouls.

Chapter Twenty-five

I look down into the water bubbling, frothing and steaming. The only thing the hot tub needs is a giant ladle. "I'm not really sure the hot tub is a good idea, Red Fish. Why don't I sit this one out?"

"Come on, it's cool." Maizy grabs my arm.

I'm not interested in making 'people soup' in a dirty commune hot tub. God only knows what kind of impropriety goes on in this place. "Actually, I just ate. Shouldn't I wait a half hour?" That should get me off the hook.

"We'll get you a set of water wings. Right Whitey?" Red Fish elbows the slick Peruvian. "Let's go, Jack."

I can only imagine the deranged hedonistic lifestyle these communal freaks share. We encircle the tub and step down on to the bench seat. Everyone drops their robes at once.

I'm naked, and to my surprise, no one else is. I immediately sit down up to my neck in the water.

"Whoa! Whoa! Whoa! Better put some shorts on, buddy. There're kids around for Christ's sake." Red Fish puts up his hands.

Red Fish is wearing Hawaiian shorts, and Maizy has on a one piece. The Peruvian is wearing surf shorts exposing a scary red tattoo of skeletons marching up the face of Machu Pichu. Scars resembling knife wounds cover his stark white back.

"I thought that…everyone was…you know?" I'm at a loss for words and swim trunks.

"This isn't Waco!"

"Okie Doke." I start to get out.

"Don't move, once was enough, thank you very much, eh, Whitey?" Red Fish elbows the jungle herb connection, who seems to be connecting on something else right now.

"We'll get you some shorts." Red Fish barks the order through his radio headset.

Below the water line, Maizy pinches my leg. She is smiling. Just what kind of a place is this? Indian music begins to spill from stereo speakers crudely disguised as rocks.

After a pair of swim trunks is delivered by an underling, we sit for a few minutes in the Jacuzzi. I let the chlorine packed steam climb into my head and fill my pores. The steam offers great relief to my face.

Everything seems to be coming together up here. There is a possible Manny connection with the fish. There is also a Peru connection, although slightly different from Flynn's' type of business, but a connection nonetheless.

Red Fish. He doesn't look Native American at first glance. He looks more California native surfer with a, not so subtle, blond comb over. I bet, that if you can go downtown and get a phony driver license you can go downtown and become a phony Native American, too.

Red Fish is in his thirties and has long since ditched the surfboard for mail fraud and arid desert real estate sales. He looks over at me several times during a senseless conversation about vegetarian fried chicken. He has a greasy, knowing smile on his face, as if he were trying to include me in his plot to fleece everyone in the Jacuzzi. During a break in a debate over paper versus plastic, I tell Red Fish about Lucy.

"I'm sorry about your sister, Bru. I haven't seen her since passing through the San Rafael halfway house. And that was two years ago. Good looking' kid I might add. Say hello for me."

"The fact that she is missing might make it difficult to say, 'hello'. Are you sure she hasn't been here?" I continue. "Maybe hanging around with a guy named Manny?"

"She's a smart cookie. She wouldn't be caught dead hanging out here, let alone with that idiot."

"How do you know Manny?"

"We met in a Bob Hope inspired jailhouse variety show, called "Shanks for the Memories". Why do you care so much about Manny?"

"He may have been the last one to see her."

"I don't know what to tell you. I haven't seen her, sorry." Red Fish has his palms up.

I choose not to believe anything he says. He has little hands. I don't trust guys with little hands.

The doors to the meditation center are open and the fires inside are stoked. We get out of the Jacuzzi. The group dries off and moves inside for what, I am told, will be a ceremony that will change my life. Maizy disappears. We take our positions on the mats, evenly spaced. The Peruvian is drooling; long strands of hair hang down in front of his face. Red Fish begins inhaling and exhaling rhythmically. His followers join in.

Maizy returns with a tray of glasses and pitchers containing a muddy brown concoction. A plastic bucket is placed next to each of us. I have a feeling that this potion isn't a thirst quencher.

I heard of ayahuasca during the trip I took to Peru several years ago. The same trip probably got me the missing person job from Christine Flynn; irony rears its ugly comb-over. I ran into several travelers who had experimented with some shamans both in the desert and in the jungle. They said that the mashed and steeped combination of jungle vines was like LSD that lasts all night along. It'll take you down to the root of the earth. I never got a chance to try it.

"You're going to see God, no doubt about it." Red Fish smiles as he drinks the contents of his glass.

I take a swig before pouring the majority of the brown muck into the bucket. No one seems to notice. I'm not going to do this while I should be out searching for Lucy.

"Was my sister here, Gabe? Was Manny with her? Did Manny take your fish?"

Red Fish rolls on to his side laughing. "How do you know about Manny and the fish?"

"Manny was here?"

"We needed to get liquid. It's not easy running a tribe without a slot machine. We simply swap the high-dollar fish with some low-rent carp and we're solid for another month and nobody knows the difference. You're killing my buzz here." Red Fish finishes his glass of ayahuasca and quickly pukes into the bucket. "Damn."

"What's the Manny connection?" I watch some of the brown liquid drip slowly off his chin. His eyes are dilated.

"Manny needed a place to stay last night. I help him out, and he moves some fish for me."

"Is he coming back?" The music has changed to a Peruvian guttural chant with loud beating drums.

"Who?"

"Manny."

"I've got no idea. Right now I'm looking for God." He pours himself another drink and downs it.

"Do you know where I can find him, Manny?" I'm pleading and at the same time smiling painfully from ear to ear.

The followers surrounding us are in various states of dysfunction. Some are puking into buckets, while others are entranced by the rhythm of the drums and pan flutes.

Red Fish shakes his head, 'No'.

I begin to laugh uncontrollably. The small dose has impacted my rationale and improved my vocabulary at the same time. I laugh, thinking about the phenomena. I notice that my legs are actually turning into vines and growing out toward Red Fish's school of followers.

Darkness boils up beneath me, cloaking the vines that are my legs in total blackness. I can't fight it. It's a violent darkness that takes control of my equilibrium. My head spins. Maizy and Red Fish are sucked into a vortex. I'm left alone in this churning black void. I'm tossed around, slammed into something solid and I'm soaking wet and gasping for air. I push off some unseen structure. I struggle to stay afloat.

There is a terrifying roar tossing me about and I can feel that I am holding something under my arm, something limp and lifeless. There is a final blow so violent and horrifying that I find myself twisting and turning, being beaten on the head and the body. I vomit and retch uncontrollably. I give in to it and I let everything go.

The darkness retreats and I'm again in the great room. I lose my balance and roll out of my sitting position, falling directly into Maizy. I stare into her eyes, still blue as the deepest ocean. She smiles and then kisses me long and softly.

Chapter Twenty-six

Maizy is wrapped around my waist, sleeping fitfully with an occasional snort and wheeze. She is naked and so am I. Was it worth it? I run my hand down Maizy's smooth soft skin, warm and beautiful. I brush my hand across her coyote tattoo. It seems worth it, but I know better. Beautiful women are like puppies. Everybody loves a sleeping puppy. When they're awake they're playful and curious, but the moment you attempt to leave them alone they start crying. You can't sleep. Soon Maizy will wake up.

I gently peel Maizy off me. I dress and slip into my shoes and slip out the door. Maizy never stirs. My senses feel heightened, a possible side effect of the drug. I can smell the fog, the flowering plants and the pine needles under my feet. The cheesy Malibu lighting casts an eerie glow over the pathways. Sounds are magnified: the beating drums, distant laughter, splashing, water dripping.

My head is clear and there is no time like the present for a little poking around. I stalk down the path looking for anything that might help with Lucy, Manny or Flynn. The redwoods tower into the sky like Greek columns. I try a few locked doors in the complex. My head parts a curtain of wind chimes. I stumble through pristine rock gardens, disturbing the fine sand. Golf courses leave rakes next to the sand traps, what do the Zen gardeners do?

I sneak past the great room where the host and his guppies are still lolling around on the mats, amongst spilled pitchers of brown muck. It's an orgy of flailing arms and legs, screaming and laugher. All the while, the Peruvian chants into a karaoke microphone like a caller at a square dance.

The moon appears in a break in the heavy sky. I move toward the entrance. I try several doors along the way, all locked except for one. I slip silently inside, closing the door behind me. The room is large. It's a lot like the great room, except this is a modern living area. A couple of sofas face a blank plasma screen. Half of the room is dedicated to office space. There is a desk with several monitors and a keyboard. It is covered with papers. There's an ashtray filled with several burnt joints and a few crumpled beer cans are scattered around the floor.

I do a cursory search of the desk and find nothing but torn off bits of paper with women's names and phone numbers. He does well. I turn on all the monitors. One of the screens is blank except for the totem. The coyote on Flynn's car is not just a coincidence. Flynn was here. He might have been a member but I doubt it. My guess is that he is doing business with Red Fish or vice versa.

Another screen has an image of a darkened bedroom with a line identifying it as "BadGirlBedrooms.com, an elegant voyeur website." Somehow I knew that Red Fish was busier than he suggested. Except for the screens, there is nothing here.

I quickly move to the cabinet beneath the plasma screen. I open a pair of doors to reveal stacks of gleaming white socks still in their bundles. They have the Costco Kirkland label. Another door reveals a stack of eight DVD players and a remote control. I press the power button on the remote. A picture snaps on. The plasma screen is divided into eight frames, each one a surveillance image. I recognize the front gate, several guest rooms where the beds are the focus, the Jacuzzi and the parking lot. There is an image of the great room. Its inhabitants are up and moving around now. Red Fish is staggering outside. He is talking into his headset. I recognize Maizy's room. The bed linens are tossed, and she is gone. Crap.

The last frame is that of me staring directly at the plasma screen. There must be a camera mounted above it. I push all the eject buttons on the DVDs. It's taking too long. Red Fish's image has just passed by one of the bedrooms and is progressing toward the surveillance room. I grab the DVDs as fast as I can and I shove them down the front of my pants. I quickly hit the power button and the screen goes black. I return to the desk and shut down those monitors as well. I ease open the door and move outside. I can hear footsteps in the gravel behind me. I'm now fully aware of my surroundings; I know exactly where I am. I can see the breezeway entrance to the parking lot. I can sense Red Fish arriving at his lair.

I round a dense stand of bamboo on a path leading directly to the breezeway. Maizy is there with the devil in her eyes and a samurai sword in her hands.

"You weren't even going to say goodbye!" She is pogoing again, this time twirling a very long samurai sword over her head. Considering her hallucinogenic state, her dexterity is simply astonishing. She's like some demented baton twirler. Maizy's eyes are dilated pinholes, not what you would expect in this half-light.

"You son of a bitch!"

"Whoa. I'm just out stretching my legs." I have no control over what I say in a break up. "It wasn't you, it was me. It was totally my fault," I plead guilty. The blather pours out from my mouth. I don't even know her. It's a male, knee-jerk reaction.

"It's a little too late for groveling, jerk face." Maizy brings the sword down in front of her, the tip of the blade at my throat.

"There's no time like the present," I say, looking for a way out. Yesterday, an oar in my face, and now a samurai sword.

"Why are you telling me now when you should have told me you had no intention to love me for the rest of our lives, when you moved your stuff into my house?"

"Huh? I think you've got the wrong guy." Her oceanic eyes have turned crazy. She reeks of vomit and marijuana.

She folds her arms, with the sword's shaft standing vertical. "You never asked me how I was feeling. You're insensitive." Maizy throws her head back and performs the most beautiful standing back flip I have ever witnessed.

"Wow. Pilates?" I ask.

"Yeah." She sweeps the sword again. "Don't try to change the subject."

I have to find a way out.

"Insensitive bastard!" Maizy lunges at me with the tip of the blade, aiming directly below my belt. The blade tears through my pants and hits the DVDs. I back up, still on my feet. Maizy stares at me in crazy-eyed disbelief. She should have run me through. She collapses to the ground and curls up in a ball. I step over her, a sobbing mess. I hate it when girls cry. I break for the driveway and for my car.

Chapter Twenty-seven

At this hour I can't do much more than think and the Ayahuasca has cut that ability way down. I drive back over the causeway and into Sausalito. I think about Maizy one more time and let it go forever. I look at the DVDs on the seat next to me. My follow-up list is growing longer. I think about the letter. It's been a while since I spoke to Dolliver.

Outside Smitty's Bar, a few drunks are sitting on the park benches. The forlorn slouch over a shared cigarette; they're fisherman, boat captains, carpenters and craftsmen. They're the divorcees who chose the boat and the bottle over the bride and the bed and they're all trying to save enough money to sail away.

I push through the double swinging doors. Inside, several TV's run sports highlights. A beat-up jukebox belts out reggae while several people sit at the bar. I recognize the guy in the red Santa coat sitting at the far end. Dolliver is arguing with the local sailboat rigging guy, Craig. Craig shoves Dolliver. It doesn't take much for Dolliver, stinking drunk, to hit the floor.

Craig sees me, so I point at him. Craig is tall and sinewy, prematurely gray. He's wearing an Aloha shirt and dirty jeans. Dolliver tries to right himself on the floor. Craig picks up a pool cue and smiles.

"Drop it, Craig." I extend my arms like a trainer, taming a circus bear. "I said, drop it."

Craig shakes his head 'No'. He lunges forward, swinging the stick, aiming for my face, but he trips, hard, smashing into the pool table. I wince and cringe as the racked billiard balls shoot off in all directions

Craig stands upright, staggers briefly, and falls flat on his face. That's two drunken bodies on the floor. It's unusual, but it's not a record. Craig curls up in the fetal position. I grab him by the back of his shirt and drag him outside into the cool Marin night. He gasps for air. I throw him on the bench. Dolliver comes out to join us.

Craig is not talking. He's still gasping when I walk back inside. The pool game is back on. Shuffle board is under way.

Lois, the bartender, has a towel filled with ice ready for me. She looks disappointed. There are no gray areas with Lois. You do your job and she'll do hers. There is no bouncer at Smitty's, just Lois. The moment you act up, she'll call you on the carpet. If necessary, the police can be here in two minutes.

Lois is delicate and barely over five feet tall. She uses a step stool to reach the top shelf. She can remember ten orders at once and can do more with a lash of the tongue than a swing of the sawed-off baseball bat she keeps under the counter.

"Is he going to be okay?" Lois asks, while pouring me a beer.

"His hangover is going to be a little worse than usual tomorrow." I answer. I press the icy towel against my face.

"I just hate to see it happen in my bar." Lois scans the room for more trouble but can't find any. "Big Marty said that Lucy is gone again. If I hear anything, I'll call you."

"Thanks, Lois."

I stare at the bottom of my beer glass. I don't remember telling Big Marty that Lucy was gone. He must have spoken to Enza. Word travels fast in this town.

I think about the ruckus with Craig. There are never any hard feelings in situations like this; no grudges, just mistakes we're embarrassed about. I put my glass down and take the bar towel outside.

Craig starts talking like he's spent the last five minutes preparing a speech. "I'm waiting for the parts, Jack. I swear. Once they come in, I'll get those new hydraulic backstay pumps installed, and you'll be ready to go. As it is right now, you're fine for day-sailing but with added pressure you can really flatten that mainsail in the light air. "Craig pleads between gasps. I hand him the towel and slide onto the bench next to him.

Sometimes people are just not on the same page. "Forget it, Craig. It's not about that right now. It's about you taking a swing at me with a twenty-two ounce pool cue." But it's not really about that either. It was about me getting beat up for the past two days.

"You all right, Dolliver?" I ask.

"Yeah." Dolliver kicks Craig in the ankle.

"Come on, Jack. This is bull," Craig pleads, blood flies out of his mouth.

"Have you seen Lucy around, Craig?" I put my hands in my pockets and stare at my truck across the street.

"I think I chipped a tooth."

"Answer the question."

"I'm serious." Craig pulls down his lower lip, exposing green and brown teeth covered in chewing tobacco.

"You would do Craig a favor by knocking them all out, Jack." Dolliver smiles and shakes his fist at Craig.

"Enough. Have you seen her?"

"Nope."

"How about a junkie named Manny?"

"Don't know him."

Dolliver sits down on the other side.

"Damn, Jack." Craig rubs his chest.

"You should've dropped the pool cue." Dolliver elbows him.

"Where are you living these days, Craig?" I ask, not expecting a straight answer.

"I got a place."

"He's living in the basement of somebody's vacation house, and they're not on vacation." Dolliver seems to get satisfaction in ratting out Craig.

With the towel stuffed behind his lower lip, Craig slurs, "Shut up Dolliver, what do you know?"

"That's enough, gentlemen." I look down at our feet. Craig is wearing worn-out leather boat shoes. He walks on the sides of his feet. I get the feeling that every step he takes is a hard one. There is no padding in his life.

Dolliver wears his worn black Santa boots but he keeps them polished as if he was waiting for the day he gets called up to the North Pole.

I'm running out of shoes. I've lost two pairs already. I am down to a pair of worn out trail runners, my painting shoes.

The door swings open next to us. Craig and Dolliver leer at a woman in her mid-thirties. Attractive, but weathered, she walks toward a beat-up old Toyota.

"She gives it up too easily," Craig remarks.

"How do you know?" Dolliver never takes his eyes off her.

"You can always tell a girl who gives it up too easily by the type of car she drives." Craig is now the teller of truths.

"She drives a piece of crap." Dolliver is confused.

"Exactly."

"Craig, get lost," I tell him. I want to go home too.

"I'm telling you, my hands are tied until I get those parts," He pleads, back on point. He is not one hundred percent all there, but he is sincere.

"Forget about it. We still have some time. I need to talk to Dolliver."

Dolliver motions like he is writing on an invisible pad. "You made the list, Craig, and it's not the nice one."

"Whatever." Craig stands to leave. He staggers a few steps then turns and walks in the opposite direction.

"I didn't need your help, Jack, but thanks anyway. It will be noted." Dolliver looks up and sends a big blast of bar room breath at the hills above town.

I stare at the same hills. We sit silently for a while. The doors swing in and out. People stagger out into the night. A few cars drive by. A Sausalito cop is doing his rounds. I can't tell who it is. I wave anyway.

"What did you hear about the letter, Dolliver?" I say, half caring now. The information will help Ellen more than me. We found Mr. Flynn. Nobody is going to Peru.

"What letter?" Dolliver is opening and closing his eyes, squinting at the lights of the houses. "You know they look like shooting stars, Jack. I can only imagine what they look like from a sleigh at fifty thousand feet."

This is the moment when I realize that I may have made a mistake in asking for help from a delusional Santa wannabe. "The Arabic letter I gave you a couple of days ago?"

"I was only kidding you, Jack, lighten up." Dolliver pulls the letter and a translation out from inside his coat and passes them to me as if we were doing it directly under the eyes of the Cali Cartel. "It's a business arrangement, money laundering, about getting rid of large quantities of cash."

"Why is an Arabic letter found among the belongings of a communications banker who works for a company doing business in Peru? Peru is a Spanish speaking country" I also squint at the house lights. I can't see the shooting stars.

"Peruvians also speak Quechan," Dolliver adds.

I'm never sure if he's being sarcastic.

"Have you ever heard of a place called Puerto Maldonado?" Dolliver asks.

"It's in the Peruvian Amazon. It's a two-day drive by truck in the dry season." I think about my visit there several years ago and the Maoist rebels who controlled most of the roads in the region. There were lots and lots of guns; lots and lots of cocoa leaf.

"It's the major boomtown for guns, explosives and cash. It's a riverside transit center where the American currency ends up after the cocoa farmers have changed it into Peruvian soles. It's where Muslim extremists can train at camps hidden deep in the jungle. It's where the Columbians do business with other criminal organizations." Dolliver rattles off the facts like he's seen it all before.

I pick up where Dolliver leaves off. "It's where someone could buy enough explosives to bring down a Jewish Community Center in Buenos Aires, back in the Nineties."

"Exactly."

"So Flynn discovers this little letter."

"It's actually a copy of a fax. We found some faint numbers on the header. It may have been sent to his fax by mistake. Once you fax, you can't get it back."

"I thought you said it was meant to be discovered?"

"I was talking out my ass. It's a fax."

"So Flynn finds this fax at his office one morning and doesn't know what to make of it. But whoever sent it wants it back and sends someone to take him out."

"Minimize the risk."

"It seems that whoever sent the fax got their man."

"But they didn't get their fax." Dolliver pulls a battered Santa hat from his coat pocket and places it squarely on his head as if he were a cowboy donning a Stetson after dispatching the villain.

"Thanks, Santa. Don't make mention about this to anyone. It will come out but I want to be in control of it when it does. There may be someone out there still looking for this."

"Come on, Jack. You're talking to a guy who sharpened his teeth at Langley."

"Good night, Santa." I get up to leave, folding the papers and putting them in my pocket. "Hey Santa, what were you and Craig arguing about?"

Santa turns his palms up. "I have no idea."

Chapter Twenty-eight

The bay is like glass. The fog beckons above the Marin headlands, waiting for the perfect moment to launch its assault on the views, the lights and the sounds. Charley is waiting for me at the dock. She's here because it is Frank's way of saying that things are going too slowly. I can feel the pressure without ever having to speak to him.

A blue heron pries mussels apart at the end of the dock. Charley makes a charge and the bird takes flight. After I pull the boards on the companionway, and without admitting defeat, Charlene follows me aboard and quickly bounds down the steps.

I toss my keys on the nav desk; the business office of the boat opposite the galley containing drawers for miscellaneous navigating tools. It faces a bulkhead which houses the electronics: GPS screen, spare hand held GPS, and radar, along with two barometers and a clock. To the right of the nav desk are the Single Side Band Radio, VHF radio, the satellite email receiver, and a weather fax. Immediately behind the desk is an electrical panel containing a circuit breaker for just about every pump, motor and appliance on the boat. The electronics required to balance and monitor the batteries and generator are also here. Anything mechanical that goes wrong has alarms and that panel is located here as well.

A note stuck to my laptop computer says, "Feed her."

I remove the translated letter from my pocket and toss it on the nav desk. I can't get into the letter tonight. If I do, I probably won't sleep. The main salon is in the same state of disorder that I left it in. Normally, at this point in an investigation, I would return to a ransacked boat with my crap thrown all over the place. Not tonight.

It proves that I just can't get involved with anything anymore. I should be digging my heels into one of the cases and getting grief for not spending enough time on the other. I should be making waves and pissing people off. Instead, I'm jerking around with one night stands, getting my face kicked in for nothing, getting nowhere. I put a couple of cups of chow in Charley's bowl. She chooses not to eat in front of me. She'll get into it after I'm asleep.

I reach into the icebox and pull out a beer. I drag the East Pacific chart onto the table. I grab my dividers from their leather case. I spread the dividers on the lat lines on the right side of the chart and make a distance of one hundred and fifty nautical miles. Each degree of latitude is sixty miles. I use the latitude lines on the side of the chart because the longitude lines vary in width as you rise and fall on the chart.

I put one point of the dividers on the mouth of San Francisco Bay. I swing the other point toward the South Pacific. The point lands somewhere south of the bay, off California's central coast. The distance between these two points represents roughly one twenty-four hour day of sailing. Holding the second point on the chart and swinging the first south beyond Big Sur, in two days I am almost to Los Angeles. It's that simple. With the prevailing north westerly winds that race down the California coast I can't help but make progress. After a three day shakedown, I can be in L.A.'s big Marina Del Rey, stocking the boat, making last minute repairs and taking on precious fuel that will speed my way through the Doldrums that guard both sides of the Equator.

From Marina Del Rey, I swing the dividers again and count off twenty days to the Marquesan port of Nuku Hiva which lies south of the Equator. In less than a month, I can be surrounded by steep emerald mountains and French-speaking Polynesians, three thousand miles from home.

I pull the French charts for the Marquesas. They're a group of towering extinct volcanoes with few sheltering bays. They've been called the world's last bastion of cannibalism. Herman Melville used them as a setting for his book *Tyree*. Gauguin's famous Polynesian women were Marquesan. Gauguin died here, but I'll just be passing through.

I pick over a few of the cruising guides that will aid me in the rules of immigration and customs. They contain detailed surveys of safe harbors, reefs and bays and local weather information. The photographs of tropical sunsets will make tomorrow's fog seem like a personal attack on me.

I remove the Western Hemisphere chart from the stack. I trace the

148

distance from San Francisco to Australia with my index finger. I ease it past the French Polynesians, the Cook Islands, Samoa and Tonga, before coming to light on Fiji. I think about the empty ocean and all the dangerous islands that sprout from its bottom. I think about the sand and the rocks and the coral that can rip a boat in two. I think about the waves that can turn steep and fierce.

I return to a particular point on the chart northeast of Hawaii. The water is thousands of feet deep here. It's a breeding ground for tropical low pressure systems that spin up from the Doldrums. It's where my father's last Pacific Cup San Francisco to Hawaii Race came to an end.

I pull the San Francisco Bay chart out from beneath the pile. The chart holds most of the bay coastline, as well as other significant landmarks like airports. I study the airports around the bay: San Francisco International, Oakland, San Jose, and Marin County. All are near the bay or even in it, like SFO. Their runways are built with prevailing winds in mind. Their flight paths carry most of the planes over water during either take-off or landing.

I follow the take-off pattern for Marin. The planes take off heading north over the lowland of the county. To drop someone over a big body of water like the Pacific, the plane would have to make a turn west. Once the package is dropped, the plane continues making left turns until its back on approach over Marin. It's a simple loop.

My guess is that the plane that dropped Flynn was a small one. Opening a door on a private jet would not go unnoticed. The flight must notify the FAA if something like that were to happen. The flight crew of a private jet would have to be in on the murder and that would be unlikely.

SFO and Oakland have minimal private air traffic. The more difficult the plan, the harder it is to pull it off. People try to keep things simple, especially murderers. My guess is that Flynn boarded another plane after landing at Marin. The plane took off and Flynn's body was dumped over Marin. The murderer was flying the plane.

Chapter Twenty-nine

I have a dream where I'm in an open boat with whales all around me on a sea of asphalt. The whales swim through the black ground, surfacing and spouting. I'm nervous, concerned that they'll rise up beneath me and drag me below the hard surface. I worry about suffocating in the darkness. I run for an island that juts from the asphalt.

Cold, damp air has spent the night creeping into every corner of the boat. I crave pulling the blanket of clouds a little closer, rolling over and waking up on a hot day. Sometimes I think it would be easier to lay in this cocoon forever. Even though the sun has been up for an hour, light barely leaks into the *Suzanne*. She rocks me gently. She keeps my whole life afloat. *Suzanne* makes it very hard for me to get out of bed. We all need a little help on days like these.

I can hear Charley barking on the wharf above. She trundles down the steps into the boat.

The swelling is way down, and the oozing poison oak seems to have succumbed to the salt water washing. I use the salt water foot pump in my head sink to wash my face. I was told that the salt water will just about cure poison oak. At least my face is almost a closed case.

"Want to make fifty bucks?" The Kid is sticking his head into the companionway, as I pull on a shirt.

"Haven't you heard of knocking?" The Kid is getting so used to everyone avoiding him that he has honed his skills at sneaking up on people. You have to keep your wits about you. I didn't even hear him get on the boat.

The Kid's a loose cannon. He's in his twenties and spent a few years in the Caribbean working on a mega yacht, saved his pennies and came home to Sausalito. He bought a small weekend charter service which included a fairly old forty-two foot sailboat. He'll boat talk you to death about the Caribbean; all girls, pirates and doe-eyed tourists. My guess is that his crewmates found his incessant chatter exhausting and took every opportunity to abandon him in some of the tropics' worst ghettos, if there are such places.

The Kid drops the name of his employer to anyone who will listen - an industry no-no - and generally alienates everyone in sight. If you mention the name Ten Zing Norgay, he'll say that he saw him at Starbucks the other day and that he says, "Hi."

"Hey, Jack. I bagged a couple of Japanese tourists for a charter today, and I told them I would send a car for them. They're at the Inn at the Tide. How about you pick them up in the Audi?"

"Sorry, can't help you. I'm on a case." The word "case" sounds better than "I'm working."

"What do you expect them to do, climb into Li'l Blue? Besides you're always on a case." The Kid is referring to his small beat-up Volkswagen pickup truck.

"Listen, Kid, I'm always on a case because it's my job."

"Okay, seventy-five bucks, and it's not 'til ten. And I would need you to lay out some breakfast pastries, croissants, coffee, that sort of thing while I get the boat ready."

"You've got thirty seconds to clear the companionway."

"Whoa. Hostility!"

"One..."

"Thanks for nothing, eh, Jack?"

I can hear the Kid drag himself off the boat like a soldier who's been shot through the leg. The reason we live here is so that we won't be bothered. He's in the wrong basin.

I fold the charts and stash them in a sliding chart drawer beneath the settee, a fancy word for bench seat. I place the tools in their proper leather case and organize the boat. I return the bag of stainless steel hose clamps to the forward cabin, sole plates replaced. I put the project on hold. The old clamps will have to hang on for a little while longer.

I come across the DVDs that I 'borrowed' from Red Fish. I put the first security DVD in my player. After it is cued up, I fast forward through hours of bedroom surveillance. The focus of this disc is a woman in various state of undress. I don't recognize her from last night or her partners, with the exception for the occasional appearance of Red Fish.

Two more DVDs are basically the same. The Red Fish appearances are marked by extreme overacting, mugging for the camera and incredibly challenging sexual positions. I'm surprised that his partners never realized that he was playing to a worldwide internet audience.

The remaining DVDs contain images of people in the Jacuzzi, and hours of uneventful meditation. The last DVD I put in is of the parking lot. This time I start at the end so that I can determine a timetable. The images on this disc are strictly surveillance. It's all time-lapse. The camera basically records an image every couple of seconds. This allows for much longer recording times. The downfall is that you may miss pertinent action.

The first image on the screen is Maizy pogoing up and down in the parking lot. I press the reverse button on the remote until the images start changing rapidly. I see Maizy walking backward to the house. This must have been the point where she left to do her begging. The light changes to sunshine overhead. The fog rolls in and out, and finally, my Audi Q7 is backing down the driveway. Manny gets out, opens the hatchback, removes an aquarium and backs toward the house. He returns empty-handed then removes a second aquarium. Water sloshes out onto the gravel as he strides backward to the house. I freeze this frame.

These are the stolen Koi fish, two aquariums worth. He loaded them in broad daylight yesterday. He must have moved the merchandise right before I saw him at the Pup and Taco, no doubt spending his new found cash on a super-sized combo meal.

I let the DVD roll some more. Two men walk backwards out of the house; one is Red Fish and the other is the Peruvian connection carrying a small duffle. They exit the frame for an instant, before a black Mercedes backs up the hill. A few more frames and the Mercedes returns, backing down the driveway. This might have been the airport run.

Was the Peruvian connection sent to retrieve the fax and eliminate Colin Flynn? Then the timing is off. The Peruvian would have already performed the murder. Unless he'd been in town longer than Red Fish indicated. I wouldn't put it past Red Fish to drop an alibi. But if the timing was right and the Peruvian just arrived, he may not be connected to Flynn at all.

More frames with darkness falling in an odd reversal of light then Manny walks backwards out of the house. He climbs into my Audi Q7 and backs up the hill. He drove backward all the way to San Geronimo where he whacked me with a two-by-four.

I get to the daylight. I freeze the frame again. Something catches my eye and I'm not sure what it is. There is a blur at the bottom of the frame going left to right. I start the DVD again, from the very beginning. I'm not quite sure of the day or the time.

I play the DVD frame-by-frame. There is an image here of something passing through the frame. It could be the top of someone's head, someone who knows which way the cameras are pointed, and someone who didn't want to be seen entering the compound. But it might just be a bug.

I watch it several times at various rates of speed to play with the resolution. Finally, I'm able to make out what I think is a black baseball cap with illegible white lettering across the front. I toss the only DVD of interest into the top drawer of the nav station. I make a mental note to have Dolliver look at it.

I take a last look around the main salon. I look at the letter Dolliver gave me last night. I don't want to get into it, especially if I am not getting paid. I toss it into the drawer. It could be my alibi.

Everything that can go flying has been put in a drawer or wedged where it won't move around. The hatches are dogged down so the water won't get in.

Chapter Thirty

There is a wonderful energy in the boat basin this morning. Sailors are preparing their boats for the day ahead, rigging their sails, scrubbing their decks. Voices drift down from riggers hanging on mastheads. Laughter carries across the surface of the water.

My father used to hoist me to the top of the mast. He strapped me in a boson's chair and cranked away. I straddled the mast with my bare feet, gently dragging them on the cold aluminum mast to keep me steady. It took him forever to jerk me up to the top.

The first time I was terrified to step into the chair. My father convinced me that I would never be a good sailor unless I went up and down that mast without a care in the world. You'd think that the higher up you got, the scarier it got, but the reverse actually happened for me. The higher I got the more fun I had. I could see out over all the other boats. I could see the Bay and the city and Strawberry and Tiburon. I could see the old dry-docked timber steamer and the anchor-outs straining against their moorings.

My job was to inspect the masthead rigging and check the tri-color for burned-out bulbs. I bent the wind vane back into place after a great horned owl used it as a perch. I was my own man. I watched ships enter and leave the lanes in the bay, and dreamt about being atop the heaving rig in the open ocean. I could've stayed up there for hours if only my father let me.

If I wanted to spend time with my father, it would have to be around the boat. My brother and sister skipped the tirades and the obscenities and spent more time with their friends. My father knew what was right, and what was good, and I would learn it all from him. I was his first mate. I looked forward to the time when I could captain a boat myself and show him all that I could do.

154

My father valued the physical work more than the quality of the work. It was all about the work and never about the finished product. He never finished anything at home, but he finished everything on the boat.

The boat had to withstand the strength of the sea. That didn't necessarily mean the work had to be done right; the end result just had to be strong. Whenever he ran out of the correct fasteners, he would use glue and epoxy. He jury rigged so many things using the wrong-sized screws I was surprised anything held together at all.

My job was to shed light on the subject: hold the flashlight. I was not there to hold the wood or the bent nails that he spent time straightening. I was a witness to the pain he caused himself. He smashed his hands on pipes, wrenches, and engine parts. They split open and bled. He worked so hard he couldn't hold his morning coffee.

He considered himself too lucky and undeserving of the fruits of his labor and his good lot in life. He punished himself with blood, and he bit his own fingers until they bled. I was there to validate his punishment. We worked into the dark of night. My hands froze, and we were late for dinner.

This morning I get to a little deferred maintenance. I remove the broken track car from the sail track and replace it with the new one. I ease out the main halyard dropping the main sail a few feet at a time. I flake the sail into an accordion pattern on the boom. I tighten the remaining track cars and check for damage. I find none. I do this slowly and carefully.

No blood. No obscenities. No pain.

Chapter Thirty-one

Charley and I make our way along the waterfront at Schoonmaker Marina. To the left are marina basins 'B' and 'C' and to the right are several commercial buildings that have great views of the boats and Richardson Bay. Beyond 'C' basin is a small sandy dog-friendly beach where the kayakers launch their boats and nannies spread blankets. This is the only beach in Sausalito open to the public and only the locals seem to know about it.

Charley is tempted to break for the water, stepping away from me, but she knows better and heels. The morning fog is breaking up over the bay and the wind is blowing lightly out of the southeast. In a few hours the wind will change directions and come from the headlands. It will gather strength and by day's end it will be blowing thirty knots across my slip. I will end my sailing day before three o'clock when the wind makes it too difficult to get back in. I'm not one to take risks with my boat and a big wind increases the risk of damage.

As we walk toward Caledonia Street, a small inlet exposes marshlands in various stages of drying. Charley knows that this is an area where she is allowed to run. Charley charges down to the waterline and spooks an egret. She cuts through the reeds with her nose down, her tail up. She bolts past me. She would be the perfect hunting dog if I was a hunter.

Further along is the site of my father's memorial, the Marin Yacht Club. The club built on a barge is the size of a four car garage. The solitary room has picture windows on both sides and a bar at one end. Two willow trees safeguard the rusty gangway.

We could have held the service at the mortuary in Mill Valley, but my father wouldn't have wanted it that way. He was a man of the people and wanted the memorial service in the clubhouse where he spent so many nights drinking and telling stories. The open casket would be proof of death.

When he died several years ago the Coast Guard lowered the basket down to his sailboat deck and I rolled his body into it. I didn't want to see him after that. I didn't want to be part of the train wreck that was his funeral, even though I was expected to be there to recount the events surrounding his death; the long helicopter ride with guardsmen who, either out of training or plain decency, attempted resuscitation of his cold body and upon landing on the roof of the hospital in Honolulu, my dead father's silver hair blew around his face, eyes closed as if he were only shielding them from the wind.

Frank had met us at the San Francisco International Airport and had been his usual macabre self. He had handled all the arrangements and made sure that I knew it. We had left Lucy messages at her place in the city but got no word. We did not hear from her until she appeared at the service.

Frank had notified a broad range of aunts and uncles, almost all of whom had the blank stare of retirement. There were old clients, colleagues and a mixed bag of lowlifes, as well as wealthy soy bean farmers from Kansas and sailors from Sausalito. Toss in a few federal and local agents using the occasion as an impromptu sting operation for parole violators.

My brother had gathered these people out of respect for my father. He had also wanted to show everyone what kind of a person my father was and how many different levels of society he operated in. Using lies and misrepresentation, my father had a chameleon-like ability to fit in every echelon. His ex-wife, who knew the truth about him, was not there. His sons were there out of necessity and his daughter was late.

Frank's wife, Pepper, took great pains to redecorate the yacht club for the somber occasion. This involved removing the Polaroid photos of topless women from the wall behind the bar and setting out bouquets of flowers. The plastic carnations in the old tequila bottles were removed for good and new carpet was rolled out over the old beer-soaked stuff. She did it for Frank, not for my father Don Brubaker.

Frank and Pepper welcomed the mourners at the door, while I stood near the coffin. I knew people would find it more difficult to engage me in conversation due to my proximity to the body. I was wildly exhausted and hung over and I didn't know what to feel. Rather than scare people off with a diatribe or shock them with my indifference, I kept my mouth shut. In the end, and all for the better, people thought grief rendered me speechless.

Dad looked stuffed.

He was never able to express his life's regrets, and I doubt he had any anyway. We didn't talk much on our last Pacific crossing. It was all business. We had a strict watch schedule and rarely interacted. Mealtime was shared but silent. We ate quickly and afterwards we either headed back on deck or to our bunks. We occasionally spoke about sail changes or the boat's condition.

Several days into the San Francisco to Hawaii race, the electrical system failed due to my father's lack of readiness and maintenance. We were left without power to operate the boat's most basic systems. Without power we were forced to hand steer. Our radio was down and we had no electronic weather forecasting.

We relied on our understanding of cloud formations and were aware of a deep low approaching, but we didn't know from which direction. On my father's directive, we unknowingly, steered a direct course for the storm's strongest winds and highest seas.

There were a few speeches, and a few toasts from the bar and almost everyone passed by his coffin. Big Marty was there as were the usual suspects from around town: the bagel guy, Lois the bartender, Dolly the meter maid, Enza's family and half the local police force. Lucy finally arrived during one of the toasts but by then the guests had burned through most of the cheap wine and the keg beer.

When the beer runs out, so do the guests. We organized a funeral convoy to Dad's final resting place: a cemetery in the rolling oak-studded hills just outside San Anselmo. Everyone arrived at the appointed time including the ne'r-do-wells, and relatives. Lucy was there too. Only one thing was missing: the coffin. Frank had been on his cell phone trying to locate the body when some of the mourners mentioned that they had seen a black Cadillac broken down a couple miles back. The mortuary Frank selected was having trouble with its hearse.

Frank would have made his father proud with his ability to take control of the situation. He borrowed the keys to a white Mercury Station wagon and went to pick him up. Frank returned in the wagon after an hour.

The mourners were sitting beneath a large oak as if they were having a picnic, drinking beer and eating potato chips. The coffin was clearly sticking out the back of the tailgate. That was about par for this family. The congregation must have thought that we were the cheapest SOBs on Earth.

It took a few minutes for the group to get back in the burying mood. Dad's funeral was the only one I ever attended where empty beer cans were tossed into an open grave.

At a brief reception following the service, Lucy laughed with the ne'er-do-wells and sang songs with her aunts. She was the life of the party. She drank heavily and was given several empty warnings by Frank, but she continued until she became a spectacle. Lucy alternated fits of shouting with sobbing and laughter. She was run down, exhausted and a little thin. Lucy was strung out.

My father was buried that day and my sister was committed the day after. I often wonder if my father were still here, would my sister be here too.

Now the yacht club lists a bit on its south end where a small sailboat wedged itself during a wild storm. When pulled out by a tug, the boat took a piece of the pontoon with it. Rust stains run down from the flat roof. Its glory days have passed, along with my father's.

Chapter Thirty-two

I decide against going to see Big Marty and lead Charley back to the boat. Dolliver is sitting at an outdoor table at the Dockside café when I arrive.

"Have you seen Shirley, lately?" Dolliver looks hung over.

"Not since I ran into her outside your house."

The Dockside café makes up the corner suite of the commercial building facing basins 'A' and 'B'. There are tables both inside and out, varnished plywood tables on a polished concrete floor. The view of the harbor is unmatched.

"Well, I don't know what you said to her, but she just hasn't been around."

"Shirley is not around because you ended it. What did you expect?"

"You know how it works? We have break up sex and then we get to have get back together sex. It is a system I learned to exploit in order to have any sex at all." Dolliver is nervously tapping his foot.

The thought of these two carnally engaged is enough to make me swear off sex forever. "Listen, she'll turn up. She's just playing hard to get."

"I hope you're right."

"In the meantime, I've got a DVD that I want you to take a look at. I am having resolution issues."

"With the DVD or your life?" Dolliver has a laugh.

"I'll leave it in an envelope in my storage box on the dock. See what you can see."

"I'll take a look."

"Shirley 'll turn up. Hang in there." I say, knowing that that is no consolation.

Dolliver nods and breathes in the cool morning air.

Charley saunters off toward the boat and I follow her. I can see from the dock that Ellen Jacobs is waiting for us.

"Don't you ever take a day off?" I ask as I climb aboard.

"This is my day off." Her feet are bare. Her shoes are on the dock.

"So you take days off during the biggest murder case in Marin history?" I open the companionway and Charley climbs below to let the adults talk in private.

"Actually, I'm working."

"So, are you here to arrest me?"

"No, I'm not. This isn't easy for me. One moment you're being very helpful with the case and the next you're doing business with the victim's wife. Now people are telling me you're going sailing today. You're not helping your own case."

"So, I'm a suspect again?"

"You're not giving us anything to rule you out. We're following this investigation by the book. You must see that your relationship with Mrs. Flynn looks suspicious? There was insurance money."

"Of course there was. I can bet you that his company had a policy on him, too. Are you checking into Evo Liquid, because you should be? And besides, I don't have a relationship with Mrs. Flynn. Is there anything else?"

Her arms are crossed again. She stares at me like someone who knows she shouldn't be here. "Sailing?"

"I'm going sailing, but I'm coming back...I hope." I leave Ellen in the cockpit and go forward to the bow.

I untie the coiled starboard jib sheet and run it back outside the rigging and through the track car. I pass it through a turn block on the deck and put a few wraps on the primary winch. I tie a figure-eight at the bitter end.

Ellen hasn't moved. "Are you going to sit there or are you going to help?"

"I'm going to help."

"Do you know how to sail?"

"No, I don't."

"Then follow my lead and I'll have you sailing in no time, unless of course you have other leads to follow?" She knows that I know her case is stalled. Either the FAA doesn't have anything regarding the recent flyovers of Tiburon or the information is stuck in the Homeland Security bureaucracy. I have more leads on her case than she does.

"Where's your partner, Stevens?"

"He's following a lead out of town."

"Let me guess, Sacramento?" I unsnap the canvas covers on the dodger's icing glass, the aluminum framed canvas cover that protects the companionway from being hit by waves.

"Let's change the subject. Let's not talk about the case. Clean slate, okay?"

"You started it by stowing away."

"The boat hasn't left the dock yet. I can still go ashore."

"Maybe you should, but you want to go sailing today because you have nothing else to do. I am going sailing either way."

Ellen looks up and down the rigging. She seems to be putting things together in her head.

"Why would I kill anybody? I have no motive unless I'm having an affair and I wanted to get Flynn out of the picture, but that's not the case. Keep looking Ellen."

"I'm not talking about it. What do I need to do?"

"Give me a minute." I scan the deck for some simple task that Ellen can perform and make her feel involved. It's been a while since I've sailed with someone on the boat. I never let Theresa sail with me after she tossed my desk chair off her balcony. Even though I could probably sail into a gale by myself I know that it's very important to keep your crew active and involved. Give them a job and they'll keep their mouths shut and are less likely to get sick.

"First, the rules." I put on my captain's hat of responsibility for a moment.

"All right." Ellen looks eager.

"Let's see." I look for visual clues on deck. It helps me remember the old safety speech. "Keep one hand for yourself and one hand for the boat. Always hang on or you will fall off. Watch your feet. There are lots of things on which to break a toe." It's all coming back now. "Life jackets are in the lockers under the seat cushions. Always look to see what is happening on deck before you come up the companionway. Be careful of the boom and any lines that might be whipping in the air. Both can kill you. Are there any questions?"

"How did you know Stevens was in Sacramento?"

"Because that's where Christine's parents live and that's where I would send a congenial guy like him. Now go forward and untie the port jib sheet and lead it back exactly like the starboard side."

Ellen gives me a puzzled expression.

"Port is left as you face the bow and starboard is right."

"Sailors have cute names for everything. Why don't they just call it right and left?"

"If you were to face the back of the boat it changes. Port becomes right and starboard becomes left."

Ellen turns to the back of the boat. I can see her doing the math in her head.

"Port is now on the right side of the boat, isn't it?"

"I got it. Port and starboard never change, no matter what direction you are facing on a boat. What do I do again with this rope?"

"There are no ropes on a sailboat." This is going to be a long day. "Just lines, until, of course, you tie them to something."

In the time that Ellen takes to run the port jib sheet I've removed the canvas winch covers and started the engine. I turned on the instrument breakers, tuned the cockpit VHF to channel two for weather and slipped the dock lines.

Ellen is ready for the next task. I ask her to pull up the fenders that are tied to the lifelines and bring them on deck. I give one blast on the air horn to alert the club rowers that we're leaving the slip. We're under way.

Chapter Thirty-three

Suzanne comes around smoothly in the flat water in the lee of the Marin headlands. Normally, a lee would mean that the land offers shelter from prevailing winds, but here behind the headlands they separate the northern San Francisco Bay and the Pacific Ocean. The wind off the pacific is compressed between the hills and the upper level winds creating strong gusts that race down the hills and into the bay. The winds get stronger as the day progresses.

As she idles with her bow pointed into the breeze, I switch on the auto-pilot and leave the helm. I'm not ready to hand the helm over to Ellen. This is the way I'm used to doing it. Dead ahead is Bridgeway, the meandering coastline of Sausalito and the tourist section of town with seaside restaurants and Inns. Along with the Sausalito Yacht Club and Spinnaker Restaurant, the ferry dock marks the port side of the Richardson Bay channel.

I prefer to wait until I get outside the channel to put up the main. The area straight ahead is known as Hurricane Gulch. I've seen winds up to thirty-five knots press down on the bay on an average day, but now the winds are calm.

I walk forward to the tack of the main and untie the sail ties that keep the flaked main from collapsing on to the deck.

I carefully check that all the lines are free from fouling. All the leads are clear, the spinnaker pole is secured to the deck and everything looks good aloft. I make my way back to the cockpit, with my eyes following the lines that are led aft for single-handing. I hoist the main with the electric primary winch.

I become so focused on the job that everything else dissolves into the background: Lucy, Flynn and even Ellen. My worries get lost in the work, the canvas, in the varnished teak and taut rigging.

Without forward momentum, the Brooks and Gatehouse autopilot faults and the boat falls off the wind. I quickly throttle up and steer her into the wind again. I ease up the mainsheet and the boom begins to swing gently back and forth. Once the bow is pointed directly into the breeze, I am able to raise the main sail completely. The new track car slides up the mast easily. I pull in on the main sheet, shut down the engine and fall off toward the city leaving Sausalito on my starboard flank.

I can see that Ellen wants to be more involved, but this is when I prefer to handle the simple tasks myself. This is the moment of disconnect. The transition from motorized vehicle to sail power is comparable to paddling into a wave on a long board, standing up on it and taking off. I stop pushing against the water with the Volvo Penta diesel and let nature take over. Let go, let wind.

I focus on the wind and the water and on the sea-traffic and on the sails. It's all forward thinking: what is the wind going to do, where is that ship going to be in five minutes, where am I going? Everything in my wake is ancient history.

I believe that sometimes certain people are put on this earth in the wrong place and they're destined to spend their whole life searching for the right place. It might be a little house around the corner, or a new job, a new family, or a whole new life across the country. Some people spend their whole lives never knowing that they should be searching for but that's okay so long as they search the horizon. They'll find the right wind and the right currents and the seabirds will follow them.

The diesel clatter gives way to the sound of the wind in the sail and the smell of the cold salty bay. I set the autopilot on a thirty-eight degree wind angle. It allows me time to leave the helm and release the break on the roller-furling jib and put three wraps of the port jib sheet on the primary winch. As the oiled gears inside the winch are turned by the powerful electric motor, the headsail unrolls from the forestay and soon billows in the strong breeze. I trim the sail until the foot is taut and the air fills the fabric.

The sailboat immediately heels over with her port rail headed for the water. The power of the increasing wind surges her forward as she is pulled into the wind. We're sailing. I watch Ellen's face light up with a smile as she grabs the high rail. Her mind is telling her that we're tipping over. She braces herself against the opposite bench in the cockpit.

"You're okay."

Standing next to the end of the boom, I check the main for any irregularities. The head and tack and clew are all in good condition; recently refurbished for a voyage that's always being pushed off.

I concentrate on the sound of the wind and water parting beneath the rising and falling bow. The air is still very cool against my face. Charley is sleeping in her bed down below. She isn't much of a sailor.

"Is there anything that I can do?" she asks as she pulls her jacket over her shoulders and zips up.

"I'll teach you to man the helm."

"I'd like that. It sounds sexy, like 'manhandle'," she says, turning her smiling face into the wind.

"Easy, Jacobs. Stand behind the wheel and grab it at ten and two." The helm is still on autopilot so the wheel turns by itself in her hands. "Do you feel it turning in your hands?"

"Of course." Ellen fights the wheel at first then gives in to the electric motor.

"Well, the autopilot is a very good helmsman. She can steer a straight line in almost any weather. You should follow her lead. Do you see how little she is turning the helm? That's exactly what you should be doing. If you follow someone who is very good and you vary little from their course then you can't help but wind up in the same place. Now, press the "off" button down on your right. The electric motor will let go and the boat will be yours."

"This isn't so hard." Ellen follows my direction and takes over the helming duties.

It doesn't take long for Ellen to be distracted by her surroundings, the light chop and the beautiful oak trees spilling into the bay on Angel Island, the grand mansions that cascade down the hills in Sausalito and behind us on Belvedere. Without knowing it, Ellen lets the boat fall off the wind and the sails begin to puff.

"Watch where you're going, Ellen."

Ellen over-corrects the wheel, and we are sent up into the wind slowing the boat to a crawl. I step behind the wheel to get her back on track.

Ellen and I are shoulder to shoulder. She is smiling, I'm sailing.

I was supposed to be filtering out all the earthly distractions and focus on Lucy and Flynn. With Ellen aboard, my only chance for doing any work depends on how much information I can get out of her. Once again, Lucy is going to take the back seat.

The wind is hovering around fifteen knots and it often creeps up to twenty- five. The fog hangs out just beyond the Golden Gate while the rest of the bay is clear. Several sailboat races are under way in the extreme east outside of Berkeley. The wall of sails blocks the view of the distant marina and Berkeley water front, of which there isn't much. I think about Cal's proximity to the water and what a nautical powerhouse it could be, its campus wedged beneath oak and eucalyptus, but its students see only politics and they overlook the beauty that surrounds it. Berkeley is Haight street in pursuit of a college degree.

The channel is clear of ship traffic but that can change very quickly. At sea, things change in an instant.

As we point the bow toward the Marina Green in the city, the wind increases as it spills beneath the bridge and quickly fills the shipping lanes. The wind brings up the chop in the bay turning a once glassy morning into a churning white-capped mess. We pass through the rivers of current where the tides and the Sacramento River meet.

Ellen is adjusted to the helm so I prepare for our first tack. I put four wraps of the lazy starboard jib sheet on the primary winch. I lock the line into the self-tailer and wait.

We're approaching the shore at the Presidio. Joggers, cyclists and dog walkers use the trails and bike along the natural shoreline. The Presidio, on the western border of San Francisco, is back in public hands after a long run with the military.

"Having fun yet?"

"I am. Shouldn't we be worried about the beach? It's coming up pretty fast. Shouldn't we be turning?"

"Tacking."

"Okay, tacking. Shouldn't we be tacking?"

"In a moment." We're still at least a half mile off shore. Sometimes the wind heads us here and we are forced to tack early, but it's still early in the day and the wind is fairly steady from the south.

"This is what we are going to do. On my word, you'll turn the boat into the wind. It turns just like a car. When you are done with the turn, you'll have to bring the wheel back to the straight position. Ready?" I remove the tail of the port jib sheet from the self-tailer. I keep the pressure on the winch, but it slips about an inch with the load. It jars the headsail.

"What was that?"

"Nothing. Begin your turn to starboard, slowly. Turn to the right."

"I'm not ready."

"Yes you are. Begin your turn, slowly," I say, as she jerks the wheel as if in pursuit of a stolen car. The bow comes through the wind. I let the port jib sheet fly and press the motor button on the starboard winch. The jib sheet races in and the tail of the jib sheet folds gently at my feet.

"Now, bring the wheel back to center." I return to my perch next to Ellen. We're too far off the wind so I bring us back on course. We're aiming for the north tower of the Golden Gate Bridge which is presently reappearing in the retreating fog.

A few more tacks will put us directly under the bridge. I like to make a few turns in the Pacific before turning to face down the Golden Gate tour boat. They get fifteen bucks from seasick tourists to see the underside of the bridge.

The incoming tide is past full strength and will soon ebb, but the force of the outgoing Sacramento River is piling up against what is left of it, creating whirlpools and chop. *Suzanne*'s sail area and sheer bulk drives us right through the slop beneath the bridge.

The bottom of the roadway is two hundred and twenty five feet above. We're dwarfed by its immensity. Nets reach out on both sides but not far enough. Many people have leapt from this bridge only to die on impact with the churning waters, but people have survived the jump too. I think about Colin Flynn's flight over Marin and the fall to his death. He might have been alive at the first impact with the trees. He might have tried to grab a limb to stop his fall. His hands were shredded.

We wave to the tourists above.

As she gazes straight up, Ellen is not paying attention again and the boat falls off the wind and drifts of course. I grab the wheel one more time and bring us back to course. The rhythmic thumping can be heard from the cars passing over the joints in the pavement above us. It has an odd hollow sound.

"How far are we going?"

"How about Mexico?" I say, standing close to her and touching her shoulder.

"That would be nice."

"A couple more tacks and then we we'll turn back. The wind is usually not as strong out here early in the day. We don't want to lose the wind and bob like a cork."

A brief moment of silence passes between us. Seagulls float above us in the high pressure air created by our sail. The rugged cliffs to our right wrap around the Marin headlands and head north to Stinson beach.

"I'm curious as to what you've been doing for the last twenty-four hours?" Ellen asks, while keeping her eyes on the Pacific.

"I've been doing lots of things, but nothing that will help you in the long run."

"You sure? People tell me you pulled a Starsky and Hutch car chase through Marin in that Suburban of yours. I hear you might be closing in on Lucy too."

"Don't believe everything you hear. Did your partner fly or drive to Sacramento?"

"Why, do you want to push him out of an airplane window?"

"Wow, not funny."

"I'm only kidding. I know you're a yacht captain, not a pilot."

"So you've done some more checking?"

"I had to. Bill is supposed to return tonight. We're not seeing a real connection with Flynn's parents and Colin's death. But that's more information than you need and definitely more than you'll tell anyone."

"I'm not so sure." I say. She gives me a little information and I'll give her a little back.

"You definitely won't tell anyone." She glares at me now.

"No, I'm not so sure there isn't a connection in Sacramento, but who would I tell?"

"How about your girlfriend, Christine Flynn?"

"Nice." I think about the grubby guy from Peru and the fax that Dolliver translated. These two bits are not going to get Ellen any closer to solving the murder either so I'll hold on to them for now.

We're approaching the steep cliffs of the rolling green headlands. We tack the boat away from the cliffs with relative ease. Ellen's turn is much smoother now. She is a quick learner. The sail becomes taut with little effort. We are now moving at about seven knots on course for the outer Richmond district neighborhood of San Francisco and the traditional Sea Cliff neighborhood.

"This isn't very difficult." Ellen says as she looks beyond the helm. "The wind is hardly blowing."

"Conditions like these lull a sailor into apathy which can lead to disaster." I recognize the shape of a container ship entering the marked channel several miles off the entrance to the bay. We'll put in one more tack before we head downwind through the Gate.

"It's really nice out here. The views of the bridge against the green hills are fantastic. It's a totally different perspective." This is the apathy that I was talking about.

"The water can be as shallow as thirty feet, which isn't much when you have the energy of thirty foot waves approaching from across the ocean. Cross the shoal at the wrong tide and during the wrong weather and you'll end up dead."

"Easy, doctor doom."

The cliffs and rocky coast of outer Richmond are quickly approaching. I can feel the wind edging up. The anemometer has been hitting twenty-two knots more consistently and gusting even higher. As the wind speed increases, so does the dread in my stomach. It's an irrational feeling I can't get rid of.

"One more tack, Ellen."

"Aye aye, captain."

Ellen starts her turn, as I release the port jib sheet and bring in the starboard. The boat heels over and heads off toward the lighthouse at Marin Headlands.

"Aren't you worried about that boat?" Ellen is pointing at the big container ship.

"When in doubt, always take its stern. Never cross in front of one of those things. They'll never stop in time."

The ship is moving from left to right. "We won't have a wide enough berth to cross in front of it so we'll aim for its stern. Once it passes us we can fall off toward the bridge and follow it into the bay."

Ellen nods and seems to be getting into it. She likes the competition. The huge ship towers right in front of us. Its dual props churn up mountains of water behind it.

"Hold on!" I say as we approach the huge wake.

We climb over its wake and pound into the trough behind it. The boat bucks hard for a moment, the sails flap and the rigging shudders.

"Okay, start turning to follow it." As Ellen turns the wheel to starboard, I keep the sails close-hauled. When she is finished with her turn we will have jibed anyway. I watch the wind indicator at the top of the mast until it crosses over the stern. The stern has turned through the wind and now the wind is crossing the boat from the opposite side.

"We jibed," I say.

At this point, I let out the main as far as it can go and quickly follow that by easing the jib. In a well crewed boat this would be the perfect time to put up the huge light spinnaker, but today the *Suzanne* is limited to two crewmembers, it would be a dangerous proposition. We'll have to be satisfied with a slower, but smoother run into the bay.

I hear the sound of running water. It's the bilge pump emptying the deepest part of the boat beneath cabin sole. The bilge pump shut offs after a few seconds. I make a mental note to check it after I finish the sail work.

The container ship quickly leaves us in its wake; its heading toward the shipping lane that turns in front of Angel Island and channels them into the anchorage past the Bay Bridge, past the Ferry building and the piers of San Francisco. We'll continue on a heading that will take us along the city's waterfront.

"Nice jibe," I say, much after the fact. I think about how dangerous sailing can get. I follow the container ship's long wake. There is nothing between us and Japan, just a big, blue, dangerous expanse.

The wind is increasing again. The anemometer is hitting consistent twenty-fives and touching on twenty-eight. I can feel it in the rigging, and

I can see it on the water. The waves are white-capping and wind is blowing cold on the back of my neck. I hear the bilge pump cycle again.

"I don't want to bury you with terminology but make sure that the arrow on the wind indicator does not get close to six o'clock. Keep the wind indicator closer to five o'clock. When it approaches six o'clock, the risk of an accidental jibe increases."

"Chief Lemley said that you've been everywhere?'

"I've been to a lot of places." This line of questioning always makes me feel uncomfortable.

"He says you're planning to sail around the world."

I watch the jib billow and puff. "I'm trying to. It's harder to leave than to do the actual sailing."

"I agree with you. Leaving the valley was tough and I didn't go very far at all. I can't understand why anyone would want to uproot themselves and travel all the time."

The bilge is on my mind. "I don't think of it so much as traveling. I think of it as not staying in the same place."

"How could you leave your job? Don't you love what you do?"

"My job is one of providing assistance during uncomfortable situations. I don't paint houses, I don't build houses, and I don't sell anything that people might want to buy. I'm hired to resolve difficult situations that are abnormal in one's normal life. The situations are painful and often leave permanent scars. So when someone asks me, 'Why would you leave?' I ask, 'Why would I stay?'"

Ellen doesn't say anything. The boat continues to rock gently back and forth on its course along the Presidio waterfront. My mind is squarely on the bilge now. I hear it pumping again.

Chapter Thirty-four

We're running downwind on a broad reach with the wind over the starboard flank. The boat is flatter now, riding down the small waves rather than breaking through them, but the boat still seems sluggish and heavy.

Ellen does a good job of keeping the wind angle right where we want it. The close waters are clear, except for a few sailboats that are making their turns out of Sausalito. It takes a lot more wind to push us rather than lift us. Our boat speed is steady at about six knots.

"Stay the course. I'll be right back."

"Where are you going?" Ellen has concern in her voice.

"I have to check a few things down below."

"Okay." Ellen gives the slightest hint in her voice of being uneasy.

I like giving a new sailor the freedom of being on deck alone. She might not understand the feeling right now, but she'll learn that being alone with the wind and the sea is a gift. It's meditative, eye-opening and even transcendent.

I take one last look at the nearby traffic and step below. Charley looks at me from her bed then buries her snout beneath her paws. I check the bilge pump meter for cycling. It registers 'ten.' It never registers ten pumps. The boat is leaking. My mind races as I reach for the floor panels. The hull can't be holed because I never hit anything. Something else is going on. I lift a floor panel to check for water. The bilge is flooded and rising. The engine is under water along with the water maker, fresh water pumps and fuel hoses. I reach into the deepening water and find the source, a through-hull is wide open and its hose is off.

I stick my head out of the companion way. "Ellen. Reach into the canvas pocket next to the throttle and remove the steel bilge pump handle. Insert it into the hole next to it and start pumping."

"This?" Her hand is on the pump handle.

"Exactly. Insert it and start pumping and don't stop until I say stop."

"Got it."

Before going below, I check the horizon. I can see a sailboat approaching our beam with the two Japanese tourists on deck. It is still a good quarter mile to the north, but it seems to be running on a collision course. It's the Kid. I can see him in his goofy captain's uniform. He looks like the Tidy bowl man. I have bigger fish to fry and so I go below.

I quickly remove a bag of wooden dowels and a mallet from beneath the companionway steps. Ellen's work on the pump has stalled the water just beneath the cabin floor. I sprawl out on the floor and jam my arm into the icy water. I find the open valve where the refrigeration unit draws water in to cool the system. It's wide open. I reach for the valve handle, but its jammed open. I shove the dowel into the hole and hammer at it with the mallet. The flow of water from the valve stops, but there is another source. The pumps are working but the water is receding at a very slow rate.

I force my arm deeper into the water. This time I aim for the water maker through-hull. My fingers are getting numb. I'm in the water up to my shoulder as I sprawl out on the floor. Same story; the valve wide open, the hose is gone and the valve is frozen. I hammer in another dowel. The water is receding, slowly. One more open valve somewhere.

I run my hands around the inside of the deep-vee hull. Hoses and pumps are everywhere. The water is dropping but not fast enough. There is another open valve. I find the heater inlet. I can feel the hose resting on the very end of the valve. The hose clamp is loose. I push the hose over the end of the nipple.

I find the last open through-hull and the hose that is supposed to be connected to it. I push the hose over the nipple. The water is falling sharply now.

Charley never moved. My upper body is soaking wet. I grab a fresh shirt and go on deck.

Ellen is pumping away and doing a great job of steering at the same time. "What happened down there?"

"I'll take over." I grab the pump. It should only take a few more pumps. "Somebody tried to sink us."

"Are you serious?"

"Several valves were jammed open and their hoses loosened. I think the down force pushed the hoses off the inlets when we hit the ship's wake back there."

"Do you think it has anything to do with Manny or Flynn?" Ellen is still thinking about the sabotage.

"Who knows, but I think I'm getting warmer." My gaze becomes fixed on the Kid. Ellen doesn't realize that the Kid is going to ram us. I stop pumping.

"We'll have to deal with that later. We've got another problem." I can see the Japanese couple on the approaching boat stuffing themselves with croissants. I watch the Kid go below. He's completely unaware of the impending collision.

We are both on the same tack and we're to his starboard, so we have the right of way. He must give way but that doesn't mean he will. I never trust another sailor.

"Ellen, I am going to take the helm for a moment, if you don't mind."

"Sure."

Ellen now sees what I am looking at. "He's getting pretty close. Can't we just go behind him?"

"We can't. That would require a jibe and I don't feel like changing course for that jackass."

The Kid should steer a course to our stern, but he's still below deck.

"Crap. He's getting close. Does he even know we're here?"

"I doubt it." I check our starboard side in the event that I have to make an evasive maneuver. It's clear. The Kid is so close now that I can see the ham on his guest's breakfast sandwich.

"Jesus. He's getting close." Ellen is nervous

The Kid and I are approaching each other at a thirty degree angle. The impact will likely scratch the boat from stem to stern, bend a few stanchions, but I am not turning.

"Do something, Jack."

I grab the air horn and give it a blast but it spits and sputters. Note to self: replace air horn.

Before I can reach for the VHF p.a., Ellen has pulled her hand gun from her purse and is unloading the magazine at the Kid's boat. The booming unsettles me. Ellen shows great poise as she steadies her firing hand with her free arm. The rounds are entering the water directly off their bow.

People do the weirdest things when they're on the water.

The Kid prairie dogs out of his companionway and lunges for the wheel. The Japanese tourists hit the deck.

"Get down!" I shout. Ellen dives for the dodger. I quickly turn the boat up into the wind, toward the city, and away from the Kid.

Ellen clings to the small deck area between the cockpit and the companionway, as spent brass shells roll all around her. The boom whips over her head and the lines lash the dodger. The noise of flogging sails against the rigging and the groaning boom is disturbing. I quickly bring in the main sheet and cleat it off.

The Kid skates right past us, never changing course. We would have collided. He heads off toward the East Bay with a wave of his hand.

"Bastard." Ellen fumes.

I gently bring the boat back off the wind. I ease the main. It takes its place on the leeward side of the boat. The jib sheet refills as I continue to fall off.

"Why did you wait so long to turn?"

"I wanted to justify the pummeling that I am going to give him on the dock."

"You're a jerk."

"I'm a jerk? He is the one who tried to kill us."

"You could have avoided him from the beginning." Ellen climbs down the stairs to the main salon.

"Great."

The jackass heads for Fisherman's Wharf, shrinking in the distance. I return the boat to auto-pilot. The automatic bilge pump has been quiet for a few minutes. When we get back, I'll have to rinse the bilge with soap and fresh water before the salt attacks the systems.

We aim for Alcatraz. The auto-pilot rights itself at one hundred and sixty degrees on the opposite tack and Ellen comes up from below. It's time to start thinking about cutting this trip short, somebody else tried to do it for us. I bring in the sails and head back toward Sausalito, leaving Alcatraz to starboard.

Ellen joins me in the captain's seat behind the helm. She looks great, as usual, as she draws her shoulders in close, her hands stuffed into her jacket pockets.

"Do you normally crash your boat into people out of spite?" Ellen is still mad.

"Not normally."

We both stare off in different directions as the boat glides toward home.

"Burr."

I take the helm and turn off the auto-pilot. "Thanks for blasting a hole in the bay back there. I'm sorry that I put you into an uncomfortable position."

"No, I'm sorry. I don't know what got into me. But you should have done something earlier."

I let it go. I don't have to explain myself.

We enter the shipping lane off Angel Island. Angel Island is the biggest island in the bay. It is encircled by a road and numerous hiking trails.

"So why did you leave the Valley? You were at the top of your game. You could have had your own team." I reach forward and ease out the main. The wind is as strong as ever.

"You make it sound like the Sacramento Valley is a hotbed of murderers. It's usually pretty quiet."

"So is Marin."

Ellen stands up in the cockpit and steadies herself against the boom. "I guess I wanted to start over."

"Was he a cop, too?"

"What are you saying?"

"I'm just saying people up and move for a lot of reasons, but the big one is a fresh start and fresh starts come after unrealized goals or unrealized relationships."

"You're very perceptive. Yes, he was."

In the distance I can see Tiburon's marina and the big white

Corinthian yacht club. The tiny island of Belvedere rises up out of the bay. It's the last barrier that channels the wind through the Raccoon Strait.

Ellen faces Sausalito. "You get excited about the job together. So you fall in love, you marry and you do everything right. You want to start a family but you wait until things calm down at work. But the work never lets up and soon you don't have time for him and he doesn't have time for you and it just gets easier not to face it. Then he finds time for someone else and you still don't have time. It's just easier to sign the papers."

"So you left town?"

Ellen reaches up to the end of the boom. "I didn't want to have to keep working with him and with everyone who knew, long before I did, that he was seeing someone else. I solved a big case and I had some clout."

"So you took your clout to Marin."

"That's it." Ellen erases a tear from her cheek with the back of her hand. "I made a promise to myself that I wouldn't let it happen again. This is my fresh start."

"So today you went sailing." I add.

"Mr. Flynn is still dead and not getting any deader."

I hand the helm over to Ellen.

I got caught up in the process of sailing, the sinking and the near collision and I forget everything else.

Chapter Thirty-five

"Can we do this again, sometime?" Ellen has a wry smile on her face. "I never knew sailing could be so exciting."

The question felt rhetorical. I just smile.

Ellen steers the boat into the wind, just south of the Spinnaker restaurant. I reel in the headsail using roller furling and the secondary winch. With the headsail in, the boat stands straight up. I reach over and turn the ignition. The small diesel fires right up. I ease her into gear.

"Ellen, I want you to steer directly into the wind. The wind indicator should be pointed directly at the top of the mast. If you fall off the wind in either direction, the main will not slide down the track in the mast, so you need to keep it straight."

"I got it." Ellen steers perfectly, using the throttle deftly.

I move forward and flake the main on to the boom. The leech of the sail slides down its track in the mast. I flake and tie the main to the boom. I motion for Ellen to fall off the wind and begin our passage through the channel to the marina.

I bring up the dock lines and the fenders from the chain locker and prepare for our arrival. We slip passed the old wooden seawall of the Sausalito Marina. To the right are the moored anchor-outs that include numerous decaying cabin cruisers and dismasted sailboats. Some are piled with bikes, potted plants and crab boxes. Most are moored in the shallows that leave them listing in the mud during the lowest tides. These moorings are illegal and are policed only by Mother Nature. When a storm blows out of the south, their lines break, and the hulks are sent to wash up on the Strawberry coastline near Mill Valley.

In the distance, I can see a group of black vultures circling a cabin cruiser anchored on the edge of the channel. This is rare. Vultures don't like the water. They can't swim like their cousins the Cormorant. They don't migrate like ducks and they certainly don't look like ducks. One single bird spirals down toward the water and disappears behind the decaying shell of the cabin cruiser. A vulture on the bay can only mean one thing: a dead seal or a dead whale. I guess that's two things.

The tide is still sluggish, the wind calm. I finish my work, quickly running the dock lines and tying the fenders to the lifelines. I take the helm.

"Do you see what I see?" Ellen asks, staring in the direction of the circling vultures. "Weird, huh?"

"Yeah. It's probably a dead seal or a whale. They get pushed up here by the tide." I don't want to ask, but I have to. "Do you want to check it out?"

"It looks like your dead whale is in the back of that boat." Ellen is pointing at a battered cabin cruiser.

Damn it. Now what? "Could be a fish or dead bird."

"Too many vultures, don't you think? Let's check it out." Ellen is a cop.

"What about my leaky hull?"

"Later."

"Right." I take the helm. Several rowers pass in the channel, driving their oars into the water. Their out-rigged white fiberglass hulls cut through the surface. The water is quiet. Voices drift over from the shoreline. A dog barks after retrieving a stick from the water off Mother' Beach at Schoonmaker Marina. Charley is standing in the companionway.

I throttle back as we approach the cabin cruiser. Green sea plants are growing on the mooring lines. Big orange barnacled fenders hang off its side.

Several black turkey vultures, with their heads hanging down, stand guard on the gunwale that surrounds the large fishing deck. A sliding glass door to the main cabin is open about six inches. All the windows are either covered in aluminum foil or dark tinting.

I throttle back as we approach the boat. This is Shirley the man-hater's boat. We're about one hundred feet away when I reverse the prop and stop the boat completely. The remaining birds alight and join their brothers circling overhead.

Ellen stands on the bow, and I join her.

"No dead animals visible."

"No." Ellen agrees.

"Do you want to call anybody?"

"No," She presses heavy brass rounds into her clip until it's full. Ellen jams the clip into her weapon.

"This is Shirley the man-hater's boat."

Ellen nods as she assesses the situation. "It doesn't look like she's been here for a while."

The dread is growing in my gut. Dolliver hasn't seen her but that doesn't mean she didn't leave town for a while.

"I'm not calling in the cavalry until I know something is wrong." Ellen doesn't want to leave this one alone.

"I agree," but I really don't. I prefer to go ashore and then call the cavalry, but in the end I understand my responsibility. "I suggest we drift up to the vessel and tie off to it."

"You go aboard and I'll cover you with my weapon from here."

"Aren't you the cop?"

"I'm not wearing any shoes and I am not going to step on that deck." Ellen has a point. The boat is covered in bird guano. "It looks like a pelican nesting ground."

"Right."

I walk back to the cockpit and touch the throttle a few times in forward. The boat moves slowly next to the cabin cruiser. I am reluctant to tie up to Shirley's boat without her permission. It's one of those maritime courtesies. Maybe terrified is a better word; reluctant might be a little weak in this situation.

A very light breeze is throwing handfuls of ripples across the water. The tide has turned and is ebbing. The cabin cruiser's stern is pointed due south and is pulling gently on its mooring line. I bring the bow alongside the other boat and kill the engine. My sailboat stops but will soon begin drifting back with the tide.

I grab a boat hook from the locker beneath the port cushion. Charley is staring at me from the companionway. I put the board across to keep Charley from getting in the way. I walk forward to the bow and, using my bowline, tie up to the cleat on the transom of the rotting boat. The bow of the *Suzanne* hangs slightly over the cabin cruiser's stern.

"Anyone home?" Ellen trains her weapon on the back of the boat.

"I doubt it. There's no tender."

"What does that mean?"

"There's no rowboat or dinghy tied alongside. There's no way for Shirley to get off the boat if she were home."

"Okay. This is the police. Prepare to be boarded." Using the barrel of her weapon, Ellen motions me aboard.

I look at Ellen. She is grimacing at the condition of the boat. Rust stains drip from the grab rails on the cabin house. Pieces of broken trim jut out from the rub rail. A huge amount of guano is pooled on the deck.

I smell the thick ammonia odor of the guano. More vultures circle overhead; to them we must smell pretty good. On a scale of one to ten - ten being enough to induce vomiting - the smell ranks around an eight. I shimmy out on the side of the stainless steel bow pulpit. I step off and land on the teak swim step. I let go of the *Suzanne* and turn toward the transom of the cruiser.

The swim step groans beneath my weight. I freeze. I don't want to end up in the water. I look at Ellen.

"Is it going to go?" She looks down at me with fear in her eyes, the gun still trained at the sliding door.

"I doubt it." There is a loud crack, and my foot sinks into the bay up to my knee. "Damn." I quickly throw my leg over the transom to save myself. My dry foot lands on the deck and immediately slips in the pool of poop. I do the splits with my crotch now pressing down on a chrome deck cleat. The swim step continues to give way and my foot sinks ever deeper into the bay. I reach out with the boat hook and grab a piece of cleat where my boat is tied, and I pull myself aboard. I'm finally standing upright on the boat, but only for an instant. My feet slide out from under me as if I were an idiot on an ice rink. I land flat on my back in the shit.

"I'll stay here." Ellen is smiling.

I watch the vultures circling overhead. They're probably going to follow me around for a week.

"Yeah, you stay there." I can feel the guano soaking my hair.

Chapter Thirty-six

There are several bumper stickers on the sliding window: "In and Out Burger" with the 'b' and 'r' removed leaving "In and Out urge" and another pleasant sticker, "Men Suck!"

"This is the Man-haters boat, alright," I announce with my back flat on the crap covered poop deck.

"Whose boat?"

"Long story." The smell is so bad now that I start to think how fragrant a rotting sheep head is. My mouth begins to water. "This is it."

"This is what?"

"A perfect ten." I scramble upright and lunge for the rail and let the contents of my stomach pour into the bay. I feel good again after a bit of retching.

I hear something stir behind me, inside the cabin, a scraping noise behind the sliding door. I turn, I wipe my chin.

"Come out, right now, hands up." Ellen shouts with authority, gun at the ready. She looks at me. "Careful, Jack."

I've got my hands up too.

"Come on out." The stirring continues until finally a huge vulture wriggles his way through the door and breaks for the air.

I'm surprised that Ellen holds her fire. Animal lover, I guess. I would have filled it with lead. I reach out for the slider with my hook again. I use it to grab the handle and pull the door open. "Oh, my god."

I lean back against the transom. "Shirley the man-hater is dead."

"Do you know her?"

"Everyone does. I suggest you call someone now."

The body is lying flat on its back. Her boat oar, broken in half, stands straight up from her torso. Her head was removed and placed between her own legs. Her arms are not readily visible.

I feel the nausea creeping up again. "Can you see this?"

"Yeah. Whoever did this…"

"…Is some messed up individual." I can't take the odor any longer. I quickly and much more gracefully step over the transom and on to the fragile swim step. I extend the hook for Ellen to take aboard. I reach for the pulpit, but the swim step gives one last resounding crack and I'm dumped under water.

The cold water freezes my head almost instantly. It's only fifty degrees, but it feels a lot colder. I use this opportunity to wash the bird excrement off my body. As I surface, I snort the salt water through my nose to clear out the stench. I feel purifying joy. I submerge one more time to get the job done. Then I breach like a playful whale, with snot and sea water shooting out of my nose.

I can see the repulsion on Ellen's face when she reaches for my hand, but I shake her off. I have to practice climbing aboard by myself. I'll be performing this ritual with some regularity in the South Pacific. I throw my soaking frame up on the deck, arm by arm and leg by leg.

"Jesus Christ." I am not sure if she is referring to my aquatic prowess or the extreme odor and filth that I was not able to erase.

"Let's go," I say, moving toward the cockpit.

"Whoa, cowboy, we're not going anywhere. We'll wait for the sheriff's department."

"I almost forgot you were a cop." I'm shaking now; my body's trying to head off hypothermia.

"You'd better get out of those clothes and try to warm up." Ellen seems sincere, pausing before dialing her cell phone.

Charley greets me at the companionway and I feed her a biscuit. I take a hot shower and change into fresh clothes in the time it takes a fire truck and several police vehicles to arrive on the beach. The Sausalito police boat and the Sheriff boat are racing toward us. Ellen is on the phone and does more listening than talking. Occasionally, she looks my way. I think we just got in trouble for our little sailing trip.

Chapter Thirty-seven

Ellen convenes with the crime scene investigators on the sheriff's boat tied alongside the *Suzanne*. The sheriffs discuss the plan of attack deferring to Ellen. There is a brief discussion with Sausalito police over jurisdiction, but they quickly retreat giving in to the two hundred yard offshore boundary. Anything beyond two hundred yards belongs to the Marin County Sheriffs and the US Coast Guard and I don't think they want the trouble anyway.

The sheriffs are beginning to get unnerved. I can hear their entire game plan, from my position on my boat.

"We appreciate everything you've done, but now we would like you to remove your boat." Ellen is thanking and asking at the same time. I can tell that she is in crime solving mode. It's as if our sailing trip never happened. I understand.

"Throw me my bowline and I'm gone."

Ellen nods at the sheriffs, and they do just that. They untie their line and toss me mine. I'm adrift in the ebbing tide. I fire the motor and back away from the scene. The captain of the sheriff's boat waves me off.

I spin the wheel and let the light breeze take the bow down. I make up enough distance to put it in forward and swing the boat toward the marina. I leave the helm and let Charley on deck. She's eager to get out.

The image of sheriffs in uniform aboard the boat is out of place but it's not like the cluster from the other night. There is a sense of solemnity about them. They're not charging around making a lot of noise. They're methodical, possibly out of respect for Shirley or the power of the sea. They're voices barely carry across the water.

I let the boat drift up against the dock. I kill the engine, jump ashore and tie off. Charley jumps on to the dock and takes off like she's late for an appointment. I plug in the shore power and phone service. I go below.

The main salon looks a little tossed from the incident with the Kid. I return the pillows to the settees.

I check the bilge. The seawater is all but gone. I can see the loose hoses where the clamps were removed. I quickly return the hoses to the valves and tighten them. I loosen the open valve handles using a wrench until they turn freely. I close the water maker valve, but leave the others open. I'll need them open when I run the boat systems while in the slip.

I return to the nav desk. I close any open drawers and straighten out my lap top. I find the Arabic letter on top of the desk. This is the translated copy, not the original. I search the drawer for the original, but it's nowhere to be found. I check beneath the benches and cushions, anywhere it might have fallen. My boat was tossed after all and Ellen tossed it while she went below during our sail. She's got the fax.

But whoever pulled the hose clamps could have spent a little extra time down here and could have found the fax too. I put on my thinking cap. I got the fax late last night from Dolliver. Ellen nabbed the original today. I was going to give Ellen the copy of the fax anyway. I was so engrossed in sailing I completely forgot, but she didn't forget. She's a good cop. She was playing me the entire time.

She used the sailing as a ruse to search my boat. That means that I'm not a suspect in her eyes because anything she found would be inadmissible. That also means she knows that I might be of some help in solving her case. All she had to do was ask.

The faxes were probably not on board when the saboteur did his dirty work. The hoses could have been loosened while I was away this morning, or even last night. The person who did it knew what he was doing and was expecting me to take the boat out.

From my vantage point on deck I can see the first county diver go into the water next to Shirley's boat. The investigators seem stalled on the sheriff boat. I don't think they're going aboard until they get that boat out of the water, or at least tied up to a dock. The vultures are still circling, but in fewer numbers.

I drag the dock hose down into the main salon and thoroughly clean the bilge, rinsing salt from all the fittings, the engine and the water pumps. The bilge pump cycles on and off until the space is clean. I quickly hose down the deck of the *Suzanne* and throw on the canvas sail covers. I cover the winches and step off the boat.

I grab a sandwich at the dockside café and wolf it down. I buy a sandwich for Ellen before returning to the busy shoreline where a group of locals gather. The number of emergency vehicles parked on shore has dwindled down to a few cruisers, one Sausalito car and Tom Ricketts. Once again, the jurisdiction issue turns any incident into the policeman's ball.

Roy is off his schooner and stands in the background while watching the action. George, an army vet who is meticulous about his boat, is on the dock with a brown paper bag in his hand. Tom Ricketts is right next to George. Tom makes the "You smell" signal by grabbing his nose and pointing his elbow at George. George watches him do it, but doesn't say anything. It's weird.

"They got positive I.D. on the body. It's Shirley. Are you going to eat that?" Tom points at Ellen's sandwich.

"Actually, it's for Ellen. There's a real sicko on the loose." Tom Ricketts is everywhere and, right now, at least seven miles from his jurisdiction.

"So you're fetching her lunch now, huh?" Tom is wearing a hound's tooth jacket and cotton khakis, a golf shirt and gleaming white sneakers. He looks like a man brought out of retirement for one last job. Everything he is wearing looks brand new. His addiction to Costco is becoming quite evident.

"She hasn't eaten all day." I say. "Besides, maybe she won't blame me for this murder either."

"When did you start trusting women?"

"I've got to start sometime. Anybody call Dolliver?" I ask, knowing too well how he's going to take the news.

"Not my case, man." Tom heads down the dock toward the Sheriff boat.

I call the hardware store on my cell and wait for Big Marty to pick up.

Big Marty answers. I give him a brief description of the situation. He isn't surprised. He agrees to track down Dolliver and bring him to the water. Dolliver usually works the tourists for photo-ops near the ferry dock at this time of day. It shouldn't take long to find him.

I follow Tom down to the dock where the deputies are towing in Shirley's boat. I'm there to catch the lines as they tie up alongside the dock. They keep Shirley's boat tied so that one has to pass through the Sheriff boat to get to it.

The coroner waits on the dock while the boats are secured. He'll wait until the crime scene guys hand it over. The sheriffs step aside as they go to work. The crime scene guys take photographs and lift fingerprints. The boat will be searched and scanned with ultraviolet to uncover blood stains. Any blood spots will be sampled, and the direction of the spray recorded.

I hand Ellen the sandwich.

She looks down at her bare feet on the dock. "I don't think I can go very far."

I look down at her very attractive feet. I forgot to bring her shoes.

We look at Tom Ricketts. Tom has one foot on the dock and one on the Sheriff boat. While he chats up with the captain, seemingly uninterested in the crime scene, the oar found in Shirley's chest is bagged and handed off the boat to be left on a waiting gurney.

We stand next to each other as she eats her lunch. I give her a few minutes to eat, but I can tell by her eyes that she is not thrilled that I'm there.

"I'll get your shoes."

Ellen nods. While she manages to squeeze the last bits of sandwich into her mouth, a piece of lettuce dangles from her chin.

"Do you need a napkin, or are you going to use the fax you found on my boat?"

Ellen grabs my arm and walks me down the dock. She wipes her face.

"I don't care that you took it, I was going to give it to you anyway," I say.

"Sure you were."

"You're going to have to learn to trust me."

"Trust is for friends. We're not friends. You're withholding evidence. You're impeding this investigation." She doesn't seem happy but she doesn't seem angry either. It is as if she expected me to hold back that fax.

"You performed an illegal search and seizure and I thought we were headed in the right direction. Had I known that you only went sailing with me to search my boat, I would have asked for a warrant."

Meanwhile, the Kid is stalking down the dock toward us.

"By holding back that information, you made me look bad."

"You made yourself look bad." I think we're having our first fight. I take a deep breath and bring down the volume. "Nobody knows you have it, and I'm not sure that it means anything anyway. Besides, when you show it to your buddy Stevens, you'll look good."

The Kid is on us and he's sucking air through his flaring nostrils. He's furious. "I should have you and your girlfriend arrested." The Kid is out of his mind.

Ellen looks at me. "What's next?"

I calmly shove the Kid into the cold San Francisco Bay. "She's not my girlfriend!"

Ellen smiles.

The Kid comes to the surface, spitting water. "I'm calling the cops."

Ellen shoves her badge into his face.

"Let it go, Kid."

The Kid paddles to the dock with an expression of loss. I help him out of the water.

The Kid nods and saunters back to 'A' basin.

Ellen's arms are crossed. "I have to go."

"Do you want to know what I know, or not?"

"Yes, I do."

"Okay, I think Flynn may have become privy to company information that turned fatal. It's in the fax. That was my only lead. Good luck."

"Flynn's death may have had nothing to do with his job. By the looks of Shirley's death, we could have a serial killer running around." Ellen is definitely keeping her options open.

"Two gruesome murders in Marin within days just don't add up," I say. "This could be a copycat. And just so we're even, Gary Dolliver, the

Sausalito Santa, was Shirley's boyfriend."

"The Man-hater?"

"Right. Dolliver didn't see her yesterday. Last night, he asked me if I had seen her. I didn't see her either. This isn't Dolliver's doing."

"Maybe it was the Grinch?" Ellen smiles.

I don't blame her for the macabre joke. She just walked out of the Valley and into two horrible murders. These don't happen more than once in a career here in Marin.

Marty pulls up to the wharf in his truck with Dolliver sitting next to him. "I'll talk to Dolliver and tell him it's okay to talk to you. He'll want you to find whoever did this."

"Thanks. Keep him from coming down here. We don't want him to see her like this."

"Yeah." I start to turn away then stop. "Was there more to Shirley's death that I didn't see?"

"I can tell you it looked like she put up a fight. It was pretty messy. We're going to check for the perp's blood, and hopefully we'll find something. Tell Dolliver she died quickly. It's likely he'll never get a chance to see the body. He's not kin."

"Call me if you think of anything that can help me on this one."

"So, I'm not a suspect on the Flynn case?"

"Not anymore."

"Why not?"

"I can't tell you. Don't worry about the shoes. I'll send someone over to get them."

She was sincere. Not about the shoes but about the lead suspect. She just couldn't tell me. If I was Ellen, I'd put Christine high up on my list of suspects. You have to have a list. You have to show the bosses that you're doing your job.

A helicopter circles low overhead. The blades shudder as it arcs away from me. I think about the basket spinning down to me from the coast guard helicopter. I had wanted to get into it myself and leave my father there on his ram shackle sailboat and just fly away.

Chapter Thirty-eight

Marty is keeping Dolliver in the car. I walk over to the passenger side window.

"What's going on?" Dolliver is shaking.

"Shirley is dead, Dolliver. She didn't feel a thing. She was murdered." I had to say it right away; no hemming and hawing. I want to get it over with.

Dolliver stares straight ahead. "Do they know who did it?" His voice breaks.

"No." I look down at the ground, anywhere but at Dolliver. I know what grief looks like.

"Can I see her?"

"They're not going to let you on the dock. They have to notify next of kin."

"They're not going to find any."

"When they don't, I'm sure they'll let you see her." I had to placate him.

"Where are they going to take her?"

"County. Do you know anybody who would want to kill her, Dolliver?" This time I look directly at him. His face is sunken, his shoulders hang down, like all his muscles let go the moment he heard the news.

"I'm the only one who loved her. Nobody wanted to kill her."

Big Marty slaps him on the leg. "You'll be all right."

"I want you to go home, Dolliver. Stay home. The police are going to want to interview you. You should be home."

"Call me when I can get Shirley back."

"It could be a while. It's a murder investigation now." I so badly want this to end. "Go home, Dolliver. Wait for the police."

"I've got nothing left." Dolliver rolls up his window.

Big Marty backs out and drives off. In the distance the coroner is placing two body bags on the gurney. The sun has dropped behind the headlands and the dock lights are going on. The 'A' basin regulars assemble themselves at the railing above the flooding tide. George is holding court as Roy stands with his arms crossed not saying anything.

George has the most ocean experience of anyone and isn't afraid to remind you. He owns a house on the hill but spends a lot of nights on his thirty-five foot vintage Swan sloop and is on it every weekend polishing, scrubbing and varnishing. George is in his seventies. He's gruff when he drinks and that's often. His wife kicks him down to his boat to sober up.

George spent his twenties greasing a destroyer in the North Pacific during the Korean War. He keeps himself in good shape, aside from the drinking. If I ever run out of a cleaning product or a specific type of grease or lubricant, he'll have it. He has everything and it's always in its proper place.

George doesn't put up with any crap except, oddly enough, for the Kid's. George has taken the Kid under his wing. Sometimes you can see them sitting at the dockside café boat talking, neither one listening to the other. They just like to tell their stories.

The café owner asks George what happened and he's more than happy to tell him it's a murder, but it's nothing close to what he saw back in Nam. The small group stares at the scene on the dock, the sheriffs' boat, the gurneys, and the CSI team working the dirty boat. I see the small ripples building on the water. I look at the hillside above us. The tops of trees begin to swirl in the wind like fields of wheat. The wind is coming up. Soon the boat will pull on their dock lines like horses at the starting gate. It's the wind calling them out.

The coroner pushes the gurney to his van, loads it, and then drives off. The remaining police leave unceremoniously. Tom Ricketts is talking to a young blonde reporter from the Journal. Bill Stevens lurches up to the dock in his cruiser. He gives me a dirty look before marching down the gangway.

It's time for me to go home. I follow Roy and George back to 'A' basin. George is listing badly after a long day of drinking. Roy gives a subtle wave and heads off. He doesn't have the patience for George. He probably doesn't have the patience for anyone and that's why he lives on a boat.

"You want to come over to the boat for a cocktail, Brubaker?" George slurs his words.

I would love nothing more than to go to George's boat and watch him drink until he pukes over the side. "I'm sorry George. I wish I could, but I have to finish putting away my boat from today's sail."

"Now, that I understand. Shipshape, everything's got to be in its place. When you go to reach for something, it's right there every time. I respect you, Jack. You've got to know that." He leans in for a hug.

I dodge him. "Thanks, George." He gets emotional when he drinks.

George and I stop at his boat. George's hands are deep in his pockets now. Not a good place for a person with enough alcohol in him to embalm a corpse. You need your arms for balance on the dock; one hand for you and one for the boat.

"You're a good man, Brubaker." George is a few inches shorter than I am. He cranes his neck back, rolling back and forth on his heels.

"You are too, George. I have the utmost respect for you." I know that this is what George wants and that's why he keeps his boat immaculate. In the distance, beyond the channel, the county diver throws his fins onto the dive boat. He removes his tank and drags it to the swim step. He'll be back in the morning doing it all over again, widening his search area.

"Hey, Jack? You ever meet my wife?" George is tearing up.

"Yes, I have."

"She is the most beautiful woman I ever met; tough as nails, too. She keeps me in line, man."

"Women do that for us."

"Yes, they do. Yes, they do." George spins around and grabs his lifelines with both hands. He puts his foot up on the toe rail and gets a foothold after several attempts.

"Goodnight, George."

"Goodnight, Jack." George pulls himself up and over the lifelines and falls head first into the boat cockpit. He is sprawled out on the hard fiberglass and coiled lines.

"Are you all right, George?"

"I'm fine. I have the utmost respect," George grumbles.

Chapter Thirty-nine

Charley is waiting for me when I get back to my boat. I pour two cups of food into her bowl and open a cold beer for myself. I walk the deck from stern to bow and inspect the hardware, deck plates and spinnaker pole.

The stainless steel bolts joining the aluminum ends with the carbon fiber spinnaker pole are corroding because of the electrolysis between metals. I'll have to remove the bolts, re-drill the pole ends and tap new bolt holes. After a while I'll have to replace the aluminum ends. This will have to be done before I make the three thousand mile crossing southwest to Polynesia.

The ocean breeze is gone. Lights are coming on all around, climbing up the hills surrounding Richardson Bay. A small cabin cruiser motors up the channel. Its bow lights reflect red and green on the glassy surface. The sheriff boat leaves the marina, towing Shirley's cabin cruiser. They're heading in the direction of the police dock.

I coil up the jib sheets and hang them on the bow pulpit. I coil the main sheet and hang it from the end of the boom. I remove the winch handles from their pockets and place them in the hardware locker. I think about the guy who tried to sink my boat. I never knew he was here. I'm starting to slip. I don't want to deal with the Flynn case anymore. It's not worth it.

"I want to find Lucy and get the hell out," I say out loud.

"I don't blame you." Tom Ricketts startles me. He's standing on the dock near the bow. "It's weird, man. You want to know what I think?"

"Yeah, I do."

"I think it's a serial killer. We haven't had one in a while. I think that the same guy who killed Flynn killed Shirley."

I've already been batting that around in my head. "Flynn was pushed out of a plane. And unless he was drugged, he knew the guy flying the plane. There is no record of him returning from Peru."

"You're saying that whoever flew him home dumped him out of a plane? Why dump him here? Why not dump him in Peru? Why go to the trouble of flying him all the way home only to kill him? Are you going to offer me a beer?"

"Sorry. Sure."

Tom goes below and grabs a beer, and returns to the cockpit like so many times before. I join him.

"You dump him near his home so nobody goes to Peru. Nobody pokes around where they don't belong," I say.

"Keep the FBI out of Peru." Tom takes a long draw from his beer.

"With this Homeland Security B.S., they've got the FBI working in the Middle East, Russia, and the Philippines. They're sticking their noses in a lot of rice bowls. If you want to keep a low profile, kill your threat on American soil. Keep the investigation here."

"I agree with you, but I'm not convinced. Two mutilations in a week spells serial killer."

"No profiler would call this a serial. What would the connection be between an upper income male High-tech professional to a female dockside sea urchin?"

"The murderer," Tom says.

"Yeah." I think about what he said. What connects these two murders, one out of a plane and one on a boat? Both victims were mutilated, but only Shirley was purposely mutilated. Flynn's disfigurement came from a fall in the woods. It may not have been intentional, but it was a lucky bonus. Shirley pissed off a lot of people. The way the body was left suggested that whoever did this to her, knew her. So who knows both Shirley and Flynn?

"Do you know anything about Red Fish?" I ask. I watch the dark shape of a burly raccoon cruise the tidal area beneath the wharf turning over rocks and plastic bottles that cling to the spoil exposed by the receding tide.

Tom Ricketts watches the raccoon a little longer before he answers.

"'Lose Weight Now, Ask Me How?' Yeah, I hear he's got a rez up on the hill in Mill Valley. He's fleecing a whole new tribe."

"I was up there last night. It's a very shady operation."

"It's out of my jurisdiction. I can't set foot on it. Native Americans police themselves and when that fails, it's a Federal issue. Red Fish is not only the chief of his tribe he's also the chief of police. I can't touch him."

"He's got an internet porn business going, as well as a Koi fish fencing operation."

"That's almost white collar. I can't say I'm proud of Gabe, but he sure is enterprising. Not bad for a guy who served a deuce in San Quentin."

"Manny was up there, too. He was the one who fenced the Koi. Apparently they get donors to give them some expensive fish. Manny fishes them out when the donors aren't looking and splits the money with Red Fish."

"Even if I was to catch Manny with the tuna, I couldn't do anything. They have to be stolen, Red Fish owns them. He's flying below the radar."

"There is something else."

"Shoot, but I sure am thirsty." Tom turns his empty beer upside down.

I step down to the galley and return with two more beers.

Tom nearly empties his right away. "I've got to get home to the wife and kids. You know how it is."

I shake my head. No, I don't.

"What were you going to say?" Tom asks.

I decide not to bring up the sinking boat incident, the saboteur that climbed aboard my boat and loosened the hoses without me knowing. "Forget it."

Tom bounces the empty beer bottle on his knee. I study his face. It's pasty and puffy. He's grabbing at everything with little self-control: junk food, beers, Costco. I think he may be in trouble.

Tom's phone rings. He wrestles it from its hip holster. He puts it to his ear. "Tom here."

I pick up his empty bottles and take them downstairs. I think about the wonderful business connections one can make in the minimum security area of San Quentin. Red Fish meets Manny and Manny introduces Red Fish to the South American connection. It's like an all-expenses paid retreat for criminals. I think about the blurry image on the computer screen. Could this image be the killer?

Tom sticks his head in the companionway, "It's time to roll.

They've got that skinny jerk Manny cornered and they're waiting for the battering ram."

"Where?"

"The Mobile Oaks trailer park in Larkspur."

"Let's go."

Chapter Forty

I park my Suburban in the 'Pup and Taco' parking lot. This is the staging area for the assault on Manny's tin-roofed domicile. Tom is already here when I arrive. He drove code two. He doesn't give a crap about the rules.

There are a couple of police cruisers from Twin Cities, Mill Valley and a beater from Fairfax. Everyone is in on this thing, not because they have to be, but because operations like this yield great experience in urban warfare for small town cops.

I'm here because I want to talk to the weasel. I want to find Lucy. I approach the small group bathed in orange sodium light. Everything east of the freeway in Larkspur was once part of the bay. The parking lot, and even the Mobile Oaks trailer park, are all built on recovered land. Most of this area still floods during the high tides and winter storms. The Pup and Taco parking lot is directly across the street from the mobile home park which explains Manny's penchant for the cheap food.

I approach Tom, who's talking to the commanding officer. The fog is filing in and the air is cooling fast. I can hear a ferry bumping the dock at the Larkspur transit center a quarter mile away. The aluminum gangway bangs into the boat. Heavy footsteps charge up the slope to solid ground, people rushing to their cars, rushing home to their wives or their husbands, to their warm homes and beautiful children.

Tom spins around. "Bru, baby! Thanks to you losing your shotgun up in San Geronimo, they called out the 'A' Team tonight." Ricketts is beaming. "That increased the fun factor for sure."

"I don't think it's that big of a deal." I'm slightly surprised and embarrassed by the size of the operation; four cars and twice as many officers.

Tom grabs me by the shoulder as if to shut me up. "We're not dealing with some cheesy pickpocket here, Bru. This guy tried to kill you. This is about public safety now, so keep your mouth shut and try to mingle. Be one of the guys." Ricketts spins around to face the guys.

"I'll try."

Tom Ricketts leans into the officer in charge while I feel the stares of the real cops. They don't like guys like me. They put the time in at the academy and the gym. They paid their admission and here Tom is giving out backstage passes to a guy like me.

Tom finishes up and walks back over to me. "You got a gun on you, Brubaker?" Tom asks in a serious tone, "Because we've got to take it now, if you do."

"I'm unarmed."

"Good. We don't want any civilians shooting the crap out of the place. You'll sure as shit get us into a lot of trouble."

Tom pulls his piece out from beneath his jacket. "We're cops, so it doesn't matter if we shoot up the place. We can get away with just about anything." It's a big gun. He releases the clip into his palm, presses the bullets with his thumb then jams it back into the grip. "We're going to air out the trailer, if that's what it takes." He brings up the weapon to his eye line, aims it at the ground then snaps it up to a row of crows sitting on a telephone pole.

Suddenly, I feel like I am surrounded by what sounds like a thousand guns getting clips jammed into grips, shot guns being loaded and pumped.

"Everybody gather around." Tom takes a knee in the huddle.

A few guys put their hands on my back. I, too, feel like one of the guys, except for the cheesy off-the-rack bulletproof vest that doesn't quite fit, leaving most of my mid-section unprotected.

"Don't you think my vest is a little small, Tom?"

"Sorry Brubaker, that's all we've got. We have to make our move on Manny, now. I want everyone to know how important it is to get in there safely. This is how it's going to go down. We're going to take three cars down the main road. Once we reach Aluminum Drive, everyone out. We march in double time and yank him out. Simple. I want everyone on the subject. He is armed and dangerous. Find the shotgun and secure the trailer.

Now, put a hand in."

Everyone sticks their gloved hands in. Tom puts his on top. "This skinny fuck, Manny, tried to kill Mr. Brubaker. Let's not let him try to kill us either."

We slowly raise our fists toward the sky, to a power greater than us.

"Now saddle up." Tom swings his hat around like it's the opening of Cheyenne Frontier Days. Everyone cheers.

Chapter Forty-one

The group of cruisers turns into the Mobile Oaks trailer park across from the 'Pup and Taco.'

Tom has his jacket off and is wearing a bullet proof vest that he keeps in his car. He also wears a black baseball cap that has 'Police' stamped in white block letters. He taps his feet like Buddy Guy. Everyone is excited, but everyone is also on edge. Tom allowed me to ride in one of the cruisers to Manny's trailer. He is reluctant, but knows I won't take 'no' for an answer.

"Hey, Tom?"

"Yeah, Bru buddy."

"Why did everyone laugh when I mentioned the vest? I'm kind of worried that it's a little too small and won't be able to catch all that lead." I yank down on it, trying to cover my vital organs.

"It's the only one we had left."

"It feels like its riding up."

Tom is looking out the window and bites his nails through his gloves. "It belongs to the K-9. It's a dog vest, buddy."

"Nice."

"Don't worry about it. By the time Manny shoots through all the other guys, he'll be out of rounds. Then you can walk right up to him and kick him in the teeth."

"I'm looking forward to it."

Tom takes on a serious guise. "Look, Jack, this is the real deal. I want you to wait in the car until we give you the all clear. We'll bring him out and put him in a cruiser. When we're busy clearing the rest of the building, you can talk to him then. You'll have plenty of face time before we put him in the gas chamber."

Tom looks me dead in the eye. "We're taking this very seriously

202

Brubaker, and so should you."

"Thanks, Tom. I'll be right here."

The main street into the park is lined with trailer homes in various widths: single wide, double wide and triple wide, all placed at a forty-five degree angle to the gravel road. Most have small gardens filled with lawn decorations. Lattice covers their foundations. Garden hoses stretch out across the main street. Pickup trucks with camper shells are wedged into car ports. A few dogs race out to the end of their leashes and are jerked off their feet.

Three police cars driving through the neighborhood have a certain effect on people. All the trailer lights that weren't on are on now. The locals are becoming restless. Portly backlit figures are crowding windows and robed citizens are coming out of their metal houses.

Tom waves his fist and the small convoy stops. He throws open his door. The officer no longer in charge and his crew in the cars behind me, join up with the main group. Now it's just me.

I'm not going to wait in this car. God forbid if Manny reaches for that Mossberg; they'll shoot his limbs off, and I'll lose my only lead. I'll be back to square one.

In a split-second decision, I'm out of the cruiser and running at the back of the phalanx. No one notices and no one cares, except for Tom Ricketts. I catch Tom's eye. He's in another world entirely. His backward glance was merely to determine if I was friend or foe. There is nothing he can do now. He carries on.

Two headless lawn flamingos guard the walkway to the front steps. Apparently, Manny took them out with the twelve-gauge. That's what led the cops here to begin with: "Shots fired."

Chapter Forty-two

The team is on the trailer hard. They rip the door off its hinges. They toss a flash grenade inside. The officers swarm in and I'm right behind them. The trailer wobbles beneath us. The place is dark and dreary and smells like cats. They find Manny in the back bedroom.

Manny, still lying in his bed, drops a PS4 controller and grabs a prescription bottle from the nightstand. He downs its contents. In what seems like nothing short of a gymnastic miracle, Tom Ricketts leaps through the air and lands knee down on the subject's chest with the barrel of his gun rammed up Manny's nose.

Needless to say, that's all it took for Manny to get the pills down. Had Tom come in a little lower, maybe with the same knee in Manny's gut, Manny would have hurled those pills like a Viennese fountain. The rest of the team secures the bedroom. I try to pull my vest down to my waist.

Tom tosses Manny on his stomach while two other guys dive in with handcuffs. One of the officers inspects the bottles by the side of the bed.

"We've got a pharmacy over here, boys: Vicodin, Oxycontin, Perco-something and some other unpronounceable class two narcotics."

"Lookie here." He holds up an empty bottle. "One very empty bottle of Viagra. Shit, this boy just took enough Viagra to keep a fifty-year old bull elephant up for a week."

The officer puts his face right in front of Manny's. "I think you meant to take these." He rattles the Oxycontin bottle. "It looks like you swallowed a lot more than you can chew, tough guy."

Manny continues to fight. "You've got the wrong guy. I didn't do shit." Manny is spitting again. A lone Viagra is stuck to his lower lip.

With lightning speed, Tom picks Manny up by the back of his neck and throws him face first against a Franklin Mint plate of Taylor Swift hanging on the wall. It shatters against his nose.

"Did you see that, he reached for my gun?" Ricketts stomps on the back of Manny's knee. Tom Ricketts is the kind of guy who would beat you up in front of your own kids.

Manny screams in agony, "Oh, my leg." You'd think it was severed by a Bengal tiger.

"That's enough. We've got a weapon to find. Five bucks to the guy that comes up with Brubaker's scatter gun!" Tom knows how to motivate the troops. He drags Manny outside.

I take a quick look around the remains of the trailer. The room is filled with piles of dirty clothes and fast food wrappers. The walls are covered with graffiti: misspelled obscenities and racial epithets. A heavy stink hangs in the air.

I decide to stay with the trailer in case they find something to tie to Lucy. The officers tear up the place. They pull out of the nightstand drawers, toss lamps, and flip the mattress. There is little room for me in the bedroom, so I go down the hall to the living area.

Through a broken window, I can see Tom push Manny into the back seat of a cruiser. I can hear Manny's skull thud against the door frame. A crowd of angry neighbors is closing in around a few cops charged with the security detail. This could turn Marin into Mogadishu in the blink of an eye.

I quickly paint the living room with light from my Maglite. Blue and red lights flash through the broken blinds dangling from the windows. The kitchen sink is filled with dirty dishes. A big half-chewed Koi skeleton is sitting on the counter. Manny didn't pawn them all.

The little metal single-wide looks likes it was decorated out of the back of the Sears Catalog. Midwestern curtains and oval rugs make it seem like the trailer might have been his parents' place. There're no pictures on the walls, nothing that identifies its original residents.

I carefully open drawers and check the refrigerator. Nothing looks like it has anything to do with Manny. A small sofa with built-in cup holders sits against the front wall of the trailer. In front of that is a varnished driftwood coffee table. Beneath the coffee table, I find several books: "Guide for Duck Hunters," "Fishing Lures and your Endeavor," and "We

Like to Hunt Birds." I can only surmise by the literature that this was once the old man's hunting cabin, towed here from the Sacramento River Delta bird fields.

Protruding beneath the sofa, the beam of my flashlight reveals a Polaroid photo. I dust it off. In the photo, Manny is standing next to Lucy with his arm around her. The expression on her face is of disgust. Her eyes are looking out of frame. She would have been a terrible poker player.

Manny is leaning into her and Lucy is leaning away. Manny is heavier here, no doubt because of the starches and carbohydrates they serve in rehab. The institutional food stuck to him like glue. It didn't take long for the horse, or the chunk, smack, junk, monkey on his back to take all the weight off again.

Lucy looks like she's pulling away from both Manny and her terrible life. Manny has a vacant expression like he's somehow content with his own.

I put the photo in my pocket, wedging it beneath my dog vest. I find my shotgun and the piece of two-by-four leaning by the front door. I leave them behind and I take one last look around the room.

Observing a crime scene depends on one's ability to isolate each of the five senses. It's like listening to music and hearing each instrument separately. I learned to listen to each sense as I grew up sailing on the bay. At sea, your senses are honed. With no distractions, you feel and anticipate almost everything. Back on land the distractions cloud my senses. Over time I have become more aware of the sensual loss and have learned to turn on my senses as I needed them.

I give the room one more pass. This time my investigative prowess lands on a huge largemouth bass trophy mounted above a fake fireplace. I pick up the two-by-four next to the door and quickly dispatch three heavy blows to the fish. The first two loosen its grip to the wall and the third sends the fish flying across the trailer. A small bundle of letters is regurgitated from its mouth onto the sofa.

Lucy's letters. I quickly shove the bundle into my back pocket.

I happily jump down from the front side of the trailer and find Tom talking with an officer by the bedroom.

Tom Ricketts is not happy with me. "I told you to stay in the car."

I nod and turn my palms up. "There's a shotgun and a section of two-by-four in there." I point over my shoulder at the front half of the single wide.

"I never saw you in there, you got me?" Tom's LED headlamp is blinding me.

I nod.

Tom turns his back to me. A Marin I.J. reporter grabs his attention. It's the same one from earlier, a pretty blonde, recent college grad named Kim. I think they might be working on a story of their own.

Manny is sitting alone in the patrol car. The scrawny freak is rocking back and forth. His long straggly hair leaves a greasy smudge on the side window. I walk around the back of the car to the front passenger seat.

The crowd of neighbors is being held back about twenty-five feet up the road. One of the officers has run police tape from the headless flamingo to a windmill duck across the street, making up the western perimeter. The eastern perimeter is delineated by police tape spanning the road between a lawn jockey and a garden gnome.

I sit down in the front seat of the cruiser. There is a plexi-glass partition separating the front from the passenger seat. Manny lunges toward the glass but his seatbelt catches him. He growls in frustration.

This is the same creep who bashed my face in twice, stole my shoes, and my car, and led me on a foot chase. I'm so angry that I can't resist jumping back there and smothering him with this Kevlar dog vest.

"Do you have any idea who I am, jackass?"

"Bite me. Eat me. Screw you!" Manny spits at the glass.

"My name is Jack Brubaker. You know my sister." I press the photo against the glass. "Her name is Lucy Brubaker. When was the last time you saw her?"

"I don't know nothing, man. I want to talk to a lawyer."

"I'm not a cop, so I don't give a shit. Do you want me to make your life easier or not?"

"Screw you!"

I stare at him. There is nothing more frightening than the Brubaker evil eye. There's a long silence as I direct my piercing gaze directly into his eyes. He's not backing down. I press the letters against the glass. "Do these look familiar?"

"Where did you get those?" Manny struggles in his seat.

"Where's Lucy?"

Manny is startled when Tom dumps the shotgun and the two-by-four on the hood of the cruiser. Manny lets out a girlish scream. Next to the shotgun, Tom drops a drug kit for shooting smack, my missing shoes, one of the headless flamingos and the broken Taylor Swift plate. Tom attempts to carefully piece the plate together. I am not sure that plate is going to make it into the evidence lockup.

Tom sees me in the seat. He slumps in frustration. He motions for me to get out of the car.

I turn to the Manson-esque small time crook. "One last chance, Manny?"

Manny refuses to budge.

"Once that Viagra kicks in you're going to be the life of the party up at County."

Tom opens the passenger door. "Get out of the car, Jack. You're going to get in trouble. Let it lay. We got him."

"We still don't have Lucy." I remove the vest and place it carefully on the hood.

"You'll find her."

Chapter Forty-three

The night desk officer makes a call for me and hands me a visitor's badge. Ellen comes downstairs to meet me.

"Congratulations on picking up Manny." Ellen looks very tired and can't manage much more than that.

"Thanks. Any leads on the Man-hater murder?"

"I can't talk about it, here. If it weren't for the fact that everyone has gone home, we wouldn't be talking to each other at all." Ellen puts her hands into her coat pockets.

"Is Tom coming?" I ask.

"Tom went home, said he'd mop up the paperwork in the morning. He said it was a missing person thing; completely out of his realm of responsibility. It's out of my realm too, but I thought I'd volunteer. Follow me."

I find it very odd that Tom isn't in on the I.D. but I let it go. I could care less if Manny ever spends a day in jail. I just want to find out what he knows about my sister.

"Thank you, Detective." I say as Ellen turns her back.

She cocks her head around, "Detective?" She smiles.

"Thank you, Ellen." I say, but much softer.

I follow Ellen down a long hall to the booking area. Several people are handcuffed to a few benches. The usual deputies work behind the cage, accepting personal belongings and evidence into custody.

There is nothing mysterious about the suspect identification process. The witness or victim looks through the window and points at the guy who did it. In this case, there are five dirt bags in a line and one of them is Manny.

The witness room at the sheriff's department is painted a grubby institutional green. It's little more than the size of a closet and brightly lit.

The ceiling is covered in water-stained acoustic tiles. There is a small window next to an antiquated intercom system.

Ellen joins me in the I.D. room and we stare at the window waiting for Manny to be led in. We're by ourselves again. I inadvertently touch her hand as I reach for the window frame.

"Excuse me. I'm sorry," I say. She must think I am flirting with her.

"Did you get anything out of Manny at Mobile Oaks?" Ellen stares straight ahead.

"Not yet, but I'll be getting my shoes back whether I want them or not." I study Ellen's reflection in the mirror. She seems more beautiful now than ever. I want to tuck her into a bed and bring her tea.

"I hear you'll be getting your Audi back, too."

"That's good news." There's a lot more uncomfortable silence. We're both tired, but there is something else going on here as well. I catch Ellen's reflection in the glass just for an instant. There is a slightest hint of a smile.

The fatigue doesn't come from working two murder cases. We get used to the pace and the workload and become accustomed to the long hours. We never get used to the drain that comes from answering the one phone call that starts an investigation, the phone call that puts us in search of the darkest side of people - the dark side that makes people steal and even murder.

I put my hand on Ellen's. We don't say anything. We are both trying to figure out what badness is behind all this: Flynn's murder, Shirley's gruesome death and Lucy's disappearance.

Normal people just don't disappear. Lucy's disappeared because of the drugs or all the misfiring that goes on inside her head.

My attention is diverted to the watch commander, who seems to be the jack-of-all-trades tonight. He notifies us that the lineup is coming in. He gives me the rules, but I already have my sights set.

The lineup is led along the wall marked with height measurements and five numbered spaces. Each guy in the lineup could be a timber-wielding junky, but only one is Manny. Each suspect is told to step forward and turn to the left, and right, and then told to step back.

An audible gasp comes from Ellen. She quickly stifles a laugh, quickly covers her mouth and composes herself. Manny's mistaken dose of Viagra has taken full effect.

Manny is a little unbalanced. He is swaying left and right, as most of the blood in his body has been diverted to his nether region. When asked to step forward, Manny turns to his left and sways forward. His synapses are not exactly firing correctly. The nearest suspect feels Manny's predicament against his leg, and his eyes become the size of dinner plates.

"Get him off me." The burly drunk in the lumberjack shirt knees Manny in the hip.

Without the slightest show of defense, Manny collapses in a heap.

The commander jumps back in, and with one latex-gloved hand, he picks up Manny and presses him against the wall.

I quickly point the finger at Manny, and the room is cleared. Manny will be taken down a separate hallway to the booking desk. He'll be stripped, searched and given a brand new wardrobe for his overnight stay.

"I've never seen a prisoner that excited about spending a night in jail before." Ellen is finally showing signs of letting loose. She giggles.

"He's lucky. The Oxycontin alternative would have killed him, but then so might the Viagra." Ellen leads me down another hallway to the interview room I was in last night.

"I can't let you in with Manny, but you can give me a list of questions for him. That's as much as we can do without getting in trouble. Manny may seem dumb but he also may have come from a place where 'civil lawsuit' is part of his vocabulary."

Ellen hands me a yellow legal pad and pen. I make quick work of it as I wait in the viewing room. Manny is led into the interview room. He's slouched over, trying not to draw attention to his erection.

Ellen joins me and looks over the list. "Good luck," she says, as she leaves the room and rejoins Manny.

Manny is sitting down with his head on the table. Ellen doesn't sit down. She leans against the door. Manny is cuffed to the table that's bolted to the floor.

I press the "Listen" button next to the one-way glass. My presence on this side of the glass is no less – maybe a little less - a policy violation than being in the interview room beating the truth out of Manny.

"Did you love Lucy?" Ellen starts right in. She puts the picture of Manny and Lucy on the table. Manny stares down at the picture on the table, his hair concealing his face.

That wasn't one of my questions.

Manny nods.

"I know what it's like. I remember the last time I saw my husband. It gets burned into your head. It's so vivid that you don't think that it will ever go away. I even remember what he was wearing. Do you remember what Lucy was wearing the last time you saw her?"

Manny nods. "She was wearing Jeans and a red sweater; the thin kind that's more like a shirt."

"Where was that, Manny?"

Manny's tears are falling on Lucy's picture. "She was going to the city. The Larkspur ferry dock."

"You took her to the ferry dock?"

Manny nods again.

"When was that?"

"I don't know?"

"Was that before you clubbed the man with the two by four in the house in San Geronimo? Where you took his shotgun and stole his car."

"Uh huh." Manny's greasy hair swings back and forth when he nods.

Ellen turns toward the mirror and smiles, mouthing 'Thank you.' "So Lucy has been gone a while?"

Manny nods.

"Was she running from someone, Manny? Was she sick again? Was she using?"

"She was always sick. She was running from me."

"Would you have gone with her if she asked you to?"

"I couldn't get on the boat. I am afraid of the water."

"She didn't ask you, did she, Manny?"

"I am afraid of the water."

"Did she seem happy to you, Manny? Was she leaving because she wanted to?"

Manny picks his head up and looks straight at the mirrored glass.

"I've never seen her happy."

The viewing room is like a dome of silence except for the gentle hum of the intercom speaker. I think about Lucy on the ferry boat. She always loved the water. Lucy wasn't smiling in any of the Polaroids she left behind. It has been a long time since I saw her smile.

Ellen lets him stew. She crosses her arms. She looks at her watch. Ellen walks around the room, she looks down at Manny.

"Manny! Manny! Did you hurt Lucy?" Ellen has her palms down on the table and is leaning over him now.

"No, I said she got on the boat."

Who does he think he is that he can even talk to my little sister? That little rat. Anger rises up in me. I feel it in my fists. I feel it in my jaw. I want to strangle him. I want to watch his life leave his face.

"Did you hurt Lucy?" She pounds the table.

"No. No!" Manny pleads.

"Where did she go, Manny? You're in serious trouble Manny. You're never going to get out of here. Where did she go?" Ellen is shouting at him now.

"It doesn't matter, she's gone. She said she was going away, that's all."

"Where?" I shout, with my fist pressed firmly against the speaker button.

Ellen spins around to face me.

Manny looks up, "I said I don't know!"

Ellen turns away from Manny and leaves the room. She enters the viewing room.

"I don't think he knows where she is." I rub my eyes of the dust from the trailer. "I was kind of counting on that dirt bag."

Ellen puts her hand on my shoulder. "Somebody knows something. You just have to find out whom. You'll find her, Jack."

"It doesn't seem like it.

Chapter Forty-four

Tom delivered my Audi Q7 to the first parking spot next to 'A' basin. He left the keys on the driver's seat. The car seems to be in good shape, except for a few scratches on the bumper where Manny slammed into the garbage cans during our brief pursuit. The interior is clean and smells like a pineapple. My running shoes, which were pulled from my feet in the abandoned house, are sitting on the floor on the passenger side. I toss them out on the ground. My shotgun is still absent, and I'm not in a hurry to get it back.

As I pull the door closed, something beneath the driver side windshield wiper catches my eye. I remove a small white parking stub. I flip it over and find a small blue stamp, "Marin County Airport." This matches the stub I found on Flynn's windshield. Could Manny have taken my car all the way to the airport after fencing the fish and before being caught at Pup 'n Taco in *flagrante delicto*?

I doubt it.

I think about the possibility that someone may have driven my car to the airport in Marin. This person might have known about the narrowing search of flight plans on the night of Flynn's disappearance. It seems unlikely that that person was Manny.

Manny stole my car at the house in San Geronimo. He drove the car to Red Fish's and stayed overnight. The following day he fenced the fish and netted some cash. He spent his take at the Pup 'n Taco where our paths met.

I turn the airport parking ticket over in my hand. It's a small airport. They don't have automated machines. There's a guy in a booth that stamps the tickets by hand. There's no time and date on the ticket. Whoever visited the airport in my Audi did so while it was in Manny's possession, or while it was in the impound lot in San Rafael. It doesn't make sense. What does make sense is that my car was recently at the site where Flynn was last seen. The ticket is another piece of evidence that doesn't bode well for me. It puts me at the scene.

Charley meets me as I lock up the car. Charley has a boyfriend, a scruffy Sheppard mix. I'm not a parent, but I can only imagine what it is like when your daughter brings home her boyfriend for the first time and he turns out to be short and fat with bad breath. I'm disappointed, but I try not to show it. I thought she would do better. I retrieve a handful of dog biscuits from the Suburban and toss them on the ground. Charley's new friend lunges toward the snacks. What a boar! I guess it's the same as paying the boy ten bucks to get lost while my teenage daughter is blow drying her hair in the upstairs bathroom.

I unceremoniously pick up my running shoes and toss them into the dumpster.

The odd-looking boyfriend lopes off to his next meal. I try to convince Charley that she was too good for him anyway. It doesn't take more than thirty seconds before he is forgotten and Charley goes on about her life. How difficult it is to earn the love of a good woman and to keep it.

I grab Charley's collar and walk her toward the boat.

Tonight the marina is a virtual ghost town where the boats are left alone to rattle their chains and clank their floorboards. The sailor who scrapes his boat and replaces the sacrificial zincs, who paints over the thinnest spots and rejoins the neediest boards as the sea mounts its nightly aggression, the sailor who stands vigil, has checked the dock lines and the rubber fenders, goes below for the night.

We lock ourselves below and embrace a hot cup of tea and curl up beneath a thick blanket. We fill our lungs with the smells of diesel, of the bilge and the sea and we hope that tonight the sea will take the night off and allow us to hold our ground until morning.

There is no traffic. The few boats that do move about at night do so in secrecy, nary leaving a v-shaped ripple. Red and green lights glide above the water like alien ships searching for life on earth. The seals are quiet and wait for the return of the fishing boats.

The muffled sound of a television drifts across the water. The Kid is watching *"When Harry Met Sally"* again. He can recite almost every line. What ails him cannot be cured, while living on the water it can only make it worse. He should be watching *"The Great Escape."*

Someone is aboard the *Suzanne*, my *Suzanne*. The cabin lights are on and whoever this person is, is not a sailor. A sailor would have left their shoes on the dock. I locked the boat before heading out to capture Manny. I send Charley in to check it out. She easily jumps from the dock steps to the deck and bounds down the open companionway. There is only silence. Charley seems to have been swallowed whole. This might be an ambush.

I mentally search the boat for anything that might make a suitable impact on someone's head. My scatter gun is locked up in the evidence room at the Sheriff's department. My Glock is in a drawer in my office. The winch handles are in the hardware locker. I could hurl my dirty sneakers at the intruder but they're already in the dumpster.

"Charley, come!" I say it in a sharp voice, barely above a whisper. She rarely disobeys me. I wait a moment. Charley does not appear.

I clench my fists and step aboard the boat. The wide beam and the heavy keel minimize the rocking as the boat feels my full weight. I move forward and look into the wide glass hatch over the main salon. I can't see anything except for Charley lying in her dog bed.

I carefully move all the way forward to the forecastle hatch. I silently drop myself into the forecastle. I silently remove a pry bar from the port locker. I open the door just a crack between the starboard head and the main salon. Charley couldn't care less. She doesn't even move. The main salon is empty.

I open the door completely and find nothing out of the ordinary. I move forward past the small table and galley. The aft cabin door is closed.

I turn off all the lights in the main salon. The aft cabin door is narrow and just short of my height. If I was to step through it, there wouldn't be room enough for me and a whizzing bullet. Instead I lie down on the floor, directly in front of the door. Light still leaks under bulkhead door. Someone is in there.

I quickly move to the electrical panel and throw the aft cabin breaker. Now the boat is cloaked in darkness. I carefully reach over, turn the knob of the door and slowly push it open.

"Oh you're good, Mr. Brubaker, really good." Christine Flynn's voice carries out from the darkness.

"Apparently not that good. How did you get in here?" I spin toward the main salon to throw the breaker and immediately hit my head on the top of the door frame. "I'm all right," I say. I don't want to give Christine the pleasure of pulling an icepack out of her purse.

I throw on the breaker and the lights in the main cabin. Charley doesn't move. "Good dog." Christine Flynn joins me in the main salon.

"Your face looks much better. I've got some cover-up for those bruises if you're interested."

"That won't be necessary."

"I'm not so sure. You're still a bit shy of your old self, but then again I've never seen you without issues with your face."

"How did you get in here?" I take a seat on the settee opposite Christine.

"Enza let me in. We were both waiting for you, but she had to leave. She said something about a longshoreman's retirement party."

"Right." I open the overhead hatch to release the mustiness that builds up in every boat. A cool breeze spirals in. I pull a beer out of the deep freeze and sit on the settee opposite the TV. I know where Colin Flynn is but I don't know where Lucy is. I think about what Manny said about her leaving on the ferry. It sounded like the truth to me. She loved the water. It makes sense, but where could she have gone?

"It was cold, so I curled up in your comforter. I apologize." Christine sits in the opposite settee.

I don't have anything to say right now.

"Ellen Jacobs isn't getting anywhere. And I am at my wit's end." Christine says, as she looks around the cabin.

"This is a difficult case. You have to give her a chance. It could take months."

Christine stares at the floor.

"Who do you think did this?" I ask.

"I don't know." She pulls her knees up close to her and rests her chin on them. Her gaze lands behind me somewhere.

Christine seems unable to move forward. Christine just lost her husband and she probably thinks that as long as his killer is out there it is her responsibility to find him or get even. What she needs to do is grieve and move on with her life. This was not a crime against her, it was against Mr. Flynn.

"What do you want me to do?" I am very tired and nearing the breaking point. Everything has turned on its head this week. I'm not gaining on anything and everything seems like it's drifting further and further away.

We sit in silence a moment. I get two more beers out of the fridge. I hear Meg Ryan and Billy Crystal's voices falling through the hatch. I can also hear a lone outboard engine straining in the distance.

I hand Christine one of the beers. "Your husband was killed by someone he knew. I believe the same person who killed your husband also killed the woman on the boat."

"How do you know?"

"I don't believe in coincidence. Two brutal murders in the same week are not a coincidence. Do you know who is behind your husband's company, Evo Liquid?"

"I know that they are based in South America."

"If you want to find out who killed your husband, you have to be very honest with me and yourself." I give Christine the same stare that I gave Manny earlier tonight.

"You know what made me dismiss any doubt I had about loving Colin?"

I shake my head.

"We were living together on Russian Hill in the city and we decided to move out to the Richmond district to save a little money. Colin rented this big, smoky U-haul truck. We loaded it to the gills. Colin just got behind the wheel and maneuvered up and around those steep narrow hills like it was nothing. I swear to God we should have wrecked, but we never did. Colin was like that. He surprised me almost every day. Just when I thought I knew him, he would pull something out of his hat."

"So do you think there is a possibility that he was involved with something at Evo Liquid that would have surprised you?"

"I'm not sure."

"Why was Colin employed as a technical engineer when his expertise was in finance?"

"Colin told me that had to do with his work status in Peru. They wouldn't let him work in a banking capacity when Peruvians could hold the same job there. They're very strict about it, so they called him an engineer. It was semantics. He didn't know anything about engineering. He was a money man."

"I believe that Colin may have received a fax from Evo Liquid in Peru in error. The confidential fax exposed Evo Liquids criminal activities. Did Colin ever mention these criminal activities to you? Did Colin ever mention going to the American authorities?

"No. He didn't tell me anything."

"How much do you know about your father's involvement with Evo-Liquid?"

"I have no idea." Christine is looking around the room now almost as if she is locating the safest escape route in the event of an abandon ship. She subconsciously places her hand over her stomach as if she herself were clenching it in her hand.

"I'm not stupid, Christine. Your father received financing from a foreign company to buy up most of the rice in the Sacramento River Delta. The more control you have over a commodity, the more control you have over pricing and profits. In exchange, your father was helping the Columbians launder cash here in the U.S."

"That's ridiculous." Christine gets up with the wave of a hand.

"You always knew there was impropriety, but you looked the other way. Your father introduced Colin to Evo Liquid, didn't he? Colin was a good guy from the Midwest. He was a moral man who was forced into a bad situation. He went to Peru and saw something that he wasn't supposed to see. My guess is that he witnessed massive amounts of cash change hands between Evo Liquid, the Columbians, and insurgents in the Peruvian jungle. He spoke up. The fax was the nail in his coffin."

"You're out of your mind, Mr. Brubaker. My father is straight as an arrow and would never be involved in anything like that. He's a little farmer from Sacramento for God's sake."

"Your father owed the Columbians. Who at Evo Liquid would have killed him, Christine?"

"I don't know. I never met any of them. They never let me near them." Christine is in the Galley now.

"You might know more than you think. Did Colin ever meet someone outside the office? Did you ever see him talking to someone you didn't recognize?"

She takes a swig of the beer and then she peers down into the bottle for answers, as if it was a Magic Eight Ball.

The boat phone rings. I pick it up. Enza is calling from the quarry. I can hear skip loaders and heavy equipment dumping and reversing in the background.

"Moonlighting?" I ask, brazenly knowing that a skip loader could just as easily bury me in a spoil heap. "I thought you were at a Longshoreman's retirement party?" I hear the skip loader again.

There is dead air, then, Enza responds. "Yeah. Whatever. Seeing how I don't have my own office, and you didn't come in today, my father was kind enough to lend me some space and his DSL. Did you know that DSL is ten times faster than a regular dial up connection? I can get ten times more work done."

"Ten times more than what?"

"Who are you talking to?" Christine reaches for the phone.

"It's Enza."

"I want to talk to her when you're done."

"It's Christine. She wants to talk to you when we're finished."

"Put her on," Enza insists.

"When we're finished. What do you have to tell me?"

"It can hold."

"No. What is it?"

"Come on, give me the phone." Christine has her hand out and is practically snapping her fingers.

Now she is snapping her fingers.

"Damn it." I hand her the phone.

Christine smiles, as she settles on to the settee. She exchanges pleasantries with Enza. Christine is stoic in describing the empty house and her lack of sleep. Then Christine looks me square in the eye, before turning away and covering the receiver of the phone. Now I start to feel uncomfortable. Christine motions for me to leave the main salon with a sort of brush-off motion. I'm not going anywhere. Then like a lion protecting her young, she bares her teeth.

I motion for her to go in the aft cabin, and she does so after delivering a serious glare.

I'm done. I am over it. She probably killed her husband. She probably learned how to fly a plane, years ago. She kept it a secret until the fateful night when she put the plane on its side, and pushed him out the door on the orders of the Columbians and her father.

I'll just give the keys to the Brubaker and Sons Investigations to Enza. She can have the business. Screw it. I'll go sailing.

I concentrate on the nav desk. I put the parking stub I found on my car on the desk next to the stub I found on the Flynn's SUV.

Using my cell-phone I call the number on the back. A startled night clerk tells me that the parking lot services the Marin airport and the charter jet providers. I thank him and swipe off the phone.

I go on deck with Charley. Charley and I walk up to the palm trees that line the wharf and stop at the railing that overlooks the basin. The Kid is no longer watching *When Harry Met Sally*. The sound of a video game leaks out of his boat and drifts across the glassy water. The wind has quelled for the night. George's boat is dark; no sign of life.

I feel a tug on my arm. My concentration is focused on the motley bunch of hulls that make up this little boat community.

Another tug and Christine hands me the portable phone, "Enza."

"Right. Enza, what's up?"

"I just checked the office messages. A friend at the Marin Sheriff's office in Bolinas called me to say that a small carry-on bag washed up on the beach."

"…and it belongs to Colin Flynn." I finish her sentence.

"Yep."

"Anything unusual about it?"

"Nope, except that his passport was in it and it had a Peru exit stamp."

"Did you tell Christine?"

"Nope."

"Good work."

"There's more." She seems hesitant to tell me.

"Okay."

"They pulled a set of prints off Shirley's oar…"

"…Yeah?"

"They're yours."

"Okay."

"They also have witnesses who say they saw you in an altercation with Shirley on the street the other day. They saw you grab the oar and push her with it. Ellen and Stevens are putting together an arrest warrant. What are you going to do?"

"I don't know yet."

"I know you didn't do it, Jack. Do you want me to call your brother?"

"Not yet. Thanks, Enza." I move away from Christine while she leans over the railing and stares down at the water, out of earshot. "Were you able to get anything out of Christine?"

"I took the "sister oppressed by a misogynistic hierarchy" approach. She may not believe in it, but she thinks I do, so I play it up. She seems genuinely frustrated about the status of her husband's case, but at the same time, she isn't hypothesizing as to who did it. It's like there's this big elephant in the room, and she refuses to look at it."

"I think that elephant may be her father."

"She's not talking about her father. It was more of a ramble. She's talking about stuff that has nothing to do with her husband: news, shopping, stupid stuff."

"She's in denial. Thanks Enza." I click off the phone.

Christine is still at the rail, shivering a bit.

"Your husband's luggage washed up on the beach in Bolinas." I have to get a case together against somebody else. The sheriff is getting his ducks in a row for target practice and they all have my face on them.

"Why would his bag be on a beach?"

"Your husband was pushed from the cockpit of a small airplane. His luggage was tossed out as well."

"No one told me that. No one told me anything."

"The sheriffs weren't going to give you any information, in the event you became a suspect."

"I didn't kill my husband and I need you to find out who did."

"I believe you, but we have to make sure that Ellen Jacobs believes you too. Have you ever been to the parking lot up at the airport?"

"Of course. That's where I parked to drop him off for the Peru trip. I park there often."

"You dropped him off in his Tahoe, but why weren't you there to pick him up?"

"He usually calls me from the plane. He never called. I called Evo Liquid, and they said it was a charter and couldn't confirm whether he was on the plane or not."

"He was on the plane. I believe that your husband was forced or lured into another plane upon returning from his trip to Peru. Then, once over the ocean, the pilot of this plane tossed his bag out the door and then…" She doesn't need to relive Colin's fall through the forest canopy. "We need to find the pilot of the second plane."

Christine seems to consider the event that took Colin's life. "I'm still paying you."

Chapter Forty-five

Charley and I put Christine into her car. I tell her that I am going to run out to the airport in the morning to see what I can uncover. Christine wants to go, but I tell her to stay home. It's bad enough that I'm still poking around the Flynn case, but if Ellen was to see the two of us together, we would both go to jail. As it is, I am almost guaranteed to be wearing an orange jumpsuit to bed tomorrow.

I open the freezer one last time and remove the last beer. The beers combined with sheer exhaustion have given me a slight buzz. This last beer should seal the deal.

The phone rings; it's Tom Ricketts. "I heard Manny was a waste?"

"Yeah. Back to square one." Tom never calls this late.

"I'm not so sure. We tore the trailer apart after you left and I came up with a box of stuff you might want to look at. I think Manny knows more about Lucy than he was letting on."

My heart skips a beat. I think of my search that netted the letters and little else. Maybe I wasn't looking for anything but the letters. I quit when I found the letters.

"When can I meet you?"

"How about tomorrow at Tennessee Valley stables? My daughter has a horse there. I've got to clean its hooves for God's sake."

"What time?" The idea that there may be some clue to Lucy's disappearance gives me hope. I want her to live her life, but I want to know where she is and why. I need to know that she is safe.

"Six o'clock." Tom hangs up.

I think about Tom and his hobbies; his daughter has a horse. I never knew. I think about the airport and the parking ticket. Tom is the only person I know who would have any connection to the airport, flying and my Audi Q7. I left it in his possession the day I chased Manny. I get it back with an airport parking stub under the wiper blade. Maybe To m is working the case and that's why he might have taken my car to the airport. He didn't want to get spotted by Bill Stevens and Ellen. They weren't the best of friends. It could all be a coincidence, but I still don't believe in coincidences.

I spread Lucy's letters out on the Nav desk. They are written in my father's uncomfortable hand, the jagged lines etched into his personalized stationery with the heading 'Donald Brubaker.' The deep blue ink is from the same pen he had for twenty years. In the last twenty years I've managed to lose sunglasses, watches, pens, wallets, jobs and gir lfriends. He never lost anything. He remembered people's names and knew where everything was. It was like everything he owned was on a flash drive and he could call them up in his head at any moment. He was sharp as a tack until the day he died.

Most of the letters contain words of encouragement and tales of my father's adventures. I read the first couple of letters, but I'm bothered by my intrusion into their private correspondence. I decide to scan the pages for places or people that might lead to a connection to Lucy's disappearance, but I find none. There is no mention of anything that would guide me to her current whereabouts; no safe houses and no mention of an underground railroad.

I remove a letter from the bottom of the stack. In it Dad mentions his preparations for the Pacific Cup; the San Francisco to Hawaii sailing race. He says the real race is in getting the boat ready for the start. He expects to leave with a few loose ends that he'll work on under way. He tells Lucy that he will be thinking about her often, and that I'll be there with him. He ends the letter by saying that he trusts me with his life and that he would never attempt it if I hadn't agreed to go with him.

I think about my father's state of mind on the day of the race start. He was very tired, rung out from prepping the boat. I told him that we didn't have to go. We could do the Transpac from Long Beach the following ye ar. My father had made up his mind. I wasn't going to get in the way of something that he had always wanted to do. We were going and I wasn't going to let him go alone.

I carefully bundle the letters and place them in a desk drawer beneath the nav desk. I place the empty beer bottles in a plastic bag and put it on deck.

I'm drowsy. I stare at the mirror in the bathroom one last time. I apply the remains of the pink fluid on my face and I down several aspirin. I crawl into my double sized bunk in the aft cabin. I'm hoping sleep will come before Ellen serves my arrest warrant.

My last thoughts before I drift off are of my father and his chaotic life and his chaotic death. Sleep is easier.

Chapter Forty-six

The wind is up again. The boat heels hard and my foul weather gear swings on its bulkhead hook. The rigging crashes with every wave and I am hanging in my lee cloth on the high side of the boat. From my position in my bunk I can see my father, illuminated by a battery operated lantern swinging from the ceiling, putting his barely legible scrawl into the log book. Dad's yellow foul weather gear is dripping wet. He rubs his face and runs his fingers through his hair. His eyes reveal a weariness that's plagued him the entire trip.

My dad uses his red flashlight to illuminate the falling barometer. He plots our position on the chart which can't be more than fifty miles from our last position twenty four hours ago. He swings the red light around toward the bilge meter. It hasn't changed. There's no electricity. He reaches for the pump handle from the bulkhead behind him. He places the handle in the jaws of the bilge pump and labors to drain the bilge. He counts aloud the number of pumps. It takes several minutes before air can be heard hissing through the line. His weathered face drips with sweat in the red light. He notes the number of pumps in the log book.

The wind is roaring through the rigging now. The boat climbs each steep wave to its crest and is thrown on its side by the strong unobstructed winds racing across the tops of waves. The autopilot, jury-rigged directly to a 12 volt battery, strains under the force of the racing air. The boat rights itself in a sort of twisting motion and plunges down the backside of another mountain of water.

I'm thrown to the cabin floor when the boat slams to a stop in the trough at the foot of another wave. My father can't hang on to the nav desk and is tossed across the cabin like a rag doll. My mind works fast as everything else moves in slow motion. The autopilot whines. I imagine the cable on the steering quadrant for the rudder snapped, wire by wire. I hear the rudder break loose and turn hard to starboard. The boat crests a wave and races down once more burying the bow into the green water. The stern stands up behind us on the chasing wave. I hear the small orange storm tri-sail tear cleanly from the mast. We're standing on our bow, pitch poling. We get tossed end over end and land flat on our back. The warm tropical water floods the companionway.

My father slams hard against the overhead when in an instant it becomes the floor. His head smashes against the grab bars, opening up a terrible gash on his forehead above his eye. He loses consciousness.

I try to wedge myself beneath the settee to keep from getting tossed around. I collide with my father in mid-air; and as quickly as I was tossed from my bunk, the rolling stops and the boat rights itself. The small boat whips back and forth with every wave.

I lunge for the galley beneath the gloomy overhead 12 volt lights. I find a soaking wet towel for my father's head and crawl back to him on the floor which is littered with canned provisions and emptied drawers. Everything that was once secured is now scattered about as if shaken loose by a massive earthquake.

I try to wrap my father's head but he's jerked from my arms when another huge wave impacts the boat. We both tumble with yet a second pitch pole of the hull. The hull stalls completely upside down as the warm sea water rushes in through the companionway, staking claim to more and more of the boat.

After a few terrifying seconds, the boat rights itself again as the heavy keel relents to gravity. The violence of the boat righting itself is far greater than that of a knockdown. The boat snaps back up with such force that everything loose becomes dangerous. Canned goods are flung around like they were shot from a gun. My father and I can no longer fight the motion.

The situation is grave. In the moment that the boat is upright, I resolve to activate the EPIRB; emergency beacon. I drag myself through the waist-deep water to the companionway where the yellow canister containing the radio beacon and strobe light is fastened to the bulkhead. I unsnap it from its holder and flip the switch. The strobe light flashes in the terrifying darkness. The main cabin is torn apart; shelves that once contained books are emptied. With every flash of the light, I can see even more damage. The small TV that was once mounted to the shelves is missing completely. My father is lying on his side in the settee, taking gallons of water in the face as the boat heaves in the waves.

As the rigging slams into the deck, there is no quiet. The rudder continues to swing from side-to-side. Suddenly, there is a new sound, a metallic creaking coming from directly beneath my feet. I think about the life raft lashed to the deck. I feel for a large flashlight in a storage space beneath the companionway steps. I find it and turn it on. With one hand I pull back the companionway cover and force myself up the few steps to assess the damage. I toss the EPIRB on the deck. Its distress signal is already being picked up by satellites and forwarded to the U.S. Coast Guard.

In the narrow band of light and blowing sea foam, I find it difficult to make sense of anything. The wheel at the helm is missing completely. Beyond where the helm should be, I trace the taut sea-anchor line with the beam of light as it disappears in our wake. The sea-anchor is like a giant canvas bucket designed to slow the boat in absurd weather. It is the only safety measure working for us right now.

The canvas dodger that once guarded the opening to the cabin below is gone. The boom is swinging wildly and the storm tri-sail is flapping like so much laundry on a line. I can't see the waves but I hear their roar. The wind is screaming. The life raft, normally mounted just forward of the canvas dodger is gone.

Through the small deadlight, I see the wreckage floating in the cabin below. I see my father tossed about with his head barely above water.

I return to the mayhem below and am determined to tie my father into a bunk. In a brief respite from the crashing waves, I make my way forward. My knees smash into the cabinets as I'm once again thrown to the floor beneath the water. I emerge to find my father face down. I pull him to my chest. I have to find a way to get some of this water out of the boat. The metallic noise continues with every smashing wave; it's the sound of stretching keel bolts, they've broken free. In less than a second, we're upside down again; this time, for good.

In the blackness, I lose sight of my father. I feel the water deepen.

The boat finally feels stable in the giant rolling seas. We rise and fall with every wave. The extreme violence of the past few minutes is gone, and the calming movement allows me to think. I call out to my father, but there's nothing. I feel something against my feet. I reach down into the waist-deep water and grab my father's jacket entangling his limp body. I pull him close to me.

Chapter Forty-seven

In the blackness, I hear the telephone ring. I reach for the boat phone.

"It's Dolliver. I looked at your security DVD."

"Jesus, what time is it?" This is crazy.

"Early. I've been up all night, so I looked at it. I toyed with the resolution..."

"Slow down. Hang on." I sit up and rub my face. What is he talking about? The DVD. "Yeah. What did you learn?"

"It's your buddy, Tom Ricketts."

"What about him?" I look at my alarm clock. It's 4:30 a.m.

"He's the guy in the hat. He's the guy trying to avoid the security cameras at the coyote place."

"Are you sure?"

"I worked with the resolution. Tom came out clear as day. I just thought you should know."

"I appreciate your help and with everything going on." I am awake now and thinking about Tom.

"Let me know if there is anything else I can do. You know me, I'll be around town. Same as ever."

"Same as ever. Thanks."

I go to my nav desk. I open the Flynn file. There are press releases and newspaper articles that had to do with the company itself. There is one news article that I didn't think pertained to the Flynn's earlier, but I might've been wrong.

I remove the downloaded article with the headline "Estate Robbery" from the folder. I scan the article about a break-in at the Marin estate of Evo Liquid's CEO. The article is of little importance, except for one thing. Thomas Ricketts' name appears as a 'Security Consultant.'

Tom Ricketts installed the cameras at Red Fish's. He knew where they were and how to avoid them, but he got lazy and got caught. Red Fish is no coincidence, either. He has to be tied into Evo Liquid through the Peruvian connection.

I remember my six o'clock meeting with Tom and I resolve to get there early. I'm beginning to think the new 'Lucy info' may not be legit.

I throw on a pair of jeans and a thick jacket. Hot tea will take too long and there isn't any food on the boat. My mouth is dry but I have a clear head. I open the companionway, and push a very sleepy Charley up the steps into the cold air.

I walk Charley to the closest palm tree and then send her back to the boat. The marina is quiet and only the fishermen on the pier are moving about. The floodlights from their boats illuminate the giant plastic crates filled with their fresh catch.

I drive the Suburban to the office. Starting a day this early calls for hardware and this may be all for naught, but Tom is connected to too many dead people. He knew Shirley and chances are he knew Flynn from Evo Liquid.

The streets of Sausalito are empty. Light from the flour dusted kitchen of the donut shop leaks out on to the sidewalk. Big Marty is at the Good Neighbor dragging barrels and ladders out to the street.

I leave the Suburban on the street and climb the steps to my office. The narrow hallway is lit by overhead fixtures. The door to my office is open a crack. The door frame is splintered. I reach into my belt for my nine millimeter Glock but it's not there. That's why I am here in the first place. I grab a fire extinguisher off the wall instead.

I believe that whoever was-or-is in there is not expecting someone to rush in behind them at 5:00 a.m. I have nothing to lose, so I kick open the door and throw the light switch.

My office was tossed. I must be getting warmer on the Flynn case. The sofa cushions are across the room. The sofa is overturned and every drawer from Enza's desk is on the floor. Enza's computer is destroyed. The telephone lines are ripped from the wall. My inner office door is hanging off its hinges.

Piles of books lay beneath overturned shelves. My desk remains upright, but my desk chair lays cut open like a gored picador. The benefit of having a steel desk is that they're hard to move and even harder to break into. The only drawer not emptied and on the floor is locked and it holds the Glock.

The face of the drawer is dented and scratched. Someone really wanted to get in it but gave up. I remove my keys from my pocket and push the small key into the lock. After some persuasion, the lock turns with a jerk of the smashed handle. The Glock is there along with a box of rounds. I release the clip; it's loaded with fourteen shiny bullets. I empty the box of remaining rounds into my jacket pocket.

There is a noise in the outer office. Someone is carefully stepping on broken glass. I quickly level the Glock at the door and slide down behind my desk.

"Jack? You all right?"

It's Big Marty.

"Yeah."

Big Marty steps into my office carrying two cups of coffee. "What in the hell happened here?"

"It looks like I stuck a nerve."

"I saw your car. You're never up this early."

"I have to meet Tom Ricketts about Lucy, but I think it might turn into something else."

"That sounds convenient." Marty hands me the steaming cup.

"I know." I pick up my torn chair. It wobbles briefly before falling over again. "Damn."

"I'll have the boys at the store fix it for you."

"Don't worry about it."

"You don't worry about it. Where's this meeting?"

"The stables in Tennessee Valley."

"You want me to call the police?"

"No, they're looking for me."

"You want backup?"

"What I want is two more hours of sleep." I look out the office window. Several green and white sheriff cruisers are quietly approaching the office. "I think it's time for me to go."

Marty and I watch the three cop cars pull up in front of the building.

"Look, Marty. Those guys are looking to arrest me for the murder of Flynn and the Man-hater. I can't let them do that. I need you to stall them for me.

"I can do that."

"Good. My meeting goes down at six. If you don't hear from me by seven, tell Ellen Jacobs where I went. Tell her to call Enza."

"Wouldn't it be better if I just went with you?"

"No offense, but you can't fit through that window." I point to the small bathroom window that leads to Smitty's rooftop.

"Right. I'll buy you some time."

"Thanks."

I push the small window open and shimmy outside, gun in hand. I take the few steps across the rooftop before leaping onto a small shed behind the bar. I jump down from the shed and onto the sidewalk.

I peek around the corner and scan the street. Bill Stevens and two deputies have left their cars and are making their way upstairs with guns drawn. I easily slip across the street to my Suburban.

Chapter Forty-eight

Tennessee Valley is only about a mile from Sausalito as the crow flies, but one has to follow the meandering coastline of the bay to get to it. After a mile of driving in the Marin Headlands, there is a break in the coast range that forms a small valley that stretches from the Pacific Ocean toward the bay.

The fog is standing still in the road ahead when I pull off the main road into a gravel area just outside the horse stables. For a moment I hoped that Tom might have Lucy but I realized that was lunacy. It wasn't going to be easy, if it were we'd have her already. I ease the Suburban behind a thick grove of redwoods. I take the powerful nine millimeter and wedge it behind my back before killing the engine. My cell phone has one bar of signal. I turn off the ringer and put it into my coat pocket.

I look over my shoulder for the Marin sheriffs as I get out of the car. I think about a career change. There must be a job out there where I don't get tossed out of bed only to meet a murderer, find my office trashed and be forced to flee the police through a small bathroom window.

In the pre-dawn darkness, I jog the paved road that ends at several large barns, riding rinks and corrals. A security light creates a fuzzy halo on the eaves of a distant barn. A black S-Class Mercedes Benz is parked beneath the orange light. It looks like I'm not the only one who wanted to own the element of surprise. I look for cover.

A murder of crows settles on a tall cedar. Their eerie cries call out to the owner of the black Mercedes. I enter a dressage ring and put some jumping fences between me and the car. Unseen horses whinny in the darkness and jostle against a metal fence. I can almost feel their heavy hooves pressing into the damp foamy earth. I sense their warm breath as I pass by their paddock on the far end of the ring.

"Where's the fax, Jack?" Tom's voice carries across the riding rink.

Two doors slam shut on the Mercedes.

I thought I had cover in the darkness. That was fast. "How did you know it was me?" I call back, carefully moving behind the jumping fences toward another barn.

"Night-vision. The good stuff. Whitey brought it up with him. You remember Whitey, don't you? He's the guy with the killer jungle vine?"

"The birth of mankind, how could I forget? How do you know about the fax?"

"A little bird told me." Tom's voice remains stationary.

"Did that little bird trash my office this morning?" I move behind the tallest jumping boards. The Peruvian's vision depends on starlight and probably the haze of the barn light.

"That was Whitey. Quite an early riser, wouldn't you say?"

I reach behind me and feel the hard plastic grip of the Glock; it feels cold and wet in the fog. I pull it out and grip it with both hands. I place one round into the security light on the barn. A shower of sparks rains down on the hood of the Mercedes. Horses stir, whinny and kick their stalls.

"Nice shot."

"Now we're even, Tom. How long have you had access to the Highway Patrol surveillance plane, Tom?"

"It's one of the perks of being a retired Warthog pilot. Aviation people are funny that way. They all want you to fly their planes. They get some weird kind of bragging rights."

I was right about the airport connection. I just didn't want to be. The logs at Marin airport showed that Evo Liquid's charter arrived at Marin but that Flynn wasn't on it. Maybe it was Tom who changed the logs. "Did you take Flynn for a pleasure flight last week? Did you try to cover it up last night with a quick trip in the Audi Q7?" I raise my gun and point it toward Tom's voice in the dense ever-whitening fog. As I come to the low railing around the rink, I step over it and move to my right.

"They say a criminal will always make one slip whether by accident or on purpose. I guess I forgot about that little parking stub and I should have done a better job trying to sink your boat."

"Knowing what I know now, I'm surprised that you had a beer with me on the boat, after you tried to sink it."

"Not as surprised as I was to see your boat in the marina. You were supposed to be doing the breast stroke to Angel Island."

"Why didn't you just shoot me?"

"I wasn't trying to kill you. I was just trying to slow you down."

"Little good that did. What about your flight with Flynn?"

I listen for Whitey. He's moving around the rink to my left but I don't think he sees me or he would have shot me.

"I took Flynn for some flight lessons over the Pacific Coast and he failed."

"He was supposed to land in the ocean with his luggage, wasn't he?"

"He was supposed to disappear forever in the current off Bolinas, but he got hung up on the landing gear. He wouldn't let go. I had to practically fly the plane upside down to shake him loose."

"You can plea-bargain. You're safer at San Quentin than with the Columbians." I say, knowing that he isn't safe anywhere.

My mind is on Whitey. Where is Whitey? The dark fog is lightening to a fuzzy gray. I'm sure Whitey is already moving toward me. I still can't see him. I keep moving.

"I'm not worried, Jack. It's you who should be worried. You woke up next to Flynn, and it looks like you killed Shirley, too. They've got some really nice prints on that oar, and you had motive. Everybody knew there was no love lost when Shirley checked out." Tom's voice is moving away from the car.

"Why did you kill Shirley?" I shout.

"I did everybody a favor and I thought it might get the boys off my case and squarely on you, which it did. Before I cut her head off, she mentioned your meeting with Santa. She said you put something on his door. I assumed it was the fax."

"Why didn't you just bust me yourself and pin Flynn's murder on me?" I continue to circle to my right and stay low along the railing. "You would have put the case in the freezer and been the local hero."

"I need the fax, Jack. It's all part of the package. It is a loose end, just like you. I'm not here to kill you. I'm here to arrest you. We're friends after all."

"Ellen's got the fax, Tom. It is only a matter of time before she zeros in on you."

"More like zeros in on you, Jack."

"You're the one moonlighting as the security pro for Evo Liquid. You work for the Columbians," I shout.

"So what if I am? Everybody moonlights in my business, but you're the shady P.I. You're the one who called me. You're the one who tried to kill me in the horse rink. "

"Evo Liquid used the commune for corporate meetings. The high-tech security system was installed under your supervision. I've got video of you on the Red Fish channel, Tom."

"Nice bluff but that's impossible. I never set foot in front of any of those cameras. Don't forget, I put 'em up. What else you got?"

"Why did you do it, Tom? You don't need the money." Where's the Peruvian?

"Ah, but you're wrong, Jack. Marin County is where the cold cash meets the white trash and I don't feel like being the white trash anymore. Do you have any idea how much it costs to put my kids through private school, with the books, clothes, donations? Do you know how boring it is to sit in a roomful of parents discussing the color of the new soccer uniforms? Nothing matters in Marin, Jack. Nobody matters. So why not spice up my life and make a few extra bucks to pay for all this bullshit."

Tom continues, "You've got no idea. These young soccer moms wear their tight little sweat suits. They shake their little asses at every opportunity. I pick 'em up for speeding, drugs, and even prostitution. People are doing things in their tract houses that would blow your mind. It's only when they get into their cars that we have a chance to bust them. You've got a community of children running amok, while one parent is in the city and the other is sitting on a yoga mat banging her tennis coach. There are tae-bo coaches, pool men, massage therapists, doctors, insurance salesmen, horny real estate agents and lesbian tree huggers all trying to get a shot at your wife and kids. It's a modern day Sodom and Gomorrah. The fences are too high and the drugs are too cheap."

"Why Red Fish?"

"He helped me out in a pinch a while back so I introduced him to the Columbians."

"What about Manny? You had to know Manny was moving the Koi." More whinnies and footsteps, moving up closer, quicker. I lie against a short fence next to a shallow water hazard.

"Manny was an informant. We tend to look the other way for the little transgressions. I was using Manny to develop a big heroin sting for the Columbians. The gentlemen that I work for don't like competition. Nobody cared about the fish."

"What about Lucy?"

"What about her? She was buying from the competition and now she's not, so everyone benefits."

"But Lucy was clean."

"She was about as clean as a comedy routine at the Apollo."

"I don't believe you."

"Who do you think has been helping her all these years? She's always been junked up."

"You son-of-a-bitch!" My grip tightens on the Glock. I turn my head, using my keen hearing to pinpoint my target. I want to blow his head clean off, but I can't. "Where is she, Tom?"

"She's gone, Jack. I sent her away. I didn't want her to end up in prison. I love her. I've loved her for years. You certainly don't."

"That's bullshit. Where is she?"

"You'll never find her. You're too busy anyway. You and your slimy lawyer brother are always too busy for Lucy. Now she's gone and you don't have to worry about her anymore."

"I swear to God, if you've so much as touched her, I will torture you." I could shoot off his foot with the Glock and get him to talk, but I would be too tempted to empty my magazine into his head.

"She's alive and getting well, Jack. She's just not here. She'll pop up again."

I can hear the movement of hooves in the soft earth, reacting at my target. I hear footsteps and heavy breathing moving fast across the ring, which is now cloaked in bright white fog. The sun is rising up behind us.

Shots ring out. I hit the ground hard and fast. Several horses appear out of the fog in a full gallop. I roll to my right as they charge past me and leap over the low rail disappearing into the whiteness. The crows light from the trees with deafening squawks.

"The weasel bastard shot me, Jack, but I got him. I got him good."

It's Big Marty.

"Stay down, Marty. How bad is it?"

"I don't know, Jack. I'm not a doctor, I'm a hardware salesman."

"Apparently, it's not bad enough." Tom shouts, moving away from us after putting a few shots in the dirt next to me.

I unleash several rounds in the direction of Tom's voice. There is only the sound of Tom running.

"Where are you, Marty?"

"In the mud and fog. Where are you?"

"Coming to you." I zero in on his response.

Big Marty is lying on his side, pressing his left hand against his hip. He has a huge handgun in his right hand. Whitey is lying in blood-soaked mud ten feet away. Half his face is missing. His body lies as if he were running along the ground, like he just fell over and died.

"What are you doing here?" I ask Marty.

"I knew there was something fishy about the whole deal. I figured I'd watch your back. I was almost on top of the skinny freak, when he spotted me."

"I'm calling 911." I pull the phone from my pocket.

"Let me do it. You find that bastard."

"Are you going to be all right?"

"Yeah, but I'm pissed." Marty presses the numbers into the phone as I quickly move toward the back of the ring

I stay low and I move toward a large gray barn that appears out of the thinning fog. I step over the rail of the practice ring and race toward the barn. I can see Tom standing in the doorway. He opens fire with his service weapon. I duck and return fire while running straight at him. Bullets whizz past my head as my return fire hits the door frame next to Tom. I watch him stagger and then disappear into the darkness of the barn.

God bless the inaccuracy of handguns.

I lean against the old barn sheathing. I can hear Tom moving on the hay-covered floor. I quickly glance inside. Tom backs toward the rear of the barn and fires a shot directly at me. The bullet blasts through the door and keeps going. Several horses kick and whinny in their stalls.

"Maybe I'll sail around the world just like you always wanted to do. I'll pick up your boat at auction when you're on death row." Tom unleashes a few more rounds at the wall between us.

"If you haven't noticed, Tom, we're in a gun fight here. I highly doubt that you're going to get away with the murders and sail into the sunset."

"You're always so negative." Tom fires another round that covers me in splinters.

"What about your wife and children?" I shout.

"They don't need me."

"How fun can it be to visit dear old Dad in San Quentin? You don't have to let it play out this way. Marty's got the entire Marin County law enforcement community on its way."

"They'll believe me before they believe you."

I turn back toward the road. The fog is gone now. In the distance, the sound of sirens rises up from the Bay. Big Marty is right where I left him, on his side covered in dirt and blood.

"Get rid of your gun, Marty." I shout, just as Tom storms out of the barn on the back of a large steaming palomino. He levels his weapon at me and fires off a volley.

"Shit." I fire two rounds before my gun is emptied. I throw myself to the ground next to the barn.

Big Marty takes over where I left, off aiming his cannon at Tom. He gently squeezes off three shots, before the last one knocks Tom to the ground. As I run to the downed cop, I reload my clip.

The emergency vehicles are just now cresting the hill. Marty tosses his weapon and collapses.

I stand over a panting Tom. I press my gun against his ear. "Where is Lucy, you son-of-a-bitch?"

Tom just smiles, as blood boils up from his coat.

Chapter Forty-nine

Marty is in stable condition, no pun intended, as the EMS guys struggle to load the big man into the ambulance. Apparently, one of Whitey's rounds ricocheted off a horse-rail and lodged in Marty's hip. Tom didn't fare as well. He was in the first ambulance and had to be resuscitated. He'll probably make it. Whitey was dead before he hit the ground.

The sheriffs have me cuffed to the back of a horse trailer. While the FBI, DEA and ATF are flipping a coin to see who gets the first crack at me, Ellen drives up in her cruiser and practically runs them over.

"Get those cuffs off him, now!" Ellen exits her car and comes out swinging.

The Feds scowl at her at first, but then an expression of recognition melts over them. I think they're remembering what it is like to be married.

"He's a witness, not a suspect."

"Well, you don't know Jack!"

There is a discussion amongst the Feds before they unlock me. They want Whitey and Tom for drugs and conspiracy. They don't even know who I am, so they let me go.

"Thank you, Ellen, but why the change of heart?" I rub my wrists. I smell like shit, again; dead bodies, bird guano and now horse manure. Where can I take a computer class?

"We finally got a court order for the CHP to release the flight records. Tom Ricketts checked out the CHP plane immediately after the Evo Liquid charter arrived. We also learned a lot about Pedro Guerrero."

"A good solid L.A. Dodger in his day," I say, without the slightest hint of sarcasm.

"The one I'm talking about is also a player in cash and drugs, not baseball."

"What made you change your focus from me and Christine, to Tom

242

Ricketts?"

"Your fingerprint wasn't the only one we pulled off the oar we found wedged between Shirley the Man Hater's ribs. Tom's was there too. I was with Shirley from the moment we found her until the moment she was bagged. Tom never touched the bare oar. He had to have touched it before, when he killed her. He made one little mistake."

"That's all it takes."

"We're going to need you here for a while, Jack."

"Yeah."

An agent hands me my vibrating cell phone.

"How are you?" Enza's voice is a comfort.

"I am okay." I watch a ranch hand lead the palomino back to the barn.

"I got a hold of your cell-phone records and traced a couple calls that Manny made."

"Thanks. I'll look at them when everything calms down."

"You don't have to. I called one of the numbers. A woman answered."

In an instant I remember my lost sister. "Was it Lucy?"

"I don't know, but I just thought you should know."

"Did you get an address, Enza?"

"It was a cell-phone. My phone guy says that the call pinged within a Santa Barbara cell, but she could be anywhere now."

"Thanks, Enza. That's something, anyway." I close the phone.

The agents are everywhere. The emergency vehicles are gone. A flatbed truck is picking up the Mercedes. The black sedan has a license plate that reads "Red Fish."

Ellen is absorbed in meetings with the Feds. I hand everyone my business card and walk away.

Chapter Fifty

Ellen's dining table looks out through wide sliding doors, a redwood deck with terra cotta pots filled with camellias, bougainvillea and geraniums. There is a peek-a-boo view of the bay between giant redwoods.

"What happened to Christine's father?" I ask Ellen.

"They put him under arrest for money laundering. The FBI and the DEA raided his offices the same day they went into Evo Liquid. They also shut down Red Fish's compound. The Evo-Liquid private jet took off for Peru empty before it could be grounded." Ellen puts the salad bowl on a small candlelit dining table. "Flynn's father was left holding the bag."

I sit down in front of the steaks that I grilled in her backyard. "What about Christine Flynn?"

Ellen sits down next to me. "She keeps coming up clean. As it turns out, she never knew her father was criminally involved with the Colombians. How crazy is that?"

"What about the Arabic connection? Puerto Maldonado? Drug money for guns?" I ask.

"As long as there is a 'War on Terror,' the 'War on Drugs' will take a backseat." Ellen sits down at the table. "The Colombians set it up that way."

I ponder the big 'War on Terror' diversion that is leaving U.S. agencies understaffed and scrambling on a thousand fronts.

"Bon appetite." Ellen smiles.

"Bon appetite." I answer. Her smile is the same one I saw on the night of the lineup. It's an innocent smile. It's her one true expression that lets you inside.

"Why did you get into this business in the first place?" Ellen asks as she cuts her entire steak into small pieces, before she takes her first bite.

"You know, if you cut off one piece at a time, your steak will stay warmer, longer."

Ellen makes a stabbing motion toward me with her fork and ignores my advice, "You didn't answer my question." She feeds Charley a tiny piece of steak beneath the table.

I consider the question a moment before answering. I look around Ellen's little Mill Valley house. The walls are painted in muted tones and the furnishings are small, but comfortable. I understand her desire to be surrounded by softness and comfort. Photos and portraits are grouped closely together on walls displaying a life beyond the crime and misery. The organization and neatness betrays the fact that she works morning, noon and night.

"When I was young I had specific ideas as to how my life was going to play out. And it didn't include working for my father. I wanted to work as a writer out of college and live a happy, safe scholarly life, but that life failed to materialize. My father gave me a few cases, which I took on only for the money. I worked the cases well, but they didn't fit in my fantasy. I was a starving non-writing writer. Rather than continue to fight against everything real that tried to attack my fantasy, I left. I retreated like a beaten army."

"Where did you go?"

"I went to Los Angeles to be a movie writer. I got tons of jobs driving trucks, and working on sets, but never writing. I worked all the time. I made great money and never wrote a word. Eventually, the jobs stopped coming my way because I never wanted to be what I was hired to do. So when my father started sending me small cases in L.A., I worked them too and resented my father at the same time. He was the person chipping away at my fantasy life."

"It sounds to me like he was helping you out when you needed it the most." Ellen puts her hand on mine.

"You're probably right, but I was a kid and I didn't see it that way. I knew the enemy was at the door. I had to flee again and that's when I went sailing. I traveled the world and saw it all. To make a long story short…"

"Too late…" There's that smile again.

"I stopped running. I stopped fighting for a fantasy. The moment I started swimming with the current, instead of against it, I began to enjoy investigating. I enjoyed the problem solving and I enjoyed helping people. If I had only stopped resisting reality sooner, I would have been much happier longer and I started writing again."

"So you're happy?"

"I'm very happy. Deep down I want to help people the way my father did. I want to solve cases that will allow people to get on with their lives. Initially, I turned my back on my father because I didn't like that he helped other people first. I don't want to be like him, but at the same time I do."

"So why are you leaving?"

"I'm not leaving. I'm looking for my sister. I'm investigating."

We eat our dinner with vigor. It's been a long time since either one of us has had a home-cooked meal. It has been a while since either one of us shared one with the opposite sex.

"Speak for yourself!" Ellen flings a piece of meat at me.

"Did I say that out loud?"

"Yep."

"Damn."

Ellen pours me a cup of coffee. It tastes a lot stronger than the tea I'm used to, but I drink it anyway.

"I'm confused," Ellen says. "I know this is a going-away dinner but it feels like a first date."

"Not a bad first date. Don't you think?"

"Not bad at all. You have a reason to stay if you want to." Ellen says as she squeezes my hand.

"You're a much bigger reason for me to come back."

"You're not just coming back for Charley are you? Maybe you have a thing for blondes."

"I have a thing for you."

"That's a very cheesy line, Jack Brubaker."

"I can't help it." I admit.

"Help what?"

I lean in and kiss Ellen on the lips.

Chapter Fifty-one

It's early, about 5:00 a.m. A black sky is turning to purple in the east. I roll up to Frank's garage and turn off my headlights. My brother's family is sound asleep. It's Saturday. I kill the engine. The only sound is that of the paperboy delivering the Marin Independent Journal from an overburdened Toyota truck.

I check under the Audi Q7 seats one more time. The empty water bottles are gone, maps are folded neatly in the glove compartment. There is a full tank of gas. I close the door, leaving the key on the seat with a quick note: "Gone to Santa Barbara. I'll call you. Drive it when you can."

I stare up at the house and family that I don't have. The big house is quiet from the laughter and crying, and occasional shouting. Eyes are dry and closed beneath warm blankets. Frank and I will never see eye to eye, but we have come to an understanding. I will spend my days searching for Lucy. I don't owe this to Frank, but I owe it to Lucy. I will find her before her money runs out.

Big Marty drives up behind me in my suburban.

"Your Dad would be proud of you." Marty pulls the big beast back on the road.

"For the Flynn case?" I ask, as we quietly weave our way back toward Sausalito on the winding back roads of San Rafael.

"Everything your father did was for you, your sister and brother. All that junk he piled up at the office and at home was for you. He saw value in everything. He knew that if you fell on hard times, you could always finish the unfinished and sell the oddities. These, in a strange way, were his gifts to you. The vision he had for his gifts was that one day you would put hard work and love into them and complete them. He was giving in a way that forced us to give in return. This was his legacy." Marty checks his mirrors and leans forward, twisting his hand on the worn steering wheel.

247

I stare straight ahead. The last person I want to talk about today is my father. It's bad luck.

"I helped your dad move that furniture up those stairs to your office. He knew you would refinish it someday. He knew it when you were five years old. Your Dad would have been proud of you for sailing again."

We finish the trip in silence. He pulls up to 'A' Basin. There are no hugs. Big Marty doesn't hug, and besides, I expect to see him again soon. I get out, he reaches over to my side of the cab and I extend my hand. He presses a mass card into my palm. There is a folded fifty paper-clipped to it. He smiles and drives away.

I turn to the boat sitting silently in its slip, heavy in the water.

Mechanical difficulties can never be forecast but can be mitigated through preparation. I have studied the route carefully. I have noted the geographic milestones: the Monterey Bay, San Luis Bay, Point Conception and the Channel Islands. I've also noted the safe havens on the west coast, of which there are only a handful. You can plan and plan for a voyage and never leave, or you can just push off.

With a clear forecast it should be smooth sailing.

Soon the tide will be flooding and I will be beneath the bridge before it turns ebb. I am pushing off in time to safely cross the bars off the San Francisco Bay.

The cloud cover is beginning to break and the small diesel motor is idling smoothly, eager to put some sea miles beneath the keel. My emotions run the gamut from sad to excited, to terrified. I am not afraid of the voyage though, or storms, or even mechanical failure, I am afraid of what I don't know.

I know the course and the waypoints on the chart, but life's waypoints can never be plotted. If I'm lucky I will recognize them as I experience them. I have to keep a good watch for the waypoints.

From my vantage point on the bow, I can see all the boats in 'A' Basin. I see Roy's, George's and the Kid's. They'll be here for a long while. They'll probably be here when I get back, whenever that may be.

I walk aft to the cockpit and kill the motor. My stomach is churning and I'm literally shaking in my boots. I consider the dock and Mt. Tam in the distance, and I consider the cold water gently moving around the boats hull. I re-start the motor. It coughs a small cloud of white smoke and churns to life. I go below.

Of course, everything is tied down. I stowed everything days ago. I check the GPS one more time. Waypoints that I entered into the computer months ago will lead me out of the bay, through the channel and south in the heavy pacific water.

I remember Big Marty's mass card in my pants pocket. I notice something different about it. I've held many throughout my life, but this one is a little bigger, a little newer. I remove the paper clip and the money. I turn the card over. It is a youthful picture of my father behind the helm of his boat. It's my father's mass card.

I pull on my waterproof overalls and Velcro them snuggly around my boots. I pull on a sweater over long underwear and then a heavy foul weather jacket. I shove my gloves into my jacket pocket. I press a wool hat down over my head. I step on deck.

Ellen and Dolliver await me on the dock. Ellen has Charley on a leash.

"You're going to call when you get to Santa Barbara right?" Ellen asks.

"Yes." Nobody knows what to say in situations like these. There is so much to say, too.

"Are you ready for the lines?" Dolliver walks to the end of the dock by the bow.

"Yeah." My eyes never leave Ellen's.

Dolliver tosses the bow line aboard, then the spring and the stern. He walks around the other side.

"Thanks for taking care of Charley. She's a good girl."

Ellen nods. She wipes a lone tear from her cheek.

"That's it, Jack." Dolliver tosses the last line onboard. When you set sail you leave nothing behind, because you never know if you'll be coming back.

I take the helm and ease the diesel into gear. *Suzanne* gently moves forward. It takes swinging on a frayed rope and aiming for the deepest part of the pond. Once you've made the leap, you have to make it again and again, for the rest of your life. And why wouldn't you?

I gently ease *Suzanne* into the channel. I quickly fall into a routine readying the boat for sail.

Ellen waves from an outside dock.

I wave back and Ellen turns away.

About the Author

Derekwadeauthor@gmail.com

Derek Wade is an American mystery writer and avid sailor. He grew up in Los Angeles and worked in the television and motion picture industry, the cattle industry and has captained a sailboat around the world. He currently lives in Missouri with his wife and three children.

**VISIT OUR WEBSITE
FOR THE FULL INVENTORY
OF QUALITY BOOKS:**
http://www.roguephoenixpress.com

Rogue Phoenix Press
Representing Excellence in Publishing

Quality trade paperbacks and downloads
in multiple formats,
in genres ranging from historical to contemporary romance,
mystery and science fiction.
Visit the website then bookmark it.
We add new titles each month!